GREAT
VILLAGE

GREAT VILLAGE

MARY ROSE DONNELLY

A Novel

Cormorant Books

The publisher gratefully acknowledges the support of the Canada Council for the
Arts and the Ontario Arts Council for its publishing program. We acknowledge
the financial support of the Government of Canada through the Canada Book
Fund (CBF) for our publishing activities, and the Government of Ontario through
the Ontario Media Development Corporation, an agency of the Ontario Ministry
of Culture, and the Ontario Book Publishing Tax Credit Program.

Library and Archives Canada Cataloguing in Publication

Donnelly, Mary Rose, 1956–
Great Village / Mary Rose Donnelly.

ISBN 978-1-77086-002-5
1. Title.

PS8607.O655G74 2011   C813'.6   C2010-907930-2

Cover art and design: Angel Guerra/Archetype
Interior text design: Tannice Goddard, Soul Oasis Networking
Printer: Friesens

Printed and bound in Canada.

MIX
Paper from
responsible sources
FSC® C016245

This book is printed on 100% post-consumer waste recycled paper.

CORMORANT BOOKS INC.
390 STEELCASE ROAD EAST, MARKHAM, ONTARIO, L3R 1G2
www.cormorantbooks.com

GREAT
VILLAGE

I

H E DIDN'T SAY A WORD TO ANYONE, NOT ONE WORD.
Thomas O'Reilly slipped into the house unseen. No one
would have known he was there except to find his barn boots
in their usual place, set side by side to the left of the woodshed
door. Crumbs of chaff, dropped from his socks, were scattered
here and there like little wayward stars across the floor Flossy'd
swept not half an hour earlier.

Just at midday as they were gathering in the kitchen, her
mother Lillian said she wondered what was taking him so long.
Whipping potatoes over the stove, her words were little more
than spilled thoughts meant for no one to wipe up.

"He's upstairs," said Flossy, who was busy placing chairs
around the table. Her mother frowned as if she hadn't heard
correctly. "His boots'r there," she added, lifting her chin towards
the woodshed.

Lillian O'Reilly stopped. "Mind the potatoes," she said, pushing the pot off the hottest part of the stove. She crossed the
kitchen and called upstairs.

"Thomas?"

She called again: "Are you coming to eat?" Her eyes traced a cool line back to Flossy.

A third time, she raised her voice. "*Thomas!*" With one hand on the banister and a pinched brow, she strained to catch his reply. There was none.

Finally, throwing her head back, she barked, "*Thom-as!*" It got him. It got all of them. She didn't ordinarily yell. What seemed like a stranger's voice from half-way across the bay returned a ragged, "Y y y ... yes?"

"Are you come for dinner?" tumbled out of her crossly.

Flossy counted to herself, one-matchstick, two-matchsticks, three-matchsticks, right up to fifteen, her exact age, before they heard, "N ... no."

That was it.

Lillian turned a hard gaze in her children's direction. Flossy and her younger brother Jimmy shifted like nervous colts, unsure of what would happen next. Her mother was waiting for the shuffled foot, an averted eye, anything that would tell her someone knew something about this and could explain what was going on with the one upstairs, what had prompted this unexpected turn — her eldest son gone to bed before dinner.

"Flossy! Potatoes!" She dashed to the stove as her mother hiked, skirt-in-hand, up the stairs, her shoes clomping out the burdened beat of lost patience. Thomas would have heard the step, the swish of the dress — she never took those stairs in better than a weary tread. The smell of burnt potatoes crept throughout the kitchen. In a few minutes their mother was back down and, without a word, dished out the potatoes with a crack of the spoon to each of their plates.

By the time they came in from the barn that night, having finished Thomas's chores, her brother still hadn't got up from his bed, then another day and another passed. It had been just two years since their father drowned in Cobequid Bay and now, without Thomas, there were only three to take a lonely place around the O'Reilly kitchen table. Nobody talked about him any more than they talked about her father. The house felt chill, though the middle of summer was already upon them.

FLOSSY O'REILLY, WELL INSIDE the door of her eighties, sat alone in her kitchen staring at the calendar on the wall without really seeing days or dates. If anyone had asked her, lost in thought as she was, she'd have said she was remembering the penny details of Monday, July 11, 1927, though she knew it would have been far more accurate to say she relived them. There she was again with her mother around the back of the old house pegging clothes to the line, legs of pants, apron strings and bed sheets thrashing at her, snapping and drying quickly in the winds picking up at the head of a rising tide on that perfect summer day when Thomas slipped into the house.

A shiver riffled across her old shoulders. She hadn't thought of that day in years, yet today it was as vivid as the back of the hand that sat upon her lap. She examined the estuary of veins and tendons, stroking her own wrist as if she might be assuring someone she loved. Who would have thought so much of their world could crumble with so little flourish? She marvelled at the mind's capacity to take such a day and turn it over and over again, searching all the edges of calamity with the futility of a blind man fingering each piece of a jigsaw puzzle he hasn't a hope of ever putting together.

Her brother Thomas, then the man of the house at sixteen, started out that day in July cutting a crop of marsh hay down along the south dike by the bay. It was an ordinary day set out between two wars and he was doing the same work he'd done each summer for two years. Sometime before noon he drove the team back to the stable, unhitched the horses and hung the harness in the usual place on a peg inside the barn door. He gave the animals water and turned them outside, then came to the house, slipped quietly from those boots and went upstairs to bed where he'd stay for twenty-four years.

FLOSSY GLANCED OUT THE back window to the field behind her house. It was going to be another hot day; a warm wind was already rustling the trees but cooling nothing. Why were they returning to her after so many years, these fragments of the past, a match struck in the memory's darkest room? It wasn't as if she'd set out to think about her brother, her mother or that innocent summer day that would so undo every last one of their expectations.

She sat up and took a deep breath. She'd been having these visitations from the dead for a couple of months now and couldn't shake the feeling that perhaps it might be her turn. Maybe everyone had at least one such warning, a week, month or year before the end. She knew she could scarcely quibble. Not many of her friends had got eighty-two good years with so little wear and tear — one weather hip and a nest of starlings fluttering in her chest when she walked uphill on her way home from McLellan's store. It was all they seemed to talk about anymore: their ailments and bit-replacements, or somebody else's. She'd never heard of people having premonitions of the end or hearing banshees wail beneath the parlour window, but then again she'd never heard even the dying talk about their dying.

Flossy O'Reilly's practical head would tell her all this was morbid imagination. "Now, stop that," she muttered. There were no banshees, only Mealie Marsh's old moggie caterwauling on a warm summer night, but Flossy couldn't quite let it be. Mealie had noticed something wasn't right. She had swept in as usual this morning, coffee cup in hand, and parked herself at the kitchen table in a sleeveless shift that Flossy hadn't seen before — a green cotton print that was bleached lighter in some sections than others with various red and purple paint splotches where body parts folded towards wet canvas. Mealie was an artist, herself bold, large and colourful, who lived a life of domestic chaos two doors away. As was her custom each morning, she stopped by to read the *Chronicle Herald.*

"I've a mouse, Flo," she announced. "Got in beneath the fridge before I could find the broom." Flossy could just imagine Mealie all in a tizzy hunting for the broom. It made her smile. As far as she was concerned, a mouse was the lesser of possible evils. Mealie's drafty old house was built by the Hills before the war and she was inclined to let everything go when she was in a painting frenzy, as she was these days in the little studio out behind her house. Leftover food sat in containers. Cans, bottles and spoiling fruit collected on Mealie's kitchen counter, virtual mouse magnets. On a couple of occasions, Flossy had been walking down to the general store towards the end of the day and noticed Mealie's door wide open to the breeze.

"You know they don't have the old wooden traps anymore — the kind you catch a finger in once you get the peanut butter on the trigger? You remember those, with the snappy wire?" She paused, glancing up. "Flo?"

"Um?"

"Remember the old wooden mousetraps with the spring?"

"Oh yes."

"You can't get them. You can only get these things that capture the mouse, alive. Then you're supposed to take it somewhere and release it." Her eyes widened, "Release it!" she said again. "Un-bloody like-ly," she cackled, her big-boned frame listing towards the wall and jiggling the table. "Bobby McLellan says they're supposed to be humane traps. If it were up to Bobby McLellan, he'd have all the mice in palliative care." She looked down at her own cat curled asleep on a chair in Flossy's kitchen. "And what are you doing here, Mister Wilde?" she stroked the cat affectionately, "You're supposed to be home working for a living." Oscar Wilde lifted his head, blinked lazily at her before going back to sleep.

"You're feeding him too well, Flo," she said, rubbing the cat's ear tenderly. "He much prefers your little tins of kitty pâté to low-cal goat kibble."

When Mealie sailed into the kitchen each morning, Flossy never knew what would be on her mind. She all but dragged the universe in with her, bits of comet dust and muck swirling behind. Mealie was at home here. In two small circles, she could pour herself a cup of coffee and fetch an ice cube from the tray in the freezer to cool it without so much as spilling a drop. Though neither of them went to the dances anymore, Mealie had always been light on her feet like that, even as she'd spread a few inches with the years. Realizing that she hadn't acknowledged her, Flossy smiled. Oscar did have a way of following the food trail. She was all but certain that cat was getting a third breakfast on the other side of the street.

"What time's the circus get in?" Mealie asked, opening up the newspaper and tapping it in the centre.

"Oh, they should be here by six, I expect," Flossy said, looking down at her coffee mug.

"Hmm," came from behind the paper.

Only Mealie would know how little she wanted these visitors. After all, Flossy'd been living on her own for well-on forty years. You could get too used to your own company to not mind the bother of someone else, getting meals on the table, being polite longer than it took to finish a good pot of tea or closing the bathroom door. When she looked back up, Mealie was watching her.

"So, what'r you stewing about, Flo?" she asked as gently as her raspy morning voice would allow. Not much was ever likely to escape Mealie's eye. She took a sip of her coffee, peering at Flossy over the brim. "Is it the Guest?"

Was it so? Could the mere anticipation of Ruth Trotter-Schaeffer's arrival today have rattled Flossy's nerves? She certainly didn't welcome someone underfoot for three weeks but there was more, much more. Flossy could hardly tell Mealie, her dearest friend in the world, she might be getting herself ready to die.

Oh, she was anxious about Ruth's visit all right, a sixteen-year-old from Ontario and her mother's idea to drop her here while she went on to some church conference in Sackville. What was a city girl going to do in Great Village for three weeks? Besides, Flossy disliked hyphenated names, thought them pretentious. And here the hyphenated youngster hadn't even arrived.

"She's not going to ask a thing about the past," Mealie said, turning down a corner of the paper so she could be sure Flossy, who had only as much hearing as suited her, could see she was talking. "When you're her age, there *is* no past."

Mealie knew Flossy altogether too well, knew how much she disliked idle curiosity, could see her fretting before she herself could. Since the sky had begun to soften through her bedroom window this morning, long before the sun peeked above its own dark covers, Flossy O'Reilly was awake and mentally bracing herself against this day — securing the shutters, gathering loose objects from the yard, locking the back cellar — as if she'd read in the paper of a hurricane chewing its way up the East Coast from Boston: Hurricane Ruth Trotter-Schaeffer making landfall at 6:00 p.m.

"Oh Mealie, you know my life, nothing happens for fifty-one weeks of the year, then it's all crammed into seven measly days. I've just a bit too much on my mind."

"You and Yahweh, Pet," she said kindly.

Of course, Mealie Marsh didn't know the half of it. She'd been away from Great Village, living in Montreal, when Marjory Trotter and Richard Archibald married seventeen years ago. Nor was she around six months later when the marriage failed, or seven months after that when Ruth was born. And that's where it got horribly muddled. Just two months pregnant when Richard left, Marjory hadn't bothered to tell him he was going to be a father. She'd promptly set up house with Jack Schaeffer, had her baby and settled into Deep Denial, Ontario, as if all this might never catch up with her. Richard returned to Nova Scotia none the wiser. As far as Flossy could tell, Marjory hadn't even told Ruth. She dabbed at a crumb on the table and deposited it on the plate in front of her.

It would never have occurred to a woman like Marjory Trotter that Flossy might continue to be friends with her former husband. Good friends. From the time Marjory first brought him around, a soft-spoken graduate student of literature, Richard and Flossy discovered a common interest in the Great Village poet, Elizabeth Bishop. It would prove the more enduring bond. Every few months or so he'd be back at Flossy's door, "the Bishop," as they called her, having got right under his skin, asking to see the old house where Elizabeth once lived, to walk the back roads and shores of the poet's childhood.

For years, Richard, Flossy and a handful of friends had been waving banners to bring some recognition of Bishop's importance to Nova Scotia where her work had been largely ignored. In a week's time they'd be hosting the charter meeting of The Elizabeth Bishop Society, right there in the Legion Hall, across from the church, in the heart of the village. Dozens of scholars from Canada, the United States and Brazil would be gathering to hear academic papers on Bishop's life and work. She and Richard shared the joy of fostering something they were sure would have a life well beyond them: the Elizabeth Bishop Society.

With such a cause to bind them, Flossy would have to admit that Richard had come to mean a great deal to her, whereas Marjory, whom she'd known for forty years, was a woman in perpetual disarray and much less her cup of tea. But surely it was never Flossy's place to tell him about the child. Of course she hadn't leaned on Marjory to tell him either. And if it wasn't any of her business, why was she distressed by it now? Because Richard would see her as having influence over Marjory, if anyone did. It was a muddle, a horrid muddle that Flossy'd been dragged into and there was no muddle she hated worse than somebody else's. It could twist her all up in a knot, just one more of those things you never talk about that grow the more you don't talk about them until you almost can't turn around in the room for what they've become.

Flossy had agreed to Ruth's visit last winter. That long ago it seemed unavoidable, like being invited to Christmas dinner on the first of July. Back then, it was to have been early in the summer for a week but that was before Marjory changed her plans four times and stretched it out by two more weeks. Honestly, it was easier to pin down a fruit fly. Flossy pulled a tissue from beneath her belt and blew her nose, and just her luck to end up now, of all times. She'd warned Marjory that Richard Archibald was going to be around, that she needed to set her house in order.

"Who?" she'd asked over the telephone, as if she'd never heard of him before.

"Richard, Richard Archibald, Ruth's father," Flossy said flatly.

"Oh," was all Marjory could squeak.

"You've got to talk to him, Marjory," Flossy warned. "Both of them."

"Yes, yes. Okay."

Before they'd ended the conversation, she repeated it: "Now, you'll talk to them?"

"I will, I promise, Flossy." But nobody knew her capacity to put-off better than Flossy O'Reilly. Marjory was a busy United Church minister and if a problem wasn't hitting her squarely between the eyes, it was somebody else's problem and she the happier for it. And now what was Flossy supposed to do with Ruth when Richard showed up? Hide her under the bed?

By this time, Flossy didn't even want Ruth around but she hadn't been able to bring herself to tell Marjory. It was actually Patricia Ruth Trotter-Schaeffer, every inch a young woman with a name a yard and a half long, after her grandmother and Flossy's long-dead friend, Patricia Trotter. They'd called the little one Patty from birth but when she turned fourteen she announced to anyone who'd listen that she preferred her second name, Ruth. Flossy would have to get used to that. She'd asked Mealie about it.

"But why suddenly change your name?"

"I hardly don't know," Mealie confessed. "Shows she's got pluck, I guess."

Pluck? Flossy turned around and sat down. At eighty-two, she thought she could do without pluck. She hadn't had a teenager underfoot in many years, too many in fact, and while she'd preferred them as a rule throughout the nearly five decades she'd taught at the Great Village Public School, she'd always been able to lock that chicken coop and head home at the end of each day. That was a lot of years ago. You could lose your fearlessness before teenagers, just as she'd lost her fearlessness for driving in Colchester winter storms.

Mealie Marsh was slim comfort. "You've always been good with kids. It'll be like riding a bicycle," she'd said, trying to assure her, but Flossy knew all too well that Mealie hadn't had a teenager around lately either, just one unruly goat that, when Gauguin had a mind to, effortlessly scaled Mr. McNutt's chain-link fence to dine on Flossy's peonies. Mealie sank her head back into the newspaper. She, no doubt, figured Flossy was just getting her worrying out of the way before the youngster got there, which she had to admit she often did. Now Flossy didn't know which was worse, putting up with Marjory, facing Richard or a teenager in the house. These young things could talk, when the mood struck, and question so much better than Flossy at their age, but they could be brash too, entirely lacking the calluses necessary to understand the answers.

"Mealie, are we to the age when all young people are going to hell in a handbasket?"

"A Gucci handbag, Pet. You bet we are," she said, turning a page.

"Is there anything they won't ask?"

"Are you kidding? Everything's out on the talk shows now."

"And do you suppose we understand anything any better?"

"Not that I've noticed."

Flossy's generation had been taught to mind their manners. They'd been cautioned to respect adults — even, lamentably, the undeserving ones. She wouldn't have asked a personal question if her life depended upon it. Yet she thought about how useless manners could be too, for those rare moments when a well-placed question might have lent a little understanding to some of the darkest days of her long life.

She looked across at Mealie's Oscar Wilde curled up in a patch of sunlight on the chair beside hers. She thought of Richard and sighed. Never would she have set out to hurt him, least of all Richard. How many young men and women had she sent off from her classroom over the years — some to wars, some to factories, some to the mines, some to unremarkable lives on farms along the bay, one or two to politics, an occasional fiddler? None was a patch on Richard Archibald. She was a fair teacher, had considerable fondness for her students, though always guarding the needful distance, even now. Richard was different. Not her student, technically, but his dogged dedication seemed to draw her more deeply into the study of Bishop's poetry. She'd always liked the poetry but he kept drawing her back to its richness. Even Mealie loved those evenings when Richard would come for dinner and the three of them would wax into the night about poetry and the artistic life over a bottle of red Jost. And somewhere along the line, she was sure the teaching door had revolved so that she was learning from him.

She looked through the window to the butternut tree at the back of her yard. A flock of starlings had swooped into it, setting the tree achatter like a schoolyard full of children. Soon the weather would break. In another month the tree would turn golden and, all in the course of a single day, drop every leaf to the ground. It was the only tree that did so between a sunrise and set. She felt sad and weary. "Courage, Old Thing," she thought. Maybe at this end of her life her store of courage was all used up.

She glanced at the sunflower clock on her kitchen wall. Marjory and Ruth would be well into New Brunswick. There was no escaping now and yet she still could not shake the feeling that her own final hour was fast approaching. All she wanted was a cardboard box down by the furnace to curl up in and to be left alone by everyone.

Oh, she had everything in order, had led a simple life really, with few chattels beyond her collection of books. Mealie Marsh, who was younger by five years and as reliable as a new galvanized pail, had agreed to tidy things up for her. Flossy had long ago instructed her on how to dispose of the house and goods — when dying never much entered her mind.

There were other things that disturbed her — things too frivolous to confide. Like the sardines she loved so well that had vanished from the shelves of the grocery store. Silly how she admired the self-sufficiency of that can with its key, reliable shape and size, the fish stacked end-to-end tight in it, their nutty taste, silver sheen and slivered bones spreading out on buttered toast. Other kinds couldn't compare.

"Ther' not making 'em 'nymore," Bobby McLellan had said from behind the counter of the general store, not looking at her, sitting on a stool, his eyes fixed on a television suspended somewhere above Flossy's head. He was seventeen and picking at a pimple beneath his left ear. Uneven teeth rested on his bottom lip.

"*Who* isn't making them? *God* not making the *fish*?" Flossy still had a teacherly voice that could put a knee into either end of a question.

"No," he said, "It was that Al Nino they had?" Bobby's inflection picked up the end of each phrase, as if he could drag you along like a tin can on the end of a string with undeniable questions before delivering the indisputable conclusion. "The warm water, like, in the ocean? Over there in Peru? It did in all the sardines; they barely got enough to feed themselves."

Bobby McLellan, Flossy realized, had just enough information in his head to make you stop asking questions but not quite enough to deliver any sense. She thought about those Peruvians. She didn't know all that much about them or *El Niño*, except what she'd read in *National Geographic*. She couldn't help imagining them all sitting around Machu Picchu in their colourful capes and bowler hats feasting on her sardines.

It was the same with maple walnut ice cream. It, too, had gone the way of the sardines. At the general store she could get a tightly wrapped sugar cone with a scoop of green mint chip on it or chocolate Oreo or pink black-cherry or tiger-striped orange and black licorice, but no plain, old-fashioned, maple walnut. Bobby had the same reply.

"Ther' not making it 'nymore."

"The Peruvians get that *too*?" It was a loop from which she could not extract herself. Four generations of Great Village McLellans had come to this: Good Walter McLellan's heir and only grandson sitting on a stool behind the cash register chewing gum and watching *Star Trek*. He couldn't be bothered with any more questions.

These things had vanished without warning. Not one, but both, in the same week. Of course they were small things, insignificant things to Bobby McLellan, but to her they were in the tradition of Thomas Aquinas's soul comforts, sweet pleasures to be indulged at times of extraordinary sadness, and now she felt even these enduring supports, however absurdly personal, had been knocked from beneath her. After all, there weren't so many pleasures left that she could count on.

Who could blame her for thinking that other things would soon be stripped away too, like life itself, and pimple-faced Bobby McLellan would say of her, should anyone inquire, "She was just in? Lookin' for stuff? Ther' not making 'em like her 'nymore."

You knew it was coming as surely as night follows day. Only a handful of her friends had made it beyond eighty-five and, for some of them, there wasn't a whole lot left to speak of. Hearing, sight, smell, past, present, they were all on the way out by then, often well before the candle itself. Take Mrs. John-Willy Fletcher in the nursing home over at Little Bass, where she was living out her last years. What a beauty she'd been in her day. Even into the better part of her later years, there was no one to cut a swath through a room quite like Clara Fletcher. Over in that home, they had to lead her around like a puppy, her elegant wavy hair combed up by a ruminant seventeen-year old. There were whiskers curling on her chin and a front tooth had vanished from Clara's once-radiant smile that nobody seemed in any hurry to replace. She didn't even know enough to find her way to the breakfast table. All she could do was stiver behind a walker and declare to anyone who'd listen, "Those Creelmans stole my chickens." Surely, there were worse things in life than death.

Flossy could see the top of Mealie's curly grey head above the jagged newspaper edge. She was gone for now, in her own world, having finally let go of the rope that was teasing Flossy out of her private swamp this morning. For the next ten minutes or so, Mealie's coffee would get cold as she finished reading the paper. Most days of the year, the two of them sat across from each other at the kitchen table like this, sometimes later in the morning, sometimes earlier, depending on the slant of the light, Mealie being essentially photoperiodic. They knew each other better than a lot of old married couples, their comings and goings, what could raise chuckles as well as hackles, but there was so much they didn't know too. So much never got spoken even in the safe orbit of a generous heart like Mealie's. She'd never told her about Richard and Ruth, couldn't bring herself to now.

Flossy thought of her brother Thomas again. She glanced up to the ceiling, almost as if he were still upstairs in that bed he lay in for twenty-four dismal years. If he'd died that day, cutting marsh hay along the south field, you could have let him go, given him a Christian burial, mourned, then somehow found your way onward. He didn't, and so from season to season and year to year she'd coddled the hope that he might one day find the will to drag himself out of that bed and resume his life as it was before.

Thomas was so much like those things locked away inside that never get talked about. You couldn't ever give them a proper burial; they weren't really living, but neither were they really dead.

II

Flossy o'reilly and oscar wilde lifted and turned their heads in unison, heavy eyes blinking to make out the shadow moving behind the screen door.

She quickly opened *The Diary of Virginia Woolf Volume V* that had fallen shut in front of her and pulled her shoulders back. She didn't like being caught dozing.

"Ah, it's you. Come in, come in," she said, pulling herself up straight and swinging her legs out from under the table. Jimmy O'Reilly was already pushing the door in with his shoulder.

"Little pair of *mackerels* there for you and Mealie, for *supper*," he said, bustling past her and dropping the fish wrapped in newspaper into the sink. Jimmy never bothered to say hello. "Looks like *Bessy's car* in over at *Lottie's* this morning," he added, motioning up the street with his head before wiping fishy hands on Flossy's clean towel. "*Passed* the *Grue* lad there going *up the road* like a bat outta *Helsinki.*"

With Flossy's declining hearing, Jimmy had worked out his own way of talking to her with a series of barked nouns and verbs. Three or four mornings a week he lumbered into her

kitchen like this, letting anything that fluttered through his mind
run right out of his mouth. He knew everyone along both shores
who was dying, gravely ill, chronically ill or mildly under the
weather and with each visit he provided an update.

From where she stood on one side of her brother, Flossy
watched a brown line of fish blood gather along the edge of the
Truro News and drip into the drain. She swallowed and looked
away. "That'll suit me fine. Thank you Jimmy," she smiled.

"I don't see Bunny *Patriquin* getting *through* the *night*," he
said, scratching the back of his neck. "The *daughter's back*,
anyway. So."

Mealie had already gone off to the studio, leaving the newspaper neatly folded on the table. She liked Jimmy well enough,
in small doses, but liked him even better when she missed his
morning rounds.

"He's a dear man who fills my head with noise," she said of
him, in confidence, her half glasses swinging from a chain not
unlike the one that kept track of Flossy's bathtub plug. "And it's
about as memorable as the inside of a bottom drawer." She
didn't have to tell Flossy. Mealie went to some lengths to protect the noise in her head and Flossy admired it. She often felt
like airing her own brain out on the clothesline beside the sour
dishcloth after her brother left. It wasn't that his chatter was mali-
cious or hurtful; he drew his own line there. Rather, it was simply
peppered with the borrowed troubles of people up and down the
shore or things not worth thinking about by tomorrow morning.

Enough. Surely she had enough scratching at the back door
of her mind without adding the arthritic joints and gas pains of
half of Colchester County. She had Marjory and Ruth — on their
way through New Brunswick by now; Richard Archibald — who
she dare not even *think* about; and scarcely one hundred pages

left in the last of Virginia Woolf's diaries. She could already see the clouds gathering, Bloomsbury disintegrating, Lytton's death, and then Roger's not two years later.

She pulled her thoughts back to Jimmy standing in the middle of her kitchen. Flossy would take the mackerel over to Mealie later. She wished Jimmy would think to drop it off himself but he was about as routinized as a Holstein cow. It would never dawn on him in a month of Sundays, though he'd drive by the house twice.

Pulling his green John Deere hat back from his forehead with one hand and his glasses off with the other, Jimmy O'Reilly wiped the sweat gathering on his brow with the sleeve of his shirt. "It's a *steamer* out there," he puffed. "I'm *sweatin'* like a *hen hauling hay.* You'll wanna get y'r *errands finished up early.*" He pushed the glasses back in place and hung the hat over the handle of the door.

There was a time when Flossy's brother would have had to take the hat off just to get through the doorway. He'd been a barrel of a man in his younger days but he was much smaller now. His wife Noreen had put him on some new diet but instead of looking better for the fifty-two pounds he'd shed, Flossy thought her brother looked rather pinched. The centre of gravity of this smaller Jimmy had somehow shifted so that he led less with the chest and a little more with his head sunk into stooped shoulders as if he were some old sweater left on a coat rack for three weeks. Everything about him was shrinking, with the exception of his nose and earlobes, and when she caught him thinking these days she noticed he'd developed a habit of chewing his tongue on the left side of his mouth.

"*Cars* on the *bridge* …" He was talking again.

"On the …?"

"*Bridge.*"

She shook her head.

"*Tourist, yesterday* from New Brunswick thought it was a *two-lane.*" They'd seen this before. The steel bridge that crossed the Great Village River in the centre of town gave the right of way to traffic coming from Glenholme but every now and again a vehicle from the other direction, impatient or distracted, ignored the yield sign and bolted across.

"And?" She waited.

"*Bumper* crunch," he said. "*Tow-truck* took the one away, so it did."

She shook her head. "Nobody's a minute to spare."

He shuffled a couple of steps in one direction as he spoke and a couple in another. Flossy sat down. Fifty-two pounds lighter or not, her brother still had the agility of a juvenile elephant in her kitchen. She pulled her feet in.

Jimmy was her only other regular visitor. Often, like today, he brought along the catch of the weir he still kept out on Cobequid Bay or sometimes the abundance of a kitchen garden he cultivated behind the retirement bungalow he'd built on the edge of the O'Reilly farm where they'd grown up together. Each year he put in enough vegetables to feed two shifts of Stanfield's underwear factory right through to November and, though he and his wife Noreen were the only two sharing the house now, Jimmy couldn't give up what he'd done every year for the better part of fifty years. Consequently, he spent his late-summer days carting Sobeys bags full of onions, beans, tomatoes and cucumbers to her and all his neighbours.

Once in the spring and again in the fall, for about a week at a time, Mealie and Jimmy would arrive in Flossy's kitchen simultaneously, he marshalled by the clock and she entirely by the sun.

She imagined the threshold of her house as an equator across which these two great planets passed. Flossy much preferred them one at a time. Jimmy was as predictable as Mealie was not. Taking her leave this morning, not twenty minutes before Jimmy pulled into the laneway, Flossy had noticed Mealie's ankle red and swollen as she walked out the door, though she wasn't limping. It was on the tip of her tongue to call her back, but once again Flossy'd been snagged by the past and her thoughts tangled like fishing line.

In that instant, it was her mother's ankle she'd seen, the exact same one, the left, thickly inflamed like that. It so surprised her to have the memory douse her concentration, even to realize she'd entirely forgotten her mother's feet, that Mealie was already halfway home before she'd had her wits about her. Was it phlebitis? Why hadn't she said something?

"They're saying *Bertie's burn pile* caught fire at *Old Barns* on Tuesday," Jimmy interrupted her thoughts. "Two *fire trucks* to put it out. Was I telling ya?"

He had told her. Twice. On Wednesday. She held up two fingers.

"Heh, heh." Jimmy looked down. He didn't mind being caught out by her. There was a seven-year gap between them and while it hadn't meant a lot for a lot of years in the middle of their lives, you can bet they were each aware of it now. The fact was, Jimmy wasn't losing much more than any of the rest of them. They were all quite capable of launching entire conversations these days without offering the listener the sliver of a clue as to what they were talking about.

"*You know* that guy who played alongside the other one in the movie with the woman who always had the hair? Oh, *you* remember him." That was Verna Fisher when they'd bumped into each other at the general store last Wednesday, badgering Flossy as if the lapse had somehow been hers. She looked back at Jimmy prattling on.

"*Fire department* doesn't take kindly to old farmers *setting fires* without a *permit*," he said.

"And old farmers don't see why they need a permit to do what they've always done."

He nodded. "You know, he's *bad crippled* with the *arthritis*." Jimmy stroked his chin. "Couldn't *chase a fire* if it was *warming* his *tea*."

"What in heaven's name is anybody setting a fire for in this heat?" She heard the crimp of impatience in her own voice. Her hearing wasn't all that bad — she had a perfectly good set of hearing aids collecting dust on the top of the refrigerator. There just didn't seem to be much of interest to listen to anymore.

Jimmy didn't answer, just raised his eyebrows and nodded his head.

"They're getting *showers* into *New Brunswick* today but it's not likely to get this far. *Crops'r* gonna be ... *useless*," he muttered, as much fret as report. He pushed his glasses back against his face.

Her brother had belatedly taken to wearing those glasses and for some reason didn't think to buy the light, fashionable wire frames. He'd got the heavy Onassis-black that blared out in front of his sun-browned face and white hair. These he worried away at, constantly pulling them off and shoving them back on again so that they were always hopelessly smudged with fingerprints and seldom sitting squarely on his face.

"*Nothin'* in the forecast," chuffed out of him. Jimmy didn't have any crops in, now that his daughter and her husband were working the farm. Regardless, he followed the weather reports and market updates scrupulously and never could get over worrying about other people's corn grown barely to his shoulder, browning from the hot winds, that should have been towering green and gold-tasselled by now.

Flossy watched her brother fumble with the glasses while getting himself a cup of coffee. She kept an eye on him to capture the crumbs of conversation. He took a mug from the draining rack by the sink, instead of the cupboard. To be sure it was clean, he yanked the glasses off his face, clutching one lens and using the other as a magnifying glass.

"*Sandpipers* are *back*," he said, over his shoulder. "Golly, they're a *spectacle*."

The coffee poured, he made for the table, slopping some over the side of the cup that he smeared across the floor with his boot. More dribbled onto the table that Flossy tried to ignore as he wiped at it with the side of his hand. He tipped the back of the chair up slightly so that Oscar Wilde plopped to the floor, sat down, hunched over his coffee and began to stir.

Ka-klink, pause. Ka-klink, pause. Ka-klink, Jimmy could sit and stir for half an hour uninterrupted, staring into space. It was the only thing that quieted him.

She waited. The clock ticked on the wall above his head to the rhythm of the spoon. Ka-klink, tick. Ka-klink, tick. Here they sat across from each other, the last of the O'Reillys, the survivors of an entire generation washed to the narrows of the twenty-first century, without a thing of any substance to say.

Jimmy shuffled his feet under the table. She tucked hers beneath the chair. He took a sip of his coffee, reached for the sugar bowl and placed most of a heaping teaspoon into his mug. What fell to the table he scooped to the floor then stirred some more. She glanced at the clock; it was eight ten on a Friday morning and he was still sitting in her kitchen. Must be something on his mind. Flossy waited. She always waited. The minute she asked him a question, Jimmy'd clam up.

Maybe Noreen was after him again about settling up the farm, which their mother had left to the two of them. He had never been able to buy Flossy out and she'd never wanted him to. She had no need of the farm now anyway, had her own little house in town and was perfectly comfortable. Though she had given him every assurance that her half would go to his girls after she was gone, Noreen wanted the property signed over to Jimmy instead. That way they, that is to say she, could decide who would get what. Every now and again, when her sister-in-law couldn't find anything else to natter about, Jimmy'd be dispatched to "talk some sense into that sister of yours."

This morning, she had quite enough on her plate. Besides, she didn't like Noreen hurrying her out one bit. It was on the tip of her tongue to say "George and Fred'll be looking for you," but she didn't want him to take offence. Not now. Especially not now when she might be on her own last legs.

Noreen made no bones about their daughters being a contest of disappointments, would go long spells not talking to one or the other of them. It had occurred to Flossy more than once that Jimmy was secretly pleased about the way she'd set out her affairs. He couldn't be seen to disagree with Noreen — knowing full well which side his bread was buttered on — but he'd always leaned towards even-handedness where the girls were concerned and never put all that much effort into changing Flossy's mind.

"Green-eyed monster," Mealie'd declare from behind the *Chronicle Herald* when Flossy'd express bewilderment over Noreen. With the bright quick eyes of a small bird, Mealie Marsh missed absolutely nothing. For sure, Flossy's sister-in-law didn't approve of Jimmy's morning visits. She put up with them because she was a late riser and grateful to have that stirring-spoon as far away from her own kitchen as possible. He was one of those men who, if they ever stopped working, would have little to occupy their days except to tag along behind their wives.

This week Noreen was in the Valley, had gone after lunch on Wednesday to help move an older brother into an apartment. She seldom left Jimmy alone for more than the time it took to make a trip into Truro. In her absence, Jimmy was going a bit to seed. His white hair was a tatty bird's nest at the back of his head, his shirtfront flecked with food and a slightly sour smell was just beginning to reach Flossy's shores. She had a foreboding that he was hoping to tag along behind her today. That was all she needed with beds to be made, groceries to get and catastrophe looming.

He scratched the lug of his ear. "When was it *mother died* there?"

"Mother?" Flossy cocked her head. Had she heard?

"Yuh, mother. When'd she *die?*"

Jimmy arrived punctually at seven forty-five each morning and was gone again before the eight o'clock news, which he listened to in his truck as he drove to the general store. There he'd warm the counter with a couple of other regulars trading news like schoolboys' marbles. Not today. George and Fred would be craning their necks up the road looking for him.

"Fifty-two," she said.

"Fifty-*two*, was it? I see." From some distant corridor of his mind he clutched at a memory of that day. He pulled the glasses off and set them on the table. "I remember it was some *cold. January* ..."

"February, Jimmy. The tenth."

"I should write this ..." He tucked his chin in and from the left pocket of his brown-checked shirt pulled out a wad of papers half an inch thick. This was Jimmy's filing cabinet. Twenty years ago he carried a pack of Export 'A' cigarettes there and before that a pouch of Daily Mail tobacco. Now it was a bundle of folded, bent and ragged bits of paper, receipts and business cards he never took the time to sort. With his head stretched back he shuffled the papers, holding them at a distance to catch the sunlight that reached in over his left shoulder. The glasses sat on the table in front of him.

"What about *Thomas?*" he asked, pulling one hip forward and plunging his hand into the pocket of his pants.

"Come again?"

With his crooked index finger, he poked through a fistful of twine, bolts, nails and chaff in the other hand. Flossy watched various loose bits drift to the floor as Jimmy paused to look up at her. "*Thomas,*" he repeated, before extracting a stub of yellow pencil from the jumble that he tucked away again. He began to write on the back of a business card.

"What about Thomas?" she asked.

"When was it he *got away* from us?" He scratched the inside of his ear with the pointed end of the pencil.

"Mighty sakes, Jimmy, what are you wanting all this for?"

He pulled the pencil out and wiped it on his trousers. "Oh, it's *Becky's* asking. They had me for *dinner* last night," he said, scribbling something onto the paper. "She wants to know *when we all died.*"

Flossy shook her head. Dear Lord. Becky was the new wife of Jimmy's grandson, his second run at marital blitz, as Mealie was so fond of saying. (The first hadn't got out of the starting gate.) She was a bouncy addition to the family, girlish for a twenty-five year old, with teddy bears dangling from her purse, who was making a point of "getting to know all the family." Flossy wasn't the least bit interested in being known by Becky.

"Was it fifty-*two*? Thomas?"

"The first time or the second?" she asked.

"The *which*?"

"First or second time?"

He looked at her. His mouth was slightly open and he pulled his bottom lip in and swallowed before answering, "*Last* ..."

"Eighth of September, fifty-one. Do you not remember any of these things?"

He shook his head before writing the date carefully on the card. Noticing the glasses, he picked them up and put them on. "What was it *got* him?"

"Pneumonia."

"Pneu ... monia," he repeated as he wrote. "How *old?* " he slurped his coffee.

"Forty. What's Becky want with all this anyway?" she grumbled.

"Oh, I can't be sure, ee-unh ..." Jimmy stalled. She watched him pull on the isthmus of skin between his nostrils, his sky-blue eyes staring off. The glasses were tilted towards his right eyebrow.

"Jimmy?" she said softly, after a couple of minutes.

"Eh?" He pulled the hand away from his face and looked over at her.

"You were saying?"

"You which?"

"Becky ..."

"Yeah, yeah, she wants to do the *family history*." He went back to stirring his coffee.

What Jimmy could have said and didn't was that Becky should let sleeping dogs lie. He ran the back of his fingers along a patchily shaven face after another few minutes of stirring and looked directly at his sister. "Don't know what *good it'll do*. So." Flossy smiled sadly. She understood. You could get too far along your own dark road to want to slog through any part of the past again. These two never talked about it. What for? Even if they'd grown up under the same roof and shared a long stretch of misery, they'd hardly sit around and chat about it now. Who among their friends sat yammering of the good old Depression? Of course, Jimmy'd gone off to the war and, no doubt, had a whole lot more he wasn't interested in chatting about.

Becky wasn't from those parts, hadn't a clue what surface she was scratching. Her new husband, Jimmy's grandson, was barely able to scrabble through the occasional dust-up with his own parents, much less the demons of an earlier generation. Besides, Becky wasn't interested in detail, and dates were simple enough to give, really. Dates were only squares on the calendar that spoke not at all of the clutter of affliction bunched up behind them. All Becky wanted was to make a chart of dates to frame and give back to them all at Christmas. Give Becky a date and she'd find a match in her mental storehouse, "Hey, that's my *sister's* birthday," she'd beam, a whisker short of jumping up and licking Flossy's face.

She glanced out the window. September 8, the day Thomas died, for the last time. Those sweet anonymous days that flutter by year-on-end, then once they're smudged with death, you can't pass another one carefree for trying. She looked back across at her brother. He was gazing at the table. She thought of her own vivid recollection catching her, not an hour earlier, of the day Thomas went to bed. Jimmy hadn't even asked about their father and she didn't offer. They never spoke of the day the date, month or year of their father's death. It was their secret, a solemn pact between brother and sister that stretched back nearly seventy years. Did he ever let his stirring-mind stray back to those times, step back inside the events of those few dates etched on the O'Reilly granite out there in the Mahon cemetery?

"Get the goddamn into the goddamned boat." Her father's voice could clutch like an undertow. She held still, resisting, the memory seemingly alive beneath her skin. She saw the face twisted with rage, his hair blown like a rag in the wind, and little Jimmy shivering in the waiting boat. Did Jimmy ever have that face rise up from his early morning dreams? Her chest thumped. She pushed her cup and the memory away, turning instead to her brother stirring his coffee in a stupor across the table.

Ka-klink, pause. *Ka-klink*, pause. She had an urge to ask him, "What is it you think about all day, Jimmy?" Maybe he had no real memory of their father — he'd only been six when William died. Did Jimmy ever think of their mother, Thomas, all the water under their family's sorry bridge?

"Don't worry, Jimmy," she said to him. "Becky'll be on to something else next week, quilting or candles." If there was one thing she could count on, it was the short attention span of these young things. "We'll send her one of those calligraphy sets they have with all the pens, anonymously. That should do it."

"I told her she should come *talk* to *you*," he said, half a grin curling up his face.

"Thanks a bunch."

Without warning he scraped the chair across the floor and was on his feet. He tucked the papers into his pocket, drank back the rest of his well-stirred coffee in three long gulps. She followed him to the door, gave him a reassuring pat on the arm.

"We'll just do like Mealie," she said to him as he punched his fist into the round of his cap. "She says a little bit of dementia can go a long way at our age."

He gave a chuckle, turned and, with a hand on the latch, looked back.

"Say, you won't guess who I seen *yesterday* over in Dickies."

"Who was that?"

"*Bubba McKeen.* Ya '*member* her?"

It took Flossy a second. "Bubba. Yes, yes, of course."

"She's down in *Parrsboro. Married* a *Trenholm* from Amherst way. She ended up a *schoolteacher* too. They've a little *place* down there. She's put on a *few stone* since she lived in these parts, so she has." Jimmy tumbled on.

"I haven't thought of Barbara McKeen in years," Flossy said wistfully. Jimmy would think this news would please her. She folded her arms across her chest.

"I was *buying* chicken feed and she *spoke* to me," Jimmy said. "I'd *never* have *recognized* her. Funny, eh?" he snapped his fingers, "*turn up* just like that after so many years?" as he stepped outside and let the door close behind him. Flossy stood and watched her brother through the screen hobble down the steps. Logie, his little sheepdog, was bouncing from window to window in the truck. Jimmy was stiff this morning, no doubt his arthritis was acting up though he never complained. He put his hat back on, rocking it on his head a couple of times to scratch or get it in just the right spot, as he gazed out over Hustler's Hill towards the church steeple before climbing slowly into his black pickup. He backed the truck onto the grass. His head turned slowly towards her, he tipped a finger above the steering wheel and drove off.

Barbara McKeen. Didn't she have enough on her mind? She watched her brother disappear down the road. He hit the pothole in front of Mealie's. Jimmy never watched the road. A cloud passed between her and the sun. What if this were her last chance to say something to him? She had an impulse to step out and wave. He'd never see.

They'd always called her Bubba. As a little girl, unable to master all the syllables of her name, it was what she'd called herself. Bubba, Patricia and Flossy were inseparable throughout school.

"*You knew*," Bubba flung the words at Flossy. It was the last thing she'd ever said to her.

Yes, she'd known. All Great Village had known. All but Bubba.

Sometimes Jimmy had an uncanny way of rubbing salt into a wound. Here she was with Richard Archibald thrumming her conscience, Marjory and the girl on their way, Virginia Woolf splintering apart and Jimmy turns Bubba McKeen up in her soup. Of course, Jimmy would have been too much younger to know of the falling out, the unique cruelties of schoolgirls. Why did people not believe that these things were none of Flossy's business? She did not make the secrets. She'd only kept them.

Well, there wasn't much she could do about Bubba. That was a long time ago. You could spend the entire second half of a life turning over the mistakes of the first if you thought there was any use in it or you had nothing better to do. Besides, Bubba hadn't stopped talking to the entire village; she'd singled Flossy out for that.

But what was she going to do about Richard? Should she call him, try to explain? And would she just leave Jimmy like that? There'd be no time to talk with the youngster here, three full weeks of someone under her feet. Did Flossy have three weeks left? It seemed too long a time to wait on the one hand, but far too short to sort out the messes of eighty-two years. She looked at the clock.

"Ridiculous," her Queen Mab voice blurted out loud. "Save your breath to cool your porridge." This voice — which sounded altogether too much like her mother's — had served Flossy well over the years, helped her sift the utterly useless from the faintly possible in her many decades of teaching and dealing with unreasonable parents. Queen Mab may even be serving her right now but Flossy was more acutely aware that she might be using up ends, her remaining few days and hours. She couldn't fritter them away. Would she go without a last word to Jimmy?

On balance, he'd been a good brother. She could say that with sincerity. It was no small thing to take his sister's part over Noreen. There wasn't a lick of malice to him. Lots couldn't say that about their brothers. Perhaps Jimmy was the kind of man never able to say the soft word but always longing to hear it.

She watched the taillights of his truck flash at the intersection as he touched the brakes and rolled around the corner onto the highway.

Queen Mab reminded her that Jimmy, like so many others she knew, much preferred to talk about everyone else's troubles. Flossy looked at the clock again. She should take Mealie's fish to her, though she didn't like to interrupt her studio time. She'd leave her a note. Maybe go find Jimmy. After. And Richard? She must call him. On the back of the envelope for the electricity bill she wrote:

Lady Partridge,

Jimmy left a mackerel for you. I've put it in the fridge.
His Lordship Wilde is still in my kitchen.

Q.Mab

SHE UNWRAPPED THE FISH AND placed Mealie's in a plastic bag. At the last minute, she put hers in as well. She dearly wished Jimmy's weir would be washed away in a rip-roaring storm; she was so tired of fish. Mealie'd be grateful enough; she was fond of mackerel and could eat twice as much as Flossy. As she walked down the hill towards her friend's house, she noticed Mr. McNutt's blinds all down, wisely hunkered in against the heat.

Inside Mealie's kitchen the air conditioner blew cold air from a box propped in the window and stuffed around the edges with cardboard. It made it harder for her eyes to adjust in the dark room. She put the fish in the fridge and tucked the envelope beneath a teapot on the counter among numerous pots and pans, dirty dishes, jars filled with paint brushes, empty bottles, milk containers, squeezed tea bags and cans. There was something sticky beneath her foot. Without thinking, she lifted the lid of the teapot. Inside, a bag floated on brown liquid with a thumbnail-sized patch of mould attached.

Flossy stilled an impulse to rinse the pot and tidy the counter. Mealie, after all, lived as she wanted. A binge cleaner, she'd tidy between spurts of artistic inspiration, going at the mess at five some morning and having it all cleared out, the floors polished, by noon. Flossy's own tolerance for chaos was much lower. A crumb-sweeper, she did a little every day, enough to keep the kitchen tidy at least. The rest she hardly noticed.

She could smell fresh paint and something else she couldn't put a finger on. As she turned to go, her eyes traced the wainscot and counters for Mealie's mouse.

"Oh," she stopped. Taking hesitant steps towards a canvas that sat propped against the wall atop a small cabinet, Flossy reached a hand out. This was new. She leaned closer, near enough to touch the picture's upper edge. She lifted her glasses to look closer still. Mealie had said she was working in acrylic and wax but Flossy hadn't seen the results.

The painting was an earthy abstract of olive and burnt sienna dragged and pitted across two-thirds of the canvas, with a suggestion of turquoise and peach peering from beneath. A red-orange horizon brightened the upper left-hand corner, then farther into the picture's maw was a volcanic energy, aswirl with smears of orange, ochre and blood-red paint. The olive reached into it, followed by a stippling of purple-blue. Flossy walked around to the other side. Mealie was calling these canvases her "Remnants." From every direction the painting was textured beauty, the kind of picture she thought a person could live with in one room for the better part of a lifetime. Her hand longed to stroke it like the irresistible head of a child.

She should go. Mealie hadn't shown her this one yet and Flossy felt intrusive, as if she'd been reading her friend's diary left open on the kitchen table, though the two women had come and gone from each other's house over the years as freely as Oscar Wilde. She stared at the picture. Mealie was working at fever pitch these days, getting ready for a show in October. She never talked about the actual work but she'd mentioned yesterday that several pictures had been hung out to dry. Always a good sign.

Stepping back outside, the heat was twice as oppressive, the light too white for the eyes. She watched the ground walking back to her own place. Beneath her feet the grass felt brittle, as if life itself had contracted and was simply waiting out the heat. Surely it would break soon.

She collected her things from the house and drove the slim stretch of road to the highway watching for Jimmy. Mealie's picture, still in her mind, brightened her mood, gave her that extra dash of optimism to go find him.

Stopped, waiting for a car at the intersection, she could see that Jimmy's truck was already gone. He'd be on his way home or down at the weir, depending on the tide. Her guests would arrive in about nine hours. She decided to go to Truro first, get all her errands out of the way, and try him at the shore later in the day. No point in chasing him now with so much to do. He might be there later. Then she'd call Richard. Get everything in order. It would be a relief by the water. She could always think at the shore.

III

BY MID-AFTERNOON, FLOSSY O'REILLY COULD DRAW A SATIS-fied line through each of the chores on her list: kitchen swept, beds made, groceries in, flowerpots watered.

With a good three hours to go before her company arrived, all that was left was to find Jimmy and call Richard, which she was studiously putting off. Then wait. Something she'd never done all that well.

"Out you go Oscar; let's get some air in our pants." She grabbed her straw hat and walking stick, nudged the cat outside and headed for the car again. A cicada whined somewhere in the butternut tree. The old Valiant was steamy inside. She opened both front windows and, as she turned the key, the engine jostled to attention.

Jimmy had given her the rusting '75 Valiant five years ago. He loved that old car too much to send it to the scrapyard where it properly belonged. She'd had to learn to drive a standard gear-shift at seventy-eight. Learn to drive, more precisely, though some would have winked behind her back at that notion. It didn't bother Flossy; mostly she never shifted out of second anyway.

A small tank on wheels, Falstaff, as she'd christened the car, was visibly crumbling in the body but staunchly reliable in the soul. In a bitter nor'easter it would start like a John Deere tractor. She patted the dash affectionately. The car lurched towards the intersection of the main street where Flossy turned right and rumbled over the metal bridge crossing the Great Village River.

The first house beyond was where dotty old Uncle Amon had died. She'd taken an early disliking to him. "Our Jimmy, here," Uncle Amon, on the O'Reilly side, would announce with a tight grin to a room full of people, his lower teeth having to hold his upper plate in place, "always lands with his arse in the buther," slapping the silent boy on the back, "don't ya Jimmy?"

It was so, but Flossy could always sense Jimmy's silent humiliation. Her younger brother had been the O'Reillys' miracle boy, the bystander to every one of the tragedies of their lives yet always himself squeaking through. At least — Flossy glanced in the rearview mirror at the cars in a tight line behind her — at least from what anyone could tell. She pulled over to let them pass.

Clusters of clapboard houses, a gas station, two general stores and the fire department all seemed Sunday-morning sleepy, though it was Friday afternoon. This kind of heat, Flossy knew, could imprison people in their homes every bit as much as three feet of snow. Most of the houses were painted white, though some of the younger people were branching into sage and taupe. (Mealie's influence there. She herself would have said green and brown.) They faced each other across the main paved road that cut an elbow through the village, a country highway known as Route 2 on maps but more commonly referred to locally by whatever lay beyond: the Road to Bass River or Economy, even Parrsboro, a town forty miles away. It was the same with other streets. Everyone called the newly named Lornevale Road, any one of the more familiar Old Post Road, the Scrabble Hill Road or the Cumberland Road for the county beyond Colchester.

It was on this road, a century earlier, that the much-loved Hiram Hyde raced his stagecoach along the mail route to Amherst. The man was so affable, and the letters he delivered so cherished, that for half a century babies would be named for him all up and down that road and clear back to Halifax.

Cheerful red geraniums poured from window boxes. Planters hung from porches. Idle swings awaited cool, unhurried evenings when men and women might rest and watch the neighbours strolling past, though few ever did. Many of the houses distinguished themselves with a modest splashing of paint here and there: a bold raspberry door, dainty lemon-yellow window frames, a royal-blue rocking chair unmoving on a porch.

Outside the Esso station loudspeakers broadcast a woman's sad song over the whine of a steel guitar. Across the street was the Bulmer house where Elizabeth Bishop once lived. Poor old Mrs. Bulmer wouldn't have liked that country music serenading her day and night. You could be thankful for some people that they were long dead and gone.

The old clapboard United Church with a huge black spire sat unavoidably in the centre of the village where the main road jogged a dogleg left. You had to turn one way or the other around it or you'd end up in the narthex. Flossy could see the spire from her kitchen window. In fact, on a close summer Sunday with the church doors open, she could hear the Chief Gougers singing "How Great Thou Art," the soloist's warble swooping across the Great Village River and up Hustler's Hill to their houses along this side of the Station Road, "Now sing my so-o-oul ..."

If she happened to be pottering in the garden just then, she would shortly after hear Mealie's windows slamming. No other tune, she'd said, could get stuck on a loop in her brain quite like that one. "I'd much prefer to hum the dial tone."

That church, St. James United, its sermons and seasons, the choir, Reverend Mumford, the literary group that met there each month, these had marked and measured Flossy's days, weeks and years for the better part of her young adult life. They'd meant nearly everything to her at one time, and now almost nothing at all. The lofty spire held not much more significance than Rick Moore's brand new grain silos, a mark on the horizon to take her physical bearings on a cloudy day. Sin and salvation seemed the senseless preoccupations of a whole other lifetime. How strange to have got so out of the habit of such a habit.

So out of the habit that she'd left Mealie explicit instructions that there'd be no service when she died. Nothing. Flossy wasn't going to let any minister who didn't even know her by name have the last word over her life. She thought of David as her foot came off the gas. When the car chugged she blinked to attention as if to reverse the memory. She pressed the gas again, refusing to wallow in that sad marsh today. Someone behind scolded her with a blast of the horn for dawdling. She was always getting that.

Beyond the church, she met two other cars and a lumber truck. When houses gave way to farmland again, she slowed to turn south off the highway and drove the gravel road towards Spencer's Point. She parked the car at the dead end, high up on the cliff overlooking the bay, and got out. She scanned the shore down towards Jimmy's weir. No sign of him. She lifted her head and took a deep breath of salty air.

Back at the car, she grabbed her walking stick and hat and made her way east along the red sand and gravel roadway that cut through the orchard of the old Spencer farm and curled down towards the shore. It was not a real road; it was truck ruts with weeds growing up between them, what the locals' pickups carved out of the sandy soil on their way to the water's edge for beer and a weekend bonfire.

A jackrabbit jumped out and bounced off in front of her as if an unsteady old woman were any threat to such sturdy legs. A dozen decrepit apple trees on either side of the narrow track, some cleaved by lightning down the middle of the trunk, others with fallen branches, seemed to all but bow as she walked past, like a band of gouty Arthurian knights pointing the way to the water's edge. In spite of their want of care, the old trees were thick with apples, dotting the grass below them and spilling onto the roadway: russets, yellow transparents, Bishop Pippins, all pocked with rusty wormholes and crawling with wasps. She could smell their overripe sweetness.

Flossy couldn't come by here without looking over to where the Spencer house once stood. Momentarily overcome by weariness, she stepped from the road then through the tall grass to a tree stump out of the sun not far from what must have been a front porch before a wayward cigarette made kindling of it all. Everything took so much more effort these days. She sat down and closed her eyes to catch her breath.

The old Spencer sisters came to mind like heat radiating up from the parched earth, as did Palmeter's Ghost who, some said, inhabited the house after the ladies were taken away. Flossy, of course, didn't believe in ghosts but there were, lamentably, some things the memory didn't have sense enough to put out. How long had that house been gone? A dozen years or more? She couldn't be sure. Time had got away from her, and there was Palmeter taking up precious memory when whole decades seemed razed altogether, like the house that once stood right there.

Dried raspberry canes arched aimlessly above the tall grass.

The leaves and browned seed heads at the top of a spindly old lilac cluster that once thrived outside the Spencer sisters' kitchen window leaned over the burnt-out hole as if to peer into all that was left of a life. A cabbage butterfly drifted from goldenrod to fleabane and back. Seated there, Flossy surveyed the scene, a perfect study of nature reclaiming its own. If she hadn't already known precisely where the house sat, she'd have missed it altogether. There was no scrap of paper, wood or metal left, no teacup shard or broken plate poking from the earth, no rusted enamel pots or cans, nothing to kick or dig out with the heel. There were only botanical clues, remnants of domestication scattered here and there, the lilac, rhubarb to the west, the yew and mock orange already reclining over the cliff.

Flossy got to her feet again and walked slowly downhill through a wooded area with a thick canopy of maple, yellow birch, larch and poplar. Beyond it, at the water's edge, she squinted out across the bay, a hand shading her eyes. Here was an old friend, a place open and predictable to gather some perspective and think things through. She looked in both directions up and down the shore again. Alone, with the tide rolling in, she leaned on the walking stick, her feet planted solidly at the water's edge, a speck of navy in a straw hat beside a vast indifference.

This was her place of rest now, in spite of the O'Reillys' long genealogy of sorrow here. She inhaled the smell of fishy waters, the most primal smell she knew. Some mornings when fog closed down the village she could smell the bay's breath through her open bedroom window. It was easy to think nothing ever happened out here, though in fact the bay and its tides were a force of unending change.

From the time her grandparents settled along here, these waters were the only means of getting to places near and far: Old Barns,

Halifax, Boston, England. It was the age of sail and you were a man blessed to get government pay as a Waiter and Watcher of Tides. Nearly a hundred great ships were built and launched from Great Village throughout the last century to sail as far away as India and Australia. They ferried passengers and goods back and forth from this very spot to all parts of Europe, Nova Scotia and the Boston States. It had even been one of the Cobequid captains who'd taken Stanley to find Livingston in the heart of Africa. The Great Village port bustled with commerce along natural north-south lines, people leaving to find work — young women as domestics and men as labourers — some returning home to marry and others to die. Vessels picking their way into this port brought manufactured goods, kerosene, molasses, rum, even exotic spices from as far away as the Caribbean Islands and loaded up again with cargo of iron ore, coal or lumber for the areas all along the Eastern seaboard.

It was all gone now, save a single line of ragged, bleached timbers where once a wharf had been. It always reminded Flossy of a prehistoric creature that washed up there and breathed its last, leaving behind the melancholy grin of a lower jawbone.

She looked behind again to the land. The cliffs were pocked with bank swallows' nests. For the better part of a century the Spencer family had kept a light right up there, above where Flossy stood, above the swallows. At first it was only a lantern set out on a post each night of the year by Afford Spencer, the son of a sea captain, to warn ships that here the land jutted out into the bay and guide his father home. Later a kerosene lamp was built into a widow's walk at the top of the house and Afford's daughters continued to keep it lit every night of the year for another forty years after their father died.

A century of nights: those poor old ducks guarding the lamp

through blizzard and gale, in sickness and health, awake all hours, watching, watching, never letting it go out, so steadfast and duty-driven. Even as they began to creak and dodder themselves, they kept that lamp lit, though ship travel had all but died, old women guarding a flame for a lover who'd long ago forgotten them. When it all got beyond them and the light, at last, went out, it was all let go, the dredging and navigational aids. All of it.

Nowadays you'd be lucky to see a boat of any kind out here from one year to the next, not a sunfish, kayak or motorboat hauled from Maine or Ontario by tourists buying up waterfront property who knew none of the dangers of those Fundy tides moving restlessly in and out of Cobequid Bay. After centuries of living along this shore, most people around there still didn't look to the water as a place of any amusement.

Everything the Spencers had dedicated their lives to, their vast fidelity, had been quietly overtaken as sailing ships and steamers were replaced by roads, bridges and a railway that made effortless what had once been near-impossible overland travel.

She looked for Jimmy again, shading her eyes in the direction of the sun. He often ran Logie along here in the late afternoon. No sign. She thought again of that day by the water as children with their father. Without so much as a word whispered between them, she'd counted on Jimmy's silence and he hadn't disappointed, young as he was. Now she couldn't shake a bit of substance out of him if his life depended on it. If he wasn't talking about the weather, it was someone's gammy hip, and if it wasn't that, it was bugs on the potatoes.

She'd always hoped to talk to his girls, knowing he never could. She might have told them about Thomas and their grandfather to warn them of what might be lurking in their genetic roulette wheel. People always said these things ran in families, but as time went on and the culture of silence persisted, it just seemed easier to let it drift. The girls were never curious anyway, never came around for that kind of talk. You could be sure Jimmy'd not say a word. He could keep a lot inside him. Too much. She wished there were something to do for him, but you never could comfort a brother.

The water was friendly today, smooth as glass. Standing by the land's lip, she'd swear it was barely moving, just breathing in and out again with each wave breaking on sand. If she didn't know in her head that close to forty feet of water came in and went out of here twice a day, she could think it was innocent as an inland lake. As far as she could see there was just shrinking or expanding glass.

"Get the goddamn into the goddamned boat." She clenched her eyes to let the breeze push the memory along but it only rose up stronger, her father's blue-red face, the veins bulging at his temple. So, so much had slipped through the floorboards of her memory over the years, why not this? She tried to outwit the recollection by calculating the years again. Did Jimmy remember? Could anyone possibly forget?

Their miracle boy with his arse in the butter. You could easily think such big men as Jimmy capable of absorbing any amount of shock, forget about them as you forgot about a sturdy stone wall or these endless stretches of shoreline, especially so when you already had a Thomas on your hands, crushed by the fears and fidgets of his own imagination. But just let the slow drip of water at the sturdy wall, the constant wash of wave against it for any length of time, you'd know differently.

Out here, you could get caught out thinking the land was the constant, the solid earth was what you put your faith in. Oh no, Flossy knew water, endlessly patient water, with time long on its side, was by far the stronger. When her grandparents first came to this area, the bay was no more than four miles across, now it easily measured seven. Whole farms and an entire baseball field had been washed away.

She looked back across the water, peaceful as a sleeping child. Nobody looking at it on such a day would ever believe how vicious it could be when it took a mind to blow up a storm. Not nice little waves lapping spume over the sand nor even picturesque whitecaps chasing each other to shore, but god-almighty breakers crashing up against twenty-foot cliffs to put the fear of God into you, ripping away four feet of embankment, gorging on mature spruce trees and spewing them out to sea. The water won every time.

A cloud of sandpipers suddenly dropped in from the north, skimming along the water's edge in perfect formation in front of her, one piece of shimmering silk lifting now, tilting left, right, like a scarf thrown into the air, that abruptly lands and begins its feverish feeding along the water's edge, all individuals again bustling along on spindle-shanks, eyes to the ground. Without warning, they spooked as a unit, lifted and glided again as one body down shore, up, up, left, right and down again. She thought of Elizabeth Bishop's magnificent sandpiper poem, how she often likened herself to the frenzied little bird searching the edge of the shore.

Now, there was another lucky-unlucky soul. Elizabeth and Thomas had started Primer class and grade one together — Flossy was sure she still had their school photo; she must pull it out for Richard. Her father died in Massachusetts shortly after Elizabeth's birth and from there her mother began an unravelling that eventually saw her committed to the Mount Hope Asylum in Dartmouth for the rest of her days. Great Village would have been Elizabeth's first memory of home where she lived a cherished few years with her mother's people, the Bulmers, until she was plucked away at seven by her wealthy Bishop grandparents and taken back to the United States. It wasn't her first loss and wouldn't be her last; it was just more of the senseless kind inflicted by adults without an ounce of common sense to them. Would she have become a poet if she hadn't left Great Village, found herself at Vassar and befriended the eccentric poet Marianne Moore? Flossy couldn't say. Elizabeth had won a Pulitzer. That was lucky. She'd also awakened one morning to find her lover overdosed in the apartment. Suicide.

Could people seem lucky to everyone else but not to themselves? She wondered if Jimmy had always been waiting for the other shoe to drop, hoping for it. She was sure Elizabeth Bishop had. Everyone else thought her brother invincible, surviving calamity, getting through that war when so many others didn't. But Flossy worried about him, worried most about the ones everyone else thought so lucky.

IV

OUT OF THE CORNER OF HER EYE, FLOSSY NOTICED THE CAR driving a little too quickly up the lane then brake in a cloud of dust.

She watched from the kitchen window as a phantom of fine particles floated from the car to the fence and the field beyond. They were here.

The sun was already lowering in the afternoon, casting an August-gold pallor over the arrivals. Getting out of the car, Marjory Trotter straightened her skirt, pulled the strap of her purse up her shoulder and pushed her curly hair back from her face. Under her arm was a Kleenex box. On stiff legs she walked around the front of the vehicle, waving to Flossy standing with the screen door open.

Halfway to the house, she hesitated and looked over her shoulder, turned and took a half-step back towards the car. Ruth Trotter-Schaeffer hadn't budged from the passenger seat, though Marjory by now had walked right up to the door and tried to open it. She set the Kleenex on the roof of the car and searched her pockets, then her purse, for her keys. Through the now-open door, words were spoken, the one in the car staring dead ahead. Flossy couldn't hear what was being spoken but something in Marjory's gestures, the hand on the hip, told her patience had been left at an Irving gas station back in New Brunswick, if not Ontario. Ruth studiously ignored her. It must have been a long, hot drive. The back of Marjory's green blouse was creased with a shadow of perspiration. Her back-split navy skirt was rumpled up to reveal the tops of stocky legs. Flossy thought there was something the teeniest bit comical in the young woman seated so defiantly in the car, her seatbelt lashing her in like Ulysses resisting the pudgy-legged Siren.

Flossy put a knuckle up to her nose to cover a smile. "Lord Wilde, I think we may have a calico on our hands," she warned as the cat slipped out the door and padded down the lane towards Mealie's. She envied this feline Houdini's nimble escapes. Oscar Wilde had been waiting for his usual gourmet white fish appetizer when Flossy returned from the shore but, whenever possible, he left human conflict to humans.

Marjory had turned away shaking her head and pushing her hair back from her face. She walked slowly towards the house. "I won't hug you," she sniffed, dragging herself up the steps to where Flossy stood, "I've just come down with a dreadful cold."

Flossy's heart sank. She always did her best to put the length of two lumber trucks between herself and people with dreadful colds, especially a summer cold, which seemed twice a betrayal. She looked back at the one in the car, the door still ajar, arms folded, staring into the field beyond. She could have sliced the misery.

"She'll come when she's good and ready," Marjory said, sniffling and pulling a tissue from the box she'd dropped on the table.

In the kitchen together, Marjory and Flossy did as they had done on countless visits over many years. Flossy began tidying the big table. She closed the two books she'd been reading: Woolf's diary and the collection of her letters. Marjory sat down next to the window, taking the same chair she did each time she came. Over at the sink, Flossy filled the kettle, took a plate from the dish rack and consulted some opaque plastic containers on the counter, lifting the lids and tilting her head to cast an imperial look into the Tupperware, as if she were waiting for the hermit cookies and butter tarts to choose from among themselves their most worthy.

As they waited for the kettle to boil, Marjory talked about the week she'd put in. To get everything finished up, she'd worked day and night, with two funerals and a mountain of reports to complete, when Ruth dropped by the office on her way to getting her hair trimmed, her beautiful red hair that was almost to her waist, the hair that everyone in the congregation adored, so elegant and feminine, the envy of all her friends. They were supposed to go together but Marjory, at the last moment, felt too busy to go.

"An hour later she prances back," Marjory cringed, "and all I heard was the secretary shriek. Flossy, it was gone. All gone." Flossy peered out the window towards the car, but was unable to get a good look at the shorn locks inside. "All but one lingering, trailing, twisted, teeth-grinding insult," she said bitterly. "Flossy, I ... could ... have ... wept," she punctuated her words with a crackling blow of her nose. "I almost cancelled this whole affair," she waved her hand.

Flossy sighed. She stepped over to the window. "Are all the kids doing that up in Toronto these days, or was it just your goat she was getting?" she asked.

"Oh, most definitely mine," Marjory sat with her tanned legs crossed. She had dropped one sandal to the floor and, as she spoke, flexed the foot from side to side like a wary cat's tail. The buttons to her blouse were pulling and she was getting a bit puffy in the face, though she'd still be considered an attractive woman. She was always on some diet or other. The first sprouts of grey were visible in the mound of hair that was side-parted and had to be pushed back from her eyes every few minutes. She sat, now, elbow on the table, one hand clasping her unruly hair, the other holding a bunched tissue against her nose. She was ill.

Outside in the dwindling light, Ruth hunkered in. Flossy squinted to see her through the screen door. The head had been shaved to within a quarter of an inch of her scalp, except for the six-inch strand braided down the back of the neck.

"Ignore her," Marjory said flatly.

"Well, I suppose it's only hair," Flossy offered. "It'll always grow back in again." She couldn't get herself too ruffled over such minor rebellions. Flossy was inclined to worry much more about the ones wearing their hair just to please someone else at that age than someone who had the pluck to shave it clean.

Interrupted by the whistling kettle, she poured boiling water over three teabags in the Brown Betty. As the water plopped into the pot, she noticed Marjory smiling as she looked around the old kitchen. Nothing much had changed in three decades, though Flossy had to admit that clutter in piles of books and magazines had left a smaller liveable space in the centre of the room. Seldom was anything perfectly square in these old houses: doorframes, window sashes, stairs, even kitchen cabinets were all in want of a clean right angle. The wallpaper was the same, with tiny flowers in regular patterns, though the colour had varied from time to time. The old black and white Enterprise wood-burning stove that caused her no little grief over the years remained the heart of the kitchen as it was in most Great Village homes, though no one cooked on them anymore. Another month and she'd be lighting it to take the edge off the cool fall mornings. In the meantime, the Enterprise provided a handy surface for books, a fern drifting over the water tank, a stack of magazines from which the yellow spines of *National Geographic* were visible, and several squatty African violets with pink, lavender and indigo flowers sitting on aluminum pie plates over the warming oven.

Marjory, no doubt, looked on these dated walls as the one thing that hadn't changed in her life, the safe harbour she could count on. But Flossy herself had changed. For one thing, she had less interest in the drama of other people's lives. A long time ago, she'd come to the conclusion that you really couldn't help other people out of their jams, and even if you only lent them a dull ear now and again you'd just as likely end up by keeping the wrong one's secrets.

"How's Thomas?" Marjory chirped.

Flossy's attention had drifted. She looked up into the bleary eyes across the table. Unable to breathe through a nose she couldn't clear, Marjory soldiered on.

"Your brother," she smiled.

"You mean Jimmy?"

"Oh, sorry Flossy." She realized what she'd done. "I always get them mixed up." She smiled. "Jimmy."

"Fine, fine." It was an error, a slip. Was it so easy to mistake the dead for the living? It could happen to anyone. But wouldn't you think, Flossy pondered, of all people, a minister might take just a bit more care? She wasn't feeling well, maybe that was it. Flossy had to think it curious, though, she could go a whole month without having Thomas float into her thoughts and there he was today dogging her every step and tripping out of everyone's mouth all around.

"They weren't going to let me in," Marjory changed the subject. "To this Sackville Conference." She'd lost the application form. "Well, that's not quite accurate either," she confessed, shifting each shoulder. "I watched it sink into the *mañana* pile on my desk." And by the time some still small annoying voice had nagged her enough to fish it out, she discovered the registration deadline long past. So determined was she to go that she sent it in regardless, only to have it returned with a form letter advising her the conference was full.

"Full? Full, my foot," she scoffed, blowing her nose. "I know better than that. There's always someone's Uncle Harold waiting to die and drop a muddy boot into someone else's holiday plans." She tossed her hair back. "There isn't a minister in the country who doesn't know it," she said. Marjory hadn't been in the business six months before confronting the wanton inconsiderateness of dying relatives.

Flossy watched her pleasure in relating the David and Goliath struggle with the conference bureaucracy. Marjory, like a few others she'd known, thrived on a little conflict at the edge of her life. "If it weren't for ..." There was always that one person out there, just one little pebble in the shoe of their perfect contentment, a past husband, an officious church board member. If that particular deer fly happened to move to Baja California, within a week there'd be another to take his or her place. They were never key people, whose support she coveted or needed, they were always somewhat disposable, just people of whom she could safely complain. It seemed entirely plausible to Flossy O'Reilly that she herself might be the next muddy boot into Marjory's holiday.

Irate telephone calls were made to the conference organizers, right to the top she'd gone, to insist upon a place on the non-existent waiting list. Then, when they finally let her in, they put her in some empty student residence in "outer Ouagadougou" on the far side of campus. "Punishment," she claimed, flicking a loose hair off her shoulder. No matter, Marjory said she preferred the relative anonymity of "self-absorbed summer students to mobs of flushed churchwomen in dream-catcher earrings wanting to share their spiritual journeys over green tea late into the night."

Flossy looked out towards Ruth, snug in the womb of the car. Just as unexpectedly as Marjory had cranked herself up over the application form, she abruptly wound down. Blessed quiet settled over the kitchen as she sat idling for the first time since she'd arrived. From a basket of fruit, she pared the peel from an orange. Then, after consuming each section, she began cutting the ribbon of rind into smaller and smaller parts until she could cut them no longer. A weary sadness fell across her features as she pursued this aimless task.

Tadpole compulsions, Flossy could see them in herself, of course, in Virginia Woolf too, and in her brother Thomas. Did everyone have them or perhaps a soft inclination? She herself recoiled over flecks and bits on the floor that Jimmy wouldn't see in four years, thought she probably preserved her good balance with the number of times she bobbed down to pick something up in a day. She was always bending behind Jimmy. Virginia, too, would get herself into fits of cleaning to keep the anxieties at bay. Before he took to his bed, Thomas had a ritual of things placed on his dresser: stones, feathers, a shell and a bullet. If you wandered in and picked something up to look at it and set it back down in the wrong place, he'd have it back before he went to bed that night. It took some kind of pressure off the brain to restore this order, or semblance of order. Flossy had never realized how hand-in-glove compulsions went with depression, a need to still the jitters with some unconnected activity, until she began to read Virginia Woolf.

Looking across at Marjory, Flossy thought she probably deserved real sympathy. She had but one rebellious child to put all her hopes in, another marriage behind her, and was caught in a career that gobbled every waking hour that she laboured away at without one ounce of love. Now she was facing the prospect of a future very much alone. And did she really imagine this would work, to dump poor Ruth here, or was this just the usual path of least resistance? It made Flossy impatient all over again. There was Marjory in her congregation, working her heart out to mother a couple of hundred people, yet missing the one who deserved it most. Without a doubt she could be exasperating but the longer Flossy sat across from her, the more she was noticing the circles beneath the eyes, the skin gnawed raw on the back of her thumbs, the shoulders hunched when she languished with her miserable little pile of slivered orange peel. Marjory Trotter had much less of the world by the tail than she cared to let on. Flossy might have touched her hand when she suddenly looked up and smiled, the face transformed.

"So, how've you been, what's new with you?" she asked.

Richard? Flossy wanted to shout, to tug that errant lock of hair, pinch her ear. Had Marjory talked to him, to Ruth? As she poured another cup of tea to steady her own nerves, Flossy could see exhaustion return, the eyes puffy and red, the nostrils raw from blowing. "You should be in bed," she reached across and felt her forehead. It was hot.

"I might lie down for a bit after my tea, if that's okay. It was a long drive."

"Do you suppose she's going to stay there all night?" Flossy asked, looking at the youngster in the car. It was still warm out. To this, Marjory confessed that Ruth wasn't entirely happy to come, that she was missing the last four games of the baseball season though the team hadn't a chance of making the playoffs. Over the course of the two-day drive, she hadn't spoken a word.

"Just like her father," she frowned.

"Which one?"

"Mmm?" Marjory looked up from her cup.

"You mean Richard?" Flossy asked.

"Jack," Marjory corrected. "She freezes me out, just like he did," she pointed outside with her thumb. "If we'd been closer, I'd have turned around, and dumped Ms. Shorn Two-Horns on him. Let Jack and The Bride deal with the attitude for a change."

Jack Schaeffer and Marjory Trotter had agreed to file their claws throughout the divorce for their daughter's sake and, from what anyone could tell, Flossy thought they'd done a better than average job of it. While Ruth saw him most weekends, Marjory said she missed having him near. Ruth hadn't forgiven her mother for the divorce, though Jack had been the one to find someone new. Marjory attributed their father-daughter closeness to shared interests but Flossy wondered if he hadn't been the more consistent parent over the years. She couldn't imagine Marjory swallowing that one easily. After all, he wasn't even related to Ruth, when it came down to it.

How many years had Jack and Marjory been apart now, three? Flossy thought back to Christmas cards; at least two, maybe three. There was a taut wet knot inside Marjory that refused to loosen, untie for good. It was Jack, and it could constrict in surprising moments. The decision to become a United Church minister, to immerse herself in a church that was so much more liberal than

Jack could abide, might have provided kindling for the marriage
to go up in flames — he was an agnostic engineer, she a feminist
reformer; he liked the laws of physics, things predictable, gravity,
that water always ran downhill, enjoyed making the decisions
and having his coffee brought to him; she wanted to talk about
consensus, Mother-God, patriarchal structures and embracing
the margins — but the match, without question, had been
Elizabeth Waverly. Marjory said she thought the single mother
who'd snagged her husband's affections had little more going for
her than motive, means and opportunity — and, possibly, that
enviably tight body.

Jack, though, could not have been a better father to Ruth.
Throughout her childhood, he had been the one to take their
little girl and five others on excursions to the woods to identify
the delicate bluebells — *Mertensia* — for the Brownie's wild-
flower badge; to glue gold sequins on wings late into the night
for Christmas concerts; or to tuck extra pink tights for dance
recitals in his briefcase alongside manuals of structural engi-
neering. A good half of those occasions Marjory was writing
make-up papers for theological college or attending church
meetings that she thought would have looked bad for her to
miss.

If Flossy could lay her hands on the photo from the first marriage, Ruth could see her father standing beside her father beside
her mother, half the breadth Jack was now and looking long
and awkward in a powder blue tuxedo, shoulder-length hair and
wide glasses. She had a fleeting vision of all the landfill dumps
of the world choking with stacks of discarded wedding photos of
first marriages.

"She thinks she's old enough to be on her own." Marjory
carried a handful of tissues from her pocket to the garbage. "I

might have agreed," she said, arguing with herself, "but something's different this summer, something's gone off with her, Flossy. I can't put my finger on it." She sat down again, biting a hangnail on her thumb, a habit left over from her childhood. Catching herself, she put the hand back on her lap.

"I'm beginning to wonder if maybe she's a bit depressed. She's kept her marks up and everything," she shook her head, "but when she didn't have camp or a baseball game this summer, she'd just sleep, sometimes until three in the afternoon."

Flossy was listening with half an ear. She hadn't been able to bring herself to call Richard when she got back from the shore. What ever would she say to him? Wasn't it Marjory's place to tell him? For days now she'd found herself on this terrible loop about him as if plucking a daisy's petals — to tell him, to tell him not, tell him, tell him not.

Ruth was unhappy; nobody had to tell Flossy that. All she had to do was look out the window but something was teasing at the back of her mind: might Marjory be creating a bigger drama so that Flossy wouldn't have the heart to ask about the other one that was pressing on *her* conscience? She shouldn't think that way. She was weary.

Could Flossy possibly feel less inclined to have Ruth? She knew they could go intolerably underground like that, kids on the cusp, living nocturnally, showing you only what they thought wouldn't arouse suspicion — oh they were clever — but leading an entirely parallel existence. Marjory said she wasn't prepared to leave her daughter alone or with her father, who thought she just needed an occasional "we're-winners" pep talk.

Ruth had no attachment to the east; this was Marjory's past. Her mother, Patricia Campbell, who was long-dead, was born in Great Village not half a mile up the Old Post Road. Her father,

Frank Trotter, lived out eighty tiresome years endlessly tracing a finger along the sharp edge of disappointment. Since the separation from Jack, Marjory hadn't talked about her father all that much. Flossy thought he'd died two years ago and she could only imagine that the death of such a chronically disjointed parent could hold but little emotion for a family that had so recently driven onto its own soft shoulder of loss. Marjory, in a high-pitched trill, once joked about taking her father to church meetings with her, his ashes still sitting in the trunk of the car. Flossy looked outside again. Maybe Frank was still there and she was going to plunk him in with her mother and the Campbells while she was here. Flossy thought there might be some poetic justice in that.

Frank and Patricia met at a Halifax hospital where she had been a ward nurse and he'd landed after taking shrapnel in Italy during the war. Four years later she agreed to marry him on condition they settle in the Maritimes so their children could be raised near her family. He'd got a university degree for his war pains and found work as a horticulture teacher at the Nova Scotia Agricultural College at Bible Hill, near Truro.

Ruth would never understand her mother's ambivalence towards Nova Scotia. Flossy thought Marjory scarcely did herself. There had been no carefree childhood for the Trotters, what with the weight of their mother's illness, which bore down on them like an enormous boulder deposited by the tide onto the middle of their kitchen table. The years passed virtually without celebration: birthday parties were forbidden because the house could never be filled with children and noise. Even an occasional friend could not be well accommodated as Patricia's bad days, always unpredictable, might fill every cranny of the house with the low thrum of pain. Gifts were bought hastily and left unwrapped in paper bags on parlour chairs because strength had failed or attention drifted.

Christmas was usually a bad time when visiting had to be curtailed and, eventually, even family church-going was abandoned, though Marjory continued to go. Meals were a spotty affair as Patricia's health deteriorated and Frank provided relief with what Flossy would always regard as barracks food. For Marjory, childhood had been a decade of peanut butter and grape jelly sandwiches supplemented with the bushels of wizened test apples her father stored in the cold cellar.

Flossy was Patricia's closest friend. The Trotters lived next door in Mr. McNutt's house. The little ones called her Aunt Flossy, as children did for all stray adults in their lives in those days, and though she had no nursing training she took on Patricia's care, guided by the patient's own skilful hand, through the final stages of the illness that had begun as a slow-advancing leukemia.

When Marjory's parents went off to Truro for one of the medical appointments that had become a regular part of each week or her mother needed to rest, she'd be sent next door to stay with Aunt Flossy. In a life lived with the steady tread of death always at their backs, Flossy became the undistracted constant in Marjory's life: the knee, the arms, the gingersnaps, patty-cakes, Beatrix Potter, beaded bracelets, candy canes and chocolate icing licked clean from glass bowls.

When Patricia died, one soft summer morning, it was as if Marjory's frayed childhood had passed away too, interred down by the bay in the old Mahon Cemetery with all the other Campbell forebears. Within a week, hardly a moment to catch their grieving breath, their father had them packed up and moved to Ontario. It took another adult to fully appreciate that Frank Trotter must have been hatching his plan and landing a new job while the last few stitches of his wife's life were quietly unravelling. Flossy bristled over the injustice of that second avoidable rupture in the children's lives. She'd probably always been compensating for it, however feebly. Marjory was twelve at the time, the boys fifteen and seventeen. She was sure it was, in large part, why she still had anything much to do with her. Guilt, even over someone else's behaviour, could have an iron grip on her generation.

Back in Ontario, where Frank had been raised, he began a job with the Agricultural College and finished out the last two and a half decades of his career researching and developing new varieties of apples.

Plump and shy, Marjory never quite fit into her new high school. It was a friendless life, doubly so without their mother since Frank's only satisfaction was long days of work. He bought the children a television to keep them company and soon there were other departures to accommodate as Marjory's brothers began to leave home.

With the better part of their adolescence in Guelph, the Trotters ended up with more ties to Ontario and so they seldom travelled back even though their mother's sisters had all married and raised families in Great Village. Marjory was the exception, cherishing an affection for Flossy and staying in touch over those many motherless years.

"I've been so looking forward to this for her," she said, reaching across and placing a clammy hand on Flossy's, "for both of you."

Flossy could see it now, Marjory's girlish emotion caught up in her own fairy tale. She was banking on some sentimental wish to bring Flossy and Ruth together. Flossy wasn't Ruth's grandmother and it would never have occurred to Marjory Trotter that a good part of the charm of those early years living next door to Flossy may have been due to the utter absence of it in any other area of her childhood.

Flossy and Mealie frequently talked about children, other peoples' children naturally. There had been no expressed regrets about having none of their own and neither felt particularly barren. Their friends spoke endlessly of their children and not much of anything else, unless it was a newly discovered hiatus hernia or the tall ships coming to Halifax. There seemed always to be one adult child in an ailing relationship and listing towards the parents, another was broke and leaning on them, and the last refused to leave the basement. More than three and you just began the count all over again. Parents think it's going to get better when they're out of diapers and they don't have to keep an eye on them every second of the day. They're so grateful when the kids marry or move in with someone else, but they're never really finished with them. Mealie says children are every bit like malaria: "Just when you think you're good and done with them they come back to give you night sweats all over again."

"Does she know?" It was out before Flossy could catch herself.

Marjory looked up, "Umh?"

"About Richard?"

Marjory pushed her hair back from her face for the seventy-seventh time as she turned and stood at the window. She rubbed her eyes. The sun was getting low, enough that Flossy had put a light on. She blew her nose once more and sighed. "That's why she's out there. I just told her. Before we got here." She leaned her forehead against the windowpane. "She said I just wanted to hurt her dad." She stood quietly for a moment. "Why does she do that?"

It wasn't a question seeking an answer. Flossy looked over the few things she'd like to tidy up before going to bed — the empty cups, plates, teapot, orange peel and crumbs. Why does anyone root around in someone else's cluttered motivations drawer, dig beneath expired coupons, string and twist-ties, the dull and useless objects pushing out the top, for a hard instrument with which to gouge the one who's inflicting pain?

Could Ruth not see that her mother was coming clean? Flossy looked up at Marjory standing at the window, staring outside, or, perhaps, at her own reflection, she couldn't be sure. It was a face disarmed, drained of colour, a face not facing its public. She barely recognized it. Who was that weary, sad creature? Could Ruth not see?

V

THEY HAPPENED IN QUICK SUCCESSION: COWS BAWLING, CAR door slamming, and Ruth scooting to the house, interrupting the Woolf diary Flossy had begun reading once again.

She pulled the screen door to let Ruth in.

"You see that?" Ruth asked, shifting her eyes over her shoulder.

Flossy looked out to the field behind the garage. The day's light was but a glow on the horizon. Not twenty feet from where they'd parked the car, three beautiful big Holsteins were craning their necks over the fence, in the exact same place they stretched across every night at about this time to eat Flossy's grass and nibble the peegee hydrangea at the corner of the garage.

In a place the size of Great Village, the country was never much farther than a few houses away, especially when the Bower lad let his cows graze along the hill that stretched behind their houses.

"Don't worry about them," Flossy motioned towards the cattle. "They're the Bishop's cousin's. They won't bother you. About this time every night they stroll by to see if the wind gods have delivered any of your grandfather's apples and just work their way up here." Flossy could see that she'd not understood as Ruth's eyebrows contracted.

"The bishop?" Ruth asked. "How's he got cows for cousins?"

"*She,*" Flossy corrected, "and they're really step-cousins, I should think."

"The *cows* are *step*-cousins?" Ruth's eyes widened.

"No, no," Flossy smiled, drawing her inside, "well, I'm not sure now, maybe they are step-cousins." Glancing out the window again, she offered, "There *is* a slight family resemblance, don't you think?" In the tangle of absurdity there was brief but palpable ease, so that Ruth momentarily forgot herself and giggled.

"Now then," she set about clarifying, "the Bishop's a poet: Elizabeth Bishop. She used to live here in Great Village. We all call her the Bishop; she wasn't *a* bishop. And the cows aren't her cousins — they belong to her step-cousin. It's possessive. He lives up that way." She gestured behind.

Looking back outside from the safety of the closed screen door Ruth mumbled, "I thought they were coming over."

"No, no. They just prefer my flavour of green, if you can call that grass green, and cows are dreadfully curious. Did you know that?" Flossy asked. "Worse than cats." Standing back and taking a good look at her, she said, "Maybe they were checking out the new hairdo. Let's have a look." As Ruth twirled, Flossy reached up and gave a small tug to the braid at the back. "Last I saw you, Ruth," she said, "you were half my size with twice my hair. Now I'm half yours with twice yours." She thrust her voice into her sentences as if she were wading through hip-deep water. "Your mother's upstairs resting. Let's get you something to eat?"

"Okay."

"And after that, we're going to raid Mr. McNutt's baking apples. We'll beat the step-cousins to them." She glanced outside. "Your mother says you're a baseball player. If I knock them off with my walking stick, you could catch them. Deal?"

"Deal."

Ruth ate her ham and tomato sandwich quietly. She was wearing long, baggy shorts, clunky running shoes that made her feet look two sizes larger than they were and a slim blue T-shirt concealing a shallow chest. She had won Richard's slender body in the genetic pairing and even without the hair, Flossy knew that face would draw gazes in the village with its lovely combination of Highland Scots red colouring and dark eyes. Those eyes were an intelligent, warm brown, her father's through and through, eyes that might have called out from the past and chastised some other, more reflective mother.

In Marjory's absence, she seemed affable enough.

Flossy was just clearing the table when Marjory came back down the stairs.

"She's taking all maths and sciences next year, then applying for university," Marjory interjected cheerfully to Flossy as she entered the room, while quietly telling Ruth, "Sit up straight, dear." She put her hand out to touch Ruth's shoulder but her daughter jerked away.

"For?" Flossy asked.

"Applying for university," Marjory repeated. "Next year," enunciating thickly before blowing her nose. Ruth had claimed her school prize for the highest average in both physics and math. "Left the boys in the dust," Marjory chuckled. The marks were already good enough to get into university — maybe she'll take medicine, she added.

"I still have Grade Thirteen," said Ruth shifting uneasily and staring at the floor. "I haven't even finished high school yet," she said, glancing at Flossy.

"Science and math will open up such possibilities," Marjory gushed. Ruth asked to be shown her room. The apples, Flossy realized, would have to wait. With a sudden inclination to shave her own head, she thought of those strange medieval saints who lived their lives up on the tops of poles so that no one could bother them as they prayed, never coming down. Wasn't it Mealie who'd read about them? She looked longingly at the Woolf books, closed in front of her, not an arm's length away. Perhaps she could take just one or two books up the pole with her — Shakespeare, Woolf, Bishop. Three, then. Oh, for a little tobacco shop or a pole to live way up on top of so that she could finish this troubling Virginia Woolf story in peace and quiet. Right away she realized she tossed and turned far too much in her sleep to live way up on top of a pole like that.

Flossy's hearing was not as good as it used to be, but you didn't need to hear a thing to detect the strain between the mother and daughter in her kitchen. She was much better talking with one person at a time, one face to watch without distraction. Even then, sense could shift with a dither of concentration. What she already knew was that something lay between these two that was deeper and darker than words spoken or lost from faulty hearing. Ruth had returned to the kitchen but she wasn't giving any ground. Flossy dearly wished they'd turn around and take their disputes back home with them.

Here it was, not quite nine in the evening, they hadn't been in the kitchen much more than two hours and she was longing to get back to her books, glancing at the clock and wishing for solitude, far removed from the little mother-daughter dust-up before her. Mathematics and physics, no doubt she'd find algebra equations pencilled on the bathroom wall. Driving all that distance and not saying a word to each other, my oh my.

She thought of her own mother. It had been many years, too many, before Flossy had taken a hard look at her mother's flat, swollen-knuckled farm hands. Those red cracked hands were nearly twice as wide as those of any other woman she'd known and they never held still until the last two years of Lillian O'Reilly's life. Yet Flossy didn't fully understand the burdens they'd had to bear while she had her mother with her.

From year to year, inside the O'Reilly gnarl, Flossy had only been able to see what those lean Depression years had meant to her alone, chores before dawn and late nights falling asleep over lesson plans, the rage digging in its sharpened talons. What her mother had held up under had been many times worse, but Flossy couldn't see anyone else's burden then and saw even less how she might be compounding her mother's. In the whirlwind of her own resentment, she hadn't appreciated a thing until it was almost too late: all those years when she might have comforted her mother, been a friend to her when she needed it most, all the things she didn't see then and couldn't make up for now.

She looked back to the two guests sipping tea at her table whose eyes would not meet, who refused to give each other that. How was it that mothers and daughters, up close like this, could see so little of each other?

VI

TURNING OVER IN HER BED, FINDING NO EASE IN QUIET, Flossy O'Reilly resigned herself to a hot and sleepless night. She was spent by the time her guests had gone off to their rooms. Weary of chatting about nothing and too distracted to pick up her reading again, her mind now refused to fold its corners down into blessed sleep.

It was always a fat roll of the dice at her age anyway. The only thing she could reasonably count on was having at least a night or two of unquiet slumbers each week. She could close her eyes but a thousand candles were blazing in her head. After watching the unhappy mother and daughter sitting around her kitchen table, thoughts of her own mother crept back to her unbidden, that most complicated of relationships. How hard it can be to get beyond the tangle of women, to know which thread to tease out and when, which to pluck, tug or shun altogether.

It had been the dead, finally, that loosened Lillian O'Reilly's tongue. Flossy's mother held her silence well into her sixties and the wonder was she unburdened herself at all. The kind of life she had endured could as easily harden a woman as make her yielding in the face of a daughter's dismay. How often had Flossy heard brittle ladies in church basements whispering, "She's made her bed, let her darn well sleep in it"?

Had Flossy not gone with her mother that chill November day they might never again have found themselves alone in the sacred arc of candour where Lillian wanted to talk and she wanted just as much to listen. And because she'd only made the decision to go to the cemetery with her as her mother was walking out the door, it seemed all the more a bestowal of grace to find themselves there together.

The two women and Jimmy had driven over to the Mahon Cemetery when the chores were finished that morning. Her mother had wanted to go for weeks, though never asking outright, and so it was left to Flossy to arrange a ride with Jimmy, who was by then married and living in the village.

Though Lillian always visited the cemetery alone, Flossy went along this time because almost overnight her capable mother had turned around an old woman. When they'd pulled into the cemetery and Jimmy shut the motor off, her mother could only paw at the door of his Ford pickup, the knuckles of her hands red and swollen from the arthritis that had descended upon her earlier that year with the ferocity of a feral cat and left her stiff, sore and incapable of clutching a needle or fastening a button. She had to be helped into and out of every piece of clothing. Seated in the middle, Flossy reached across and released the lever that swung the door open. Perched there at the edge of the seat, hunched in her brown winter coat, Lillian hesitated. The ground, Flossy could see, was a long way down.

"Jimmy, move," she said, jabbing her left elbow into her brother. By the time he'd slouched aside and she dashed around the truck to help her mother, Lillian had squirmed to the ground.

"I'm going with her," she said to him through the open door. "Suit y'rself," he said, shrugging his shoulders then nestling them back into the truck seat and pulling his hat forward over his eyes. One thing you could count on with Jimmy, he could always sleep.

Flossy followed Lillian, who'd set out unsteadily across the field of graves like a toddler just finding her legs. She was headed towards the far end of the cemetery. As she got closer to where her mother had stopped, Flossy could see her bent over the grave and brushing particles of red sand from the crevices of letters carved into the granite, despite the soreness of her fingers. She slowed. That long after William O'Reilly's death, the gesture seemed an absent-minded tenderness, as if he were still close enough to sweep straw from his jacket as he stomped into the house ruddy and grateful from a frosty winter's evening at the barn. Had it been twenty-five years since they'd laid him there?

With one hand on the granite, her elbow taut, Lillian leaned against her husband's grave. Flossy could see she was gathering herself, waiting for her breath to return, as she so often did now at the kitchen table after the smallest chore, draining the water from the potatoes on her better days or hoisting the kettle from the pump to the stove. That walk across the cemetery ground was not so easy anymore on thick legs with one ankle swollen overtop of the shoes Flossy had laced up for her an hour earlier.

In her spry years, Lillian would contrive to come here alone. From the highway in, it was a half-mile walk along the old cemetery road, dusted in Colchester red sand, the grass then as now heaving between wagon-wheel ruts, to the graveyard sleeping in a grove of maple, white pine and spruce. When they were little, her mother would dole out chores to Flossy and Jimmy to be done while she was away — sweeping the kitchen, emptying the

ash can, filling the kindling box. Their Uncle James would drive
her to the end of the cemetery road on his way to the village
and she'd walk the distance in for her solitary visit. Uncle James
avoided cemeteries whenever possible and, when the children got
a little older, they did too.

Though the leaves had fallen for another year, Lillian and
Flossy were still considerably sheltered from wind off the bay in
this refuge. It wasn't good enough for her mother to see the stone
among the many others in the graveyard, from a distance; she
wouldn't have had to make all that effort to get out of Jimmy's
truck for that. No, Lillian had to bend and touch the chill stone
for it to count. Even before looking down at the names, Flossy
thought her mother could tell by the distance she stood from
the maples growing along the south edge and the graceful white
pines along the east, which was his, give or take a few feet. She'd
take her bearings like an aging crow, scanning the tree line for
a curved white pine with a broken leader that struggled behind
the rest.

There had always been an angular comfort in returning to
this lonely spot for Lillian O'Reilly. She seemed not at all
offended by the signs of decay, old man's beard spreading over
ailing spruce and dying lilac like hoarfrost, the creeping charlie
growing up around the stone of her husband's grave, nor the sand
and wind that would take such pains to wear away his name,
like her memory of him.

Reflecting on her mother's life, Flossy thought those visits were
Lillian's way of holding on to something of William, feeling the
slab of granite, keeping the plot weeded, as if she might be doing
a small kindness for him still, something he'd not be expecting,
like sewing a hole in his pocket before he'd thought to mention
it was there.

"Hard as it was to lose him, I wouldn't have him back."

Though she never expected to hear the words, they did not surprise Flossy.

"Oh no," Lillian sucked the thought in with a little gasp of air. Her mother just needed to see where he was now and again, needed to see the permanence of the place, his few feet of space, sinking on two corners, in relation to all the other souls laid there.

The maple trees had grown into a massive wall of intertwined gray branches in the decades since he'd died, though you couldn't have seen it so clearly from year to year. And death had been greedy in their midst. Newer graves were stretched out four times beyond where they'd laid him.

Flossy looked at the stones of the others near her father's grave, unable to ignore names and dates. Great Village's Mahon Cemetery was a good size, established by the Presbyterian Scots who settled along the bay. Some of those lichen-crusted stones went back a hundred and fifty years. To William's left was a Bungay headstone. The Bungays had settled out Montrose way on one of the more remote farms this side of Portaupique Mountain. A son, who had been a year or two ahead of Flossy in school, was still there living on the same unyielding wood lot, last she'd heard.

"How was it Mrs. Bungay died?" Flossy asked.

Lillian was still staring at her husband's grave. "Old age."

Flossy thought about that a few minutes. "Couldn't have been that old, Mah," she said. "Sam Bungay was with Thomas in school."

"Whatever Doctor Rushton didn't know, he pretty much called it old age," she nodded. "You'd be surprised, Flossy, people were a lot older back then." Flossy turned in the direction of the doctor's own monument, not far from where they were standing, a granite angel with a chip off the top of one wing. He had once been as revered as King George in their household but that was a long time ago and a lot of water had passed beneath the Great Village bridge since then.

Mrs. Bungay's death hadn't rung in the ear quite the way word of a death would just after they'd lost William. You could easily develop a sensitivity to dying, an irritating itch like hives that turns up every now and again in a different spot when you least expect it.

To the south lay Hiram Hyde McKay. Now, Hiram her parents had known well.

"Sold us our first calf and a brood sow just when we were married," Lillian said of Hiram, "and could have asked quite a bit more for them. He was as good as they come. Would tell you where to dock a lamb's tail or break a piglet's wolf teeth and the sex of every one of your chicks." Hiram farmed more successfully than most in those parts, with two sturdy sons to help him. They said he split his foot with an axe just about the time William died, though Flossy and Lillian remembered him coming by the house to pay his respects, but never had it looked at until it was too late. He was just the kind of man to put more faith in his uninterrupted good health than doctors.

Among the fellow-departeds in her father's row was a small mound whose headstone held two names, "Charles and John-Calvin, cherished angels." Flossy would have reached out and stroked this one but didn't want to risk the memory disturbing her mother. She thought, instead, about the two people whose graves flanked her father's as she pulled wisps of brown and brittle grass from behind his stone. He'd known them both. When you're going about your business hale and hearty, you never think much about who it is who'll be keeping you company in the local grave-yard. Great Village was a small place when you looked around, so the chances were good that you were meeting up with your left or your right regularly at Sunday service or in McLellan's store as you bought molasses, tea and sugar. You'd never enter-tain the thought, when someone was selling you a bushel of oats, that this might be the man you'd eventually be mingling your dust with. It wouldn't be healthy. People were made to live, not dwell on their dying.

"Never easy to live with." Lillian seemed to be talking to her-self. A damp breeze was building from the north. It was a day running to icy when the sun ducked behind the clouds. Flossy wondered if they shouldn't be going. She didn't want her mother to catch cold.

Lillian pulled her coat tightly around herself and felt for a button at the neck that wasn't there. "If I'd known the kind of man he was, I'd never have married him," she said, this time directly to her daughter, her lips screwed tight into a little beak. She worked her bottom lip as if in silent prayer or rehearsing what next she wanted to say.

"You surely wouldn't have been the first to think that way, mother."

"I never told anyone that before, Flossy," she said in a near-whisper, then added, "and I wouldn't want Jimmy or Thomas to know." She folded the weeds in her left hand down into a smaller bundle. They were always careful about what they said in the house with Thomas upstairs in his bed, as if he were a small child that needed to be shielded from the truth. "It's as well we don't know, I guess, or weddings would be scarce as hens' teeth." Flossy caught a softening in her mother's eye. Lillian, she thought, had got into the habit of talking to herself, to William, out here with only the wind and a few gulls to chide her back. In this Valley of Death she was free to say all the things she should have said in the fifteen years of their marriage. Now, for the first time, it seemed, she was allowing her daughter to listen in.

"Some of the women around here got the drinkers, or the ones too quick with a backhand. Some the loafers — though they didn't usually last long; some couldn't stay in their stalls ..." She stood looking down at William's grave. "If you had a bad spot like that in your man you'd think the other bad spots would be easier to contend with," she raised her head to her daughter, "but they're all about the same in the end, Flossy, even him." She tapped his headstone with her toe then looked up and around as if she were just now noticing the dozens of other graves surrounding them. She pulled herself up to her full height, chest out, and stood like Moses at the foot of the mountain. "They're all out there on their own sandbar. Unreachable."

"Was he different ... at first?" Flossy inquired hesitantly, not wanting to ask too much for fear her mother, like all the other times, would quickly shy from this kind of talk.

"Oh, I can't say as I recall." Ah, there it was, gone, brief as a match. Flossy chastised herself for rushing in with her questions. She longed to know more about her father, who died when she was thirteen, but so often Lillian got this far into the story of him, wooed to this very threshold of recollection, when suddenly the loaves had to be turned in the oven or the clothing brought in from the line. Lillian stood a long while looking down at the grave, her eyes flickering back and forth.

"I thought it set in shortly after Thomas came," Lillian began, her voice low and calm, "but it could well have been there all along."

Flossy reached to take the weeds her mother held.

"I was the one with stars in my eyes. Thomas was a crier and William detested the sound of that crying and yet he wouldn't let me go to him either. I'd just get him fed and settled and I'd have to adjust to William's sulking for ignoring his order. I was spoiling the creature. Got so I had to hold the child away when his father was near, so William wouldn't be in a temper. He even took offence to the nursing. For pity's sake, Flossy, he'd never have said such a thing of the mare and her colt."

An old church pew set at the edge of the cemetery served as a resting place and Lillian made her way over to it. "They can be a different man all out in front, when they're making their way into your affections," she said, squatting and dropping heavily onto the bench, "than the broody one that sets up house." Flossy watched her mother closely. "You see him courting, you see him with a different coat on, all colourful, bright and gay." She shook her head, still looking out at the field of headstones in front of her. "You don't know what he has inside, Flossy, what he's thinking, what he's thought all along about your family and friends that'll come pounding out some day when a little rage pushes him past caring. You don't know how he'll be when you're turning the last of the flour sack out, when he's crushed an ankle under a wagon wheel or tossed the final spade of earth over his mother." Her red hands were on her lap. She turned the left over and twirled the wedding band back and forth.

"I've never wished him back, not one minute." Lillian must have realized how hard it sounded because she cast an eye at Flossy as if expecting to find judgment there. She sat down beside her mother and tucked her hand inside Lillian's elbow. She leaned close to keep them both warm.

"Why him?" Flossy asked. "Was he good to you, at first?"

"The pick of the Truro lads, he was," she said, nodding her head.

They had met in Truro and, from the look of their wedding portrait, Flossy gathered there may have been some choice, for Lillian Davison had once been a beauty, though the picture bore but slight resemblance to the corrugated features of the woman beside her now.

"He had no end of work in him, going off in the winter to cut wood. We needed the money. There were a lot of things I could count on but an awful lot I couldn't."

Flossy nodded. Her mother was a chickadee eating grain from her hand. She didn't want to ask too much, scare her off, so rare were these moments when Jimmy and Thomas weren't near and her mother talked.

"A solitary man," she continued, "solid as oak, Flossy," slapping the bench with the flat of her hand. "It was as lonely out there as if he'd died in our marriage bed."

No wonder Thomas took up such a soft place in her, the firstborn, her favourite, so soon the companion his father was not. Flossy could see it would have made things worse between them. A baby needed his mother, whereas William could give the impression he needed little more than someone to keep his tea and porridge hot, his potatoes on the boil and boots clean.

She could remember her father going off to sleep every night just after his tea. He'd be snoring in the bedroom off the kitchen by the time she and her mother got all the dishes done up and Jimmy to bed. In the morning he'd be up before everyone else and begin his day as if he were a man living alone. There was no keeping pace with him. As a boy, Thomas had been the only one to try, and fail miserably.

"Never talked about his family when I was getting to know him, only a couple of funny stories about his parents. He'd more likely tell you about the antics of his brothers and his mates. All he'd say was his mother was a saint and his father a fair and decent man, but that no one had ever helped him from the time he was seven. The ones who think they raised themselves? They've conveniently forgotten they had a mother, and I can tell you for sure that father of his was neither fair nor decent."

Flossy could remember William's brothers and sister sitting like granite lumps around the kitchen after the funeral, virtual strangers to the children. They had her father's critical glare, looking with cold disdain on all who'd gathered.

"They're the kind to watch out for," she continued. "The ones with no past to speak of. Anyone could tell by the lines on his mother's face that it had been a hard life and there's nothing much worse, Flossy my girl," she said, raising a cold finger, "than a hard Irish life."

Might not poor old Grandmother O'Reilly with the wary eyes have warned Lillian about this son of hers? Might she not have taken the younger woman aside and said "he's a deep dark well you'll never see the bottom of"? You could count on the Davisons to warn her mother against marrying an Irishman, Flossy knew that from one of her aunts, but Lillian had only resented it and defended him the more.

If only Lillian had had her own mother near or any of her sisters perhaps she'd have been able to ask them, knowing they would know or, at the very least, the listening would have been born of concern, not curiosity. Was it this way for all of them? Was he peculiar or did they all withdraw after a time? Two years, six years, a decade? Did they all eventually shove you away from them or had she done something to betray him? Maybe Lillian had broken some filament of trust unwittingly, as one steps through a spider's web that breaks across the face before you can see it, something fragile, carelessly torn, that was hardly even perceived until you were looking over your shoulder at it, something completely beyond her understanding to repair. If so, how did William come to be so unforgiving that he could not let her back in, not spoken his disappointment, not given her half a breath of a second chance? Flossy longed to shout it out in this valley of granite: "Could a woman never make her man love her again?"

You couldn't put those things into a letter to your mother. Each one sent home was undoubtedly read by everyone who could read for six houses in each direction. There was no way that Lillian could get her mother's ear alone; people around would all be wondering why they couldn't read the letter, Tommy Jenks the postman having told everyone along the line that Fenton and May Davison's Lillian had a letter come through that day. When any of the Davisons came out to the farm, on the rare occasions they did, Flossy and Jimmy stuck to the table like spilled jam.

"And Thomas, the way he was with him ...?" She shook her head. "He was only a boy, for Mighty Sakes," she said. "You remember what he was like, Flossy. William expected him to learn something once and never forget it."

"Oh, I do." Her father hadn't taken the same disliking to the younger two. It was too bad for Thomas, doubly so because, unlike the others, he adored his father and wanted nothing more than to be close to him. Thomas was awkward and accident-prone. He spilled pails of water, broke handles, bashed knees and fingers trying to take shortcuts, doing things in a hurry to please. And never did. Yet it was, above all, the clutter of his words that infuriated her father far more than all the rest: sound so often foundering on the shoal of his thought, stuttering or tumbling from the boy incomprehensibly.

The sheer unpredictability of it, the mystery of its absence some morning followed by hours of jerking, knotted stammers, fell on William's ears as patent wilfulness. And Thomas cried. It wasn't punishment that went so hard on him; he could take a strapping. It was humiliation. There he was, poor boy, doing his best to muddle along, caught between two warring continents yet understanding nothing of it, no one explaining a thing, knowing instinctively that abandoning his mother was the only way to his father's shore and not entirely willing to turn from the sole beacon of kindness in his life. It was a terrible and impossible sea upon which to set adrift so sensitive a boy.

"You knew he'd never talk to James."

"I knew he didn't," said Flossy, "I never knew why." Lillian's older brother, James Davison, lived two farms up the road from them. After Thomas took to his bed, James did what he could to help them get by, finishing the hay that year, the oats and wheat and planting them until their own Jimmy was able. The woodpile, too, was always magically replenished by kind Uncle James. They wouldn't have survived otherwise.

"The year Thomas was a baby," her mother began, "we had a bad April storm. Thomas wouldn't have had more than three months to him, took a cold and then a fever. I wanted William to take us to Dr. Rushton. He wouldn't, said it would put some fight into the boy. Thomas grew hotter and hotter and I was scared. I begged William but he turned hard. I was at my wit's end when James dropped by, like an angel of mercy. Straight away he took the two of us to the village. Dr. Rushton said Thomas wouldn't have lasted the night. William never spoke to James again. Wouldn't have him in the house."

"I never knew, Mah."

"And you shouldn't've," she said. "It wouldn't have made you feel any better about your father." Staring towards her husband's grave, Lillian blinked a couple more times, then said, so softly

Flossy almost missed it, "Sure didn't make me feel any better about him." She clasped her elbows with those raw, inflamed hands pulling her arms in as if she could fold a bitter memory back inside herself.

So that's where the divide had been struck. Flossy had to look away to hold her own thought. That was where her mother lost faith in her father; anyone would. From then on Thomas had become their sacrificial lamb, the unsuspecting booty in a war waged half a dozen times a week between them. They all bore witness to it.

"He was a good worker and that's all he was," she said, as if she needed to find something redeemable. It was true. William would have made an enviable hired hand. He had no end of energy for work. After her father died, Flossy remembered they'd all been afraid. With someone else in the house, a capable man, her mother could share the burden of the fear of not surviving. Not that they'd speak about it, but at least there'd be someone else there to brace the back against. Thomas, even before he'd taken to his bed, never had his father's appetite for work. Slight and nervous, he wasn't made for it. He couldn't have gone off to the woods to cut trees without one falling on him. They'd had to wait for Jimmy to grow up for that. In the meantime, their survival had been in Lillian's hands, as it turned out, quite literally so.

But the end, when it came, none of them could have foreseen. Lillian may have thought she knew her husband, knew what to expect after fifteen years but it was dismally clear she'd underestimated William O'Reilly. Hadn't they all? Flossy knew this was where her mother would make the motions to be going home.

William's death was still intolerable to think about. And so, Lillian O'Reilly came to this place to clear and tend the grave site but made every effort to put his dying from her mind. They never spoke of it. None of them. Never had. Her mother wiggled herself forward from her seat and planted both feet on the ground, and she slowly heaved herself up. Flossy grasped her elbow until the old woman was steady.

William's death was another thing for Lillian Davison O'Reilly, Great Village's finest milliner, to stitch tightly into the seam of her hard life, the seam of forgetting. She would much sooner have pushed a needle into the palm of her own hand and drawn it through to the other side than think of how they'd lost him.

"We'd best be going. Jimmy'll want to be getting on."

The dead, the living, Flossy thought, were ever connected: gone but never gone. Grief collided with their living day in and day out; they moved over each other like tide on land, and the survivors, if they could be called that, were utterly incapable of pushing the one back from the other.

She watched her mother pull a frayed handkerchief from her pocket and wipe her nose and eyes; she wrapped her loss tightly inside her winter coat and held it close with one hand at her neck, limping back among the graves to where Jimmy sat asleep in his old pickup truck.

VII

MEALIE MARSH PLANTED HER RUMP IN ONE OF THE RICKETY lawn chairs with badly woven plastic straps that they'd picked up for two bucks at last year's Bass River Baptist Church bazaar.

This Saturday morning, she and Flossy had set them out along the shoreline of Cobequid Bay below the cliffs at Spencer's Point. The tide had turned, offering a good hour of fishing. Mealie didn't fish but Flossy knew she'd always jump at the chance to come out early to sketch.

This part of the shoreline was crammed with boulders pushed back against ledges of sandstone close to the cliffs but nearer the water's edge, smooth stretches of hard-packed sand wove red swathes among the blue-pebbled beach. Mealie rocked her substantial frame from side to side, squeezing the aluminum struts solidly into the sand. Once in place, she withdrew a sketchpad and her battered wooden box of charcoal and pencils from the canvas bag she always toted around with her.

The bottom of the bag, an unappetizing coffee-pot brown, was the kind of thing Mealie'd never notice, though a delicate lilac line, which she'd just pointed out at the water's edge on the far side of the bay, could fascinate her for hours. She gazed at it with singular unselfconsciousness, her lips parted and soft with the pleasure colour always gave to her.

Mealie didn't just see colour in the refracted light of her coffee cup that danced on Flossy's kitchen wall; colour was her language. She studied it: in the sky, fields, water and trees, the shadows on houses, in hair, on skin and in eyes. Flossy thought that Mealie probably perceived colour with far more intensity than all the rest of them and she had a primordial passion for red. Her earliest memory, she'd once confided, was of a pair of red fuzzy socks, a gift from distant relatives, that she refused to take off. Her mother'd had to peel them from her in the middle of the night as she slept. Flossy thought Mealie's relationship with red might have been her most enduring. Whenever she dressed for a gala opening, there would always be a flash of red somewhere, at her neck, dangling from ears, across her shoulders or on her feet, sometimes all together.

Flossy reached for a Thermos by her chair, twisted the top and poured them each a cup of coffee. Mealie turned in her direction to speak; their eyes met.

"Hmn?" Flossy leaned towards her.

"Sleep?" Mealie enunciated carefully. When she was tired, Flossy didn't hear as well.

"Not so much," she shrugged.

On a morning as foggy as this, the barns, fields and forests normally discernible along the bay's far shore from Noel to Maitland were no more than a blueberry wash above that pure lilac line. The pinky waters appeared lighter than the aluminum cloud mass loitering above.

"It's manic-depressive," Mealie muttered. Raising her voice so

Flossy could hear, "it's bipolar, the bay," lifting an eyebrow and pointing with her chin. "Don't you think?"

Flossy nodded. She watched as Mealie nosed the various pieces of charcoal and pencils around the wooden box that she'd set on a small tripod between them, nudging the cool blues and sober purples towards her and pushing the party colours out of the way. It was that kind of day.

The ends of Mealie's fingers and thumbs were always brownish-black, as was the length of her little finger, which she used to smudge charcoal. As a result, there were often hieroglyphs at intervals beneath her eyes, on her chin or along her nose that Flossy did her best to tidy up; the acrylic on her eyelid and hair would have to wear itself off. Mealie kept a cloth with her to clean her hands but seldom took the time to get it out of the bag. Now mattered, mattered most. There had always been a characteristic urgency about her sketching, a need to snatch what she saw. That was, no doubt, why they still had her teaching the Life Studies classes at the Truro Teachers College at seventy-six. And she was young at heart; no one could ever guess Mealie's age.

If Flossy ever wanted to get somewhere on time with her, though, she generally avoided the early morning or late afternoon because Mealie couldn't resist a warm cast of light. Invariably you'd be stopped in her van on the side of the road while she disappeared into a ditch to sketch a milkweed pod she'd noticed or the mist hovering above an inlet. Though they were both a good age by now, Mealie was surprisingly agile. Flossy had to give her that. Never one to apologize for a delay — Mealie didn't allow for regret — she simply expressed gratitude, fully expecting a compact of enthusiasm.

"Thanks, Pet, had to get a closer look there. They're all fugitive this time o' day — light, colour," she'd say. Like so many things they'd known in their lives, beauty didn't hold. It wouldn't be there on the way back and you couldn't always take the time to wipe your fingers in the right place.

The two friends seldom made it to Spencer's Point together anymore, though they both loved this sheltered spot and clucked endlessly about coming more often. It was far enough from the highway that most of the sounds of people coming and going about their Saturday chores vanished to the roll of surf, seagulls and *Aida*, which played softly on the cassette recorder by Mealie's leg. She was quite sure the fish were drawn to all Verdi's operas, but *Aida* in particular.

"Like herding goats," Mealie said, picking up the end of a conversation they'd been having in Falstaff on the way over. "Remember the time Jimmy found Gauguin on the cab of his pickup and couldn't get him down?" She cackled and slapped her thigh. It made Flossy smile too. Her knuckle went to her nose. Jimmy was parked right in her driveway and was more than a bit wary of that surly old goat who stood his ground and stamped his front foot in warning when her brother tried to shoo him down. She was relieved that Mealie had given the goat to the Clarkes down in Economy who already had a couple of their own. On a damp day, with winds coming off the bay, she was sure she could still smell that musty old billy from two doors away.

Mealie was talking about her students, naturally, from the summer school session at the college "You can see it in the first week, Flo, maybe the first day," she said. "They either have it or they're wasting their time." She took another sip from her cup, "And mine." After introducing herself on the first day of classes, it was Mealie's custom to place a fat-bellied eggplant on her desk for the students to sketch.

She raised her hand and flourished it like a sword above her head. "Essence, essence," she hissed, as if her Life Studies students were standing right in front of her now, ankle deep in Cobequid waters. "Most of them couldn't capture essence if it tripped over their easels and fell plump as an ostrich into their laps." She shook her head. "They're so dreadfully careful." Some of Mealie's charges wanted to be thought of as artists. These, she claimed, were the hardest to get at and the ones who had to make every wee stroke count. Mealie was happy if a stroke in a hundred caught precisely what she saw or maybe something better.

"If I wanted an eggplant," she'd say to them, her voice sounding every bit like the county grader rumbling down the Station Road as she slapped the vegetable's purple-black paunch, "I'd put *this* on the kitchen table. What more can you see? *Flog* it!"

Flossy knew what Mealie was doing this morning. She wasn't so preoccupied by her students. In fact, by times she could seem indifferent to their success or failure. It didn't mean she wouldn't work hard with them, wasn't encouraging or duly sympathetic about truant children or unsupportive spouses. No, Mealie above all was convinced that a real student didn't even need a teacher; in fact, most teachers would hold them back, and the rest were without a doubt putting in time. This morning's dismay over students was all for Flossy's benefit. Mealie was working the row ahead of her, double-digging and softening the soil so that Flossy might come up behind and find the ease to talk about what had been so much on her mind over the last few weeks.

If only it were so simple.

Mealie wanted her cavalry to charge, seize something, an angle, a line, a spirit, anything. She always said you had to know how to waste to be an artist. Take a cleaver to the work, toss and begin again. Some just didn't have it in them. "Move on, move on," she'd marshal her pupils, twenty pairs of eyes gazing at a model shifting in her seat every minute, "don't finish."

Flossy longed to do just that. She wanted nothing more than to grasp this private moment and tell Mealie about Richard, whom she expected to walk through the door any day now. She was sure Marjory hadn't told him. The very thought of it made her weak. With the first Elizabeth Bishop Society meeting next Saturday and Richard among the organizers, it was all but certain he'd drive up from the Valley to make sure the arrangements were in order at the Legion Hall, maybe even today. Flossy imagined him wandering in, as he always did when he was in the village, with Marjory and Ruth right there.

"Hello Richard, you remember Marjory. Oh, and here's your daughter." She closed her eyes; she thought she could feel the blood rushing through her arteries. It would serve Marjory Trotter right. Flossy should have got after her years ago but she much preferred to stay on good terms with both of them while ignoring the little problem of Ruth. Now, the little problem was a grown-up problem that had arrived on her doorstep. Mealie never had too much to say about Marjory Trotter but she didn't make a point of staying around when she was in town either, not like Richard's visits. All she'd say was, "How do ya suppose, on a planet as big as this one, those two ever found each other?"

Flossy had a pretty good idea. They were young, had gone to university together and were paired up on dates because they were the only two not already paired up with someone else. (For some reason, she thought of all those poems Elizabeth Bishop had written and left unfinished over the years. All of them awaiting their final couplet.) As graduation approached, the weddings tumbled along and all the couplets were swept up in a torrent of love all around. They too made plans for the future. Who, after all, really wanted to be free and twenty-three? Flossy'd never observed much spark between them but in those days of chaste expectation perhaps everyone expected passion to ignite sometime after the wedding. They had only lived together long enough to realize it wouldn't, and, most ironically, for her to become pregnant. Richard, Marjory was to discover, and of course confide in Flossy, was homosexual. Back then, Marjory confessed she hardly knew what it meant.

So many things didn't matter anymore, but Flossy's friendship with Richard did. What if she were to go suddenly like Lavinia Gamble, sitting up in her armchair with half a glass of apple juice in one hand, *Jeopardy* on the television, and all of this came out after she was gone, no opportunity to give her side? Poor Lavinia hadn't even spilled the juice. What would Richard think? And Mealie? Would even a good soul like Mealie Marsh try to find some generous light in which to see this, see keeping Richard's daughter a secret from him all these years? If anybody could see beyond what was seeable, it was Mealie.

It had always been one of her finest qualities that she thought so differently from everyone else. Flossy counted on it. Among her students, Mealie adored the lean wolves that drifted into her classes, kept their heads low, watched and circled hard for three months, drew like demons, then vanished. They weren't mewling for marks. She knew they'd be turning up in the galleries in a decade or two, she said, if they didn't starve first. Not, sadly, her usual students who arrived punctually, brought muffins, attended every class, laboured for accuracy and scratched out nice pictures. (The only thing they did well, she'd cackle, was pay their tuition.) In fact, the older Mealie got, the more she said she wondered if art, seeing actually, could ever be taught, perhaps a small measure of technique early on, pointing out true north, but the ones who had it, had it long before they'd stepped over the threshold of her classroom. As for watching, she said you either did or you didn't.

But Mealie was forever calling Flossy's attention to things: colour, shadow, pattern, shape, tone, emotion. She could teach you what to look for in something beautiful to appreciate it even better. Looking out across the water again, she could see that Mealie was right about the bay. It *was* manic-depressive, something she'd perhaps felt more than thought. Nor was this the first time Mealie's observations had lent her own feelings words. When the day was fine out here at the shore — Van Gogh sky reflecting off the water, sun shining, dancing diamonds on the surface — it was painfully spectacular, harsh to the naked eye. And when it wasn't, like today with a fog brooding over it, this was the saddest, most godforsaken beautiful place she knew.

And Flossy had to admit she preferred this melancholy palette. It was, in all things, richer. You couldn't see to the back of green on a day like this; blue was anchored on each horizon with flecks of purple; olive clods of fresh-ploughed earth sported lilac highlights and red could crawl inside you like blind obsession. She breathed deeply of the morning's salty air. Every colour she knew had deeper saturation, energy, in the half-light of this gathering note of sadness. It made her look up close, attend, made her grateful to be alive. On the sunny, glowing days, she more easily forgot such gratitude.

The women had settled themselves near a channel gouged into the floor of the bay. This was Flossy's preferred fishing spot. The channels weren't visible from shore and if you weren't from these parts you'd hardly believe they were there. Great fissures, carved like a river deep into the basin's floor, allowed the tide a stealthy return to encircle sandbars then suddenly flood the entire bay. The bottom of this one was a good fifteen feet below where they were seated. It would wander another half mile east, running an oxbow to the land before hooking north to collect the flow of the Great Village River as it emptied into the bay. All along the edges of those channels and for twenty feet on either side lay a dangerous bed of gumbo that you could sink into up to your knees. Muck, Marjory and Richard muck.

"Mealie," Flossy began, "did you ever get yourself into something that was messier than you imagined, then not know how to get yourself out?"

Scratching her wrist, Mealie thought for a moment. "Well, I guess that pretty much sums up two marriages gone south, Pet." Her wry look met Flossy's eye, waiting for the elaboration and when it didn't come she went back to her sketching. Flossy watched her hand dodge across the page.

That eye. Thomas might have noticed it first from the few pictures and sketches Mealie brought home early on. She had an eye for sadness, he'd said, though never to Mealie directly. He wouldn't have wanted her to take it badly. Flossy was sure Mealie already knew this about herself. In fact, she'd have laughed. At the several shows of her work over the years in Halifax at the Northgrave Gallery, Mealie said there'd always been one, at least one, kind older woman in a white blazer standing patiently at a little distance with a purse clutched between tummy and bosom to first apologize then ask if perhaps she'd ever painted any happy pictures.

The American tourists that arrived by the busload at the gallery run by the Cobequid Arts Collective rarely chose Mealie's abstracts. They preferred pictures of lighthouses with lupines or colourful fishing boats at Peggy's Cove, keepsakes of their trip to Canada. Nevertheless, if there was but one soul among five buses of tourists who liked her brooding lines, Mealie was amazed to discover the buyer paying any price she asked. Initially it puzzled her. Then she claimed it gave her insight into the depth of sadness among the well-heeled. "The poor, at least, still have their illusions to keep them warm."

Flossy watched the swallows sweep low, tilt and roll after flies along a wide ribbon of water in the bottom of the channel, agile brown stars tumbling over white, snatching a dragonfly and darting away. Drifts of sandpipers fluttered in, dropped and scurried along the water's retreating edge, plucking grains of sand from the wet land or creatures too small to be seen, indifferent to everything including the tide drawing them away from the women with each gentle lap. They both stopped to watch. The birds were catching breakfast, a layover on their annual migration from the Arctic to wintering grounds in Argentina. Flossy loved such creatures of the edge, pitiful knock-kneed runners with the courage every minute to chase alongside the vast and dangerous unknown for pickings of grain and grace.

The Bishop's Pipers, she thought, remembering Elizabeth Bishop. She told Mealie about the Bishop's cousin's cows. Mealie listened attentively, her wholesome wide face looking particularly happy this morning.

Flossy decided to try again. "But did you ever do something for one person, a kind of favour, that ended up hurting another you never intended?"

Mealie leaned back and kicked off her sandals. She pushed her heels into the sand.

"I'm sure I have, Flo. You know better than most how I can shoot from the lip before thinking where it'll land."

Flossy looked away. Normally it was peaceful out here, comfortingly predictable. The place she came to settle her mind. The fog and clouds would burn off by noon on such a day. Here, sitting near the water, the rhythmic breathing of the ocean in and out, like some primal parent they could lean against, the women could be still. For well on two decades now, this shoreline had been a good place for Flossy and Mealie.

Today, though, was different. Fumbling with her fishing hook, Flossy held some pieces of squid at arm's length. "Mealie ...?" As with old friends, she didn't need to finish every thought.

Placing the charcoal pencil against her stomach, Mealie leaned out over the sketchpad laid across her knees and sewed the squid onto Flossy's hook.

"You're losing your nerve, Flo. Fish can sense these things," she said, as softly as Mealie's voice ever got.

"Why is it I can't even impale a piece of dead squid anymore?"

Mealie walked to the edge of the water and rinsed her fingers as her friend cast the line. A clean whir above their heads ended in a delicate plop precisely into the water in the centre of the channel. Flossy stood to draw in the slack.

She wore her fishing attire today, a navy dress and a grey sweater buttoned at the neck, which differed from her everyday clothing only in the straw hat and black rubber boots that reached almost to her knees and drubbed against her calves when she walked across the sand. Mealie, curly hair tufting out beneath a baseball cap, was in beige capris, with a charcoal smudge down her thigh, a blue and white checkered shirt and blue flip-flop sandals. The two had been here since seven.

Usually these mornings by the bay brought relief from the summer heat, but this month with the unrelentingly high temperatures there was little more than a moist warm stillness as if the air were stalled above them. From the look of it, she might have expected rain, but Flossy had a feeling they wouldn't be getting any anytime soon. It was plain muggy. She longed for a good wet old Maritime day.

When they first began coming to Spencer's Point after Flossy had retired from teaching and Mealie could find a free morning from her art classes, the two would drive down here, already dressed in their bathing suits, for an early swim in the bay, one as big as the other was tiny. The locals took to calling them the Big and Little Dippers and they served both as weathervane and considerable entertainment to those living along the bay within sight of Spencer's Point.

"It's here, Vickie."

"What's that?"

"Winter. The Dippers ain't going in today," Russel Corbett, Jr., from behind his new birthday binoculars, would announce to his wife standing over the stove stirring Red River Cereal. It, indeed, marked a finale of sorts, or a beginning — time to light the wood stove — when the women stopped swimming in the fall. It was not the literal change of season, of sun crossing equator, but an end to the draw-you-out days, when it was so much more pleasant to be outdoors than in.

In those times, the Dippers could stand a brief swim in the cold Cobequid waters up until the end of September and start up again for Queen Victoria's birthday in late May. In more recent years they gave up swimming altogether, declaring the frigid Fundy waters an assault to the aging central nervous system.

First thing this morning, Flossy had placed her fishing rod outside the back door. When Mealie dropped by with scones and a basket of freshly picked tomatoes she noticed the rod and the can of squid beside it. She wouldn't have been expecting a fishing excursion, particularly when there were guests in from Ontario, but Mealie had learned long ago that when Flossy put that rod out you either joined her or got right out of the way. Mealie dropped the food on the kitchen table and hiked home to gather her bag and sketch pad. Flossy picked her up in Falstaff.

"I'm too old to be putting things off," she said as they sneaked off like teenagers who'd just crawled out of an upstairs window. Neither of them was much interested in the fish she might catch as Jimmy kept both of them well supplied from his weir. But fishing wasn't always about fish.

Mealie was good about hanging around, waiting for Flossy to find the words to render sense to her worries and even patient when she couldn't. She didn't get bothered about many things these days, but when Flossy did she really did. Not like Thomas, of course, whose fears and imaginings from an upstairs bedroom could keep him awake all night and the rest of them skittering to protect him from any whiff of genuine bad news.

In spite of her best efforts, this visit from the Trotters was proving resistant even to Mealie's ministrations. She'd told Flossy the kid should be staying at her own place; that they wouldn't find her for three weeks among the flora and fauna taking over the kitchen. Mealie scraped her back from side to side against the chair's plastic straps.

"Here," Flossy said. Mealie leaned towards her and Flossy scratched between the shoulder blades.

"A little to the left, lower. Oh, right there. Right there," she straightened up again, a gap-toothed smile stretching across her wide face. "That's much better. Thanks Flo," she said. "I think that's just about the only thing I miss about my last husband," she chuckled as her hand arced along the sketchpad. "Company got in okay, then?"

"Oh yes." Flossy answered quickly then slumped into silence. Sitting a little farther back in her chair, Mealie waited. Flossy was well able to talk a good spontaneous hour about psychological realism in Shakespeare, Hopkins cadences echoed in Bishop or Woolf's detachment from plot, but when it came to articulating the contours of her own fine feeling, dipping a finger into the warm wax of her heart, she was at a perfect loss.

"And?" Mealie prodded gently.

"Well," she tended to swallow her first step when laying out bad news, "the youngster shaved her head just before they left. She doesn't want to be here and hasn't spoken a word to her mother since they arrived, maybe since Ontario."

"Pluck," Mealie chuckled, stopped sketching and picked up her coffee.

"Pluck," Flossy agreed, rolling her eyes. "Mealie?"

"Un-huh?"

"Do you suppose if I were to live up on one of those poles like the Polish saints, you'd be able to send me a book now and again?"

"Take your fishing rod; we'll cook up something." She looked over at Flossy, "They weren't Poles, Flo, they were saints on poles. The Stylites."

"What if you toss and turn a lot in your sleep?" Flossy asked.

"They'd be on a bit of a platform, I'd think," she said, frowning. "Be too hard on the arse to sit on a pole all the time, even for a saint."

"You must be right." They both returned to their pursuits. Flossy cast her line again, then worked it back in. She hadn't caught anything. Two healthy, fat sneezes from Mealie reminded her of Marjory's cold.

"Oh, they've brought us some Ontario bugs, too."

"The spattered-on-the-bumper kind, or the sick-in-bed kind?"

"Very sick-in-bed."

Mealie shook her head. "Some people just don't know when to stay home." She turned the page and looked through her wooden box for something. When she didn't find it, she withdrew a purple and a blue and began shading one on top of the other. She was aiming for that line. Flossy looked across the bay.

"Mealie, do you remember Bubba from school? Bubba McKeen?"

She looked across at her. "I remember the McKeens," she said, reaching for the Thermos, "I haven't thought of Bubba in years." She offered Flossy more, filling her cup, then her own. Cradling the mug with two hands she rested each elbow on an arm of the chair. "Frizzy hair, slight …?" Flossy nodded. Mealie was five years behind the rest of them, but with only two rooms in the Great Village schoolhouse, they'd all shared the same class at one time or another. For a moment Flossy thought it funny that they both still imagined Bubba as a skinny twelve year old, though she had to be well into her eighties too. It was the betrayal of age: though they were all more or less developing what Mealie liked to call 'a case of the dwindles,' they didn't feel a day over thirty inside their heads.

"Jimmy bumped into her this week."

"Oh yeah? Wasn't she the one raised by her grandparents?"

Flossy knew she'd remember. No one from around those parts with any memory was likely to forget. The McKeens were an early Scrabble Hill family. Bubba's father was a sea captain, when sailing was still a thriving industry on both sides of the bay, just about the time Flossy's own parents married. On one of his trips to Boston, Bubba's father met a woman he brought back to Great Village to marry.

Not so long after, the newlyweds were helping out at a barn-raising bee. This was when Mrs. McKeen was carrying Bubba, their first child. Just when the barn's structural timbers were in place and everyone sat down to dinner, a single beam slipped, came down and struck Bubba's father on the back of the neck, killing him instantly.

Her mother collapsed, took to her bed and went into early labour, giving birth to little Bubba at the home of her in-laws, who were preparing to bury their son. No doubt the McKeens had their reasons, but they removed the child and told Bubba's mother that her baby hadn't survived either. When she recovered enough to travel, she was encouraged to return to her own people in Boston, broken-hearted and twice bereaved. Bubba grew up in Great Village knowing her grandparents as her mother and father. It took a lot of collusion to keep such a big secret in a small place where everybody's business is everybody else's. The secret was kept for many years but somehow Bubba found out and it wasn't the grandparents who told her.

"She never spoke to me after she found out," Flossy said.

"You were her friend."

Flossy nodded.

Leaning back in her chair, Mealie looked off towards the far side of the bay. Flossy put the fishing rod down. How many times had they come out here in all the years they'd been friends? How often had they taken a cup of tea of an evening and sat watching the shifting summer sky over this same bay from the back porch of the O'Reilly homestead when Flossy lived there, the same land, the same barns along the far shore, the same fields, cliffs, water, moon, sun, stars and there was always something out here they hadn't noticed before, some new way of looking at it all. Mealie might point out a blush of colour creeping across the mudflats or the evening sunlight painting the marsh greens golden, something neither of them had seen before or seen in just that way.

"It'd be awfully hard to know," Mealie finally spoke, "which would be the greater kindness: to tell her or keep it from her, Flo."

"But how do you know, Mealie? How's anybody supposed to know?"

"Can't," she shook her head. "Some things you just gotta trust your best instincts," she sipped her coffee, "then trust how they turn out."

There were only brief moments in a lifetime, Flossy was convinced, when people genuinely opened their hearts to each other, got anywhere behind the fortifications. And they were holy flashes, though she'd never seen them happen in a church. Mealie had made every effort to tease out her tatted worry and if there was ever a breach into which Flossy could take a small step today, knowing compassion's long reach would be there, it was here and now, with Mealie Marsh, her dearest friend. But Flossy could not; she just could not bring herself to.

Was she like Jimmy that way? Here she sat quietly beside Mealie Marsh, her oldest, most accepting and forgiving friend, fully determined to talk about everything but what was bleeding her concentration. It was her own unfinished poem, her elusive couplet. Flossy just could not bring herself to bare her soul, did not have the words.

VIII

FLOSSY WAS TEMPTED TO REACH OVER AND STILL THE impatient knee jiggling beneath the kitchen table.

Bored with the conversation around her, Ruth Trotter-Schaeffer had picked *The Diary of Virginia Woolf Volume V 1936–1941* from a pile of books nearby. Her long, freckled hand stroked the cover as if to remove an invisible layer of dust. She opened the first few pages, read quietly and sometimes looked up, variously listening to and ignoring the others around the table — her mother Marjory Trotter, Mealie Marsh and Flossy O'Reilly.

Talk and more talk. Ruth fidgeted. At first she scratched her newly shaved head, then twirled the remnant, the single braided strand that hung down her neck. The three older women talked of many things — of Marjory's church, the peonies her mother once grew, the arts collective, hot flashes, weather, traffic on the road to Bass River, Mealie's art show, the old Trotter home. They swung from topic to topic through a forest of conversation. Every now and again Ruth yawned loudly.

Tomorrow morning, Sunday, Marjory would be leaving for the conference on *Spirituality for a New Millennium*, something she said she'd been "dreadfully looking forward to." It was being held at Mount Allison University.

At a lull in the conversation, Ruth asked, tapping the cover of the Woolf diary, "Wasn't she the one who went crazy and killed herself?" She had to ask it twice since Flossy's thoughts were elsewhere. "Didn't she go crazy and kill herself?" she asked again, this time loudly while looking at Flossy and flashing a half-smile that belied the pleasure of dropping a biographical tidbit.

Flossy knew her sleepless night was catching up with her, though she was not too tired to notice the darkening iris of Mealie's alert eye. She looked away from the others towards the screen door, outside for a moment, to what promised to be another scorcher of a day. The cloud cover had moved off and the August sun was already hard and white. Beyond the door a wind devil touched down and did a pirouette in her garden, tossing up a vortex of dry leaves, pitching the purple coneflowers, black-eyed Suzies and daisies in one direction and as quickly throwing them back. The lace curtains billowed in like sails through the open window. She could hear the mourning dove's regretful call.

Flossy glanced back at Ruth, "That's right," she nodded and smiled. How careless were the young in their handling of the Limoges of literary lives, Flossy mused as she looked down at the amber tea in the bottom of her cup and rubbed her thumb along the end of the teaspoon on her saucer. Ruth was a tender shoot, well yes. And Woolf? Woolf was a writer, so naturally her life public property. Even more so since she was a dead writer and one who had plotted her own demise like everything else in that finest of literary imaginations. Her life, her torment, the tenuous grip Mrs. Woolf held on her sanity from year to year were now the feeding ground of the acned critic, countless undergraduate speculations and doctoral theses "not worth a fiddler's fart," as Mealie was so fond of saying. It was open season.

The compassion of the young is wintry, so entirely unfurled in tiny buds along the length of their wiry branches. There she sat, this fresh-faced child-woman, softly speckled like a fawn, smooth-skinned, stroking the strange shorn head, with no more schooling in the sufferings of the human mind than Little Miss Muffet.

"Virginia Woolf suffered all her life from depression," Mealie interjected in an uncharacteristically solemn voice, as if she were sitting in the third row of Mattatall's Funeral Home, not right here in Flossy O'Reilly's kitchen. There was a tightening in Mealie's body, Flossy noticed, the shoulders pulling forward, the hands suddenly reaching for her knees. In a big alert woman, it was the mother-lion instinct with the first whiff of predator in her nose.

Ruth, with all the strength of a young woman's good imagination, could scarcely comprehend the depth of friendship that Florence O'Reilly had cultivated with Virginia Woolf throughout the years. Never mind that one was long dead, how irrelevant to genuine friendship. Like herself, Mrs. Woolf had been a lonely creature at heart and this had made her a most beloved and sympathetic companion, sitting right beside Flossy in this very kitchen. In her imagination, Mrs. Woolf came regularly to tea in that loose, frumpy brown coat she wore in life and most likely in death. Since the first of her journals was published in 1977 and the letters two years before that, Flossy had been reading all Virginia Woolf's writings in order, using the diaries and letters as a hub and picking up all the other works on the radius as they were mentioned — novels, essays, reviews, biographies. As she parsed together Woolf's writings year by year, she'd felt a growing affinity for that anguished mind and now the life was nearing its end. (Of course, Woolf had actually died over fifty years ago, yet Flossy felt as if she were dipping her bread into this grief as freshly as if Jimmy had delivered the news that morning — this with a house full of guests surrounding her like a cocktail party.)

In fact, Mrs. Woolf lived next door to Flossy far more substantially than old Mr. McNutt, whose most pressing concern was a two-cent increase in the price of creamed corn at the general store or Mealie's cat pooping in his backyard, never a kind word to say about anyone or anything. Now that seemed senseless. Much better to surround herself with the deliciously catty Mrs. Woolf, that incisive mind, polished wordcraft, even, dear God, the tongue that could garrotte a lesser mortal with one gilded flap. At the very least Flossy was determined to choose an entertaining senselessness, not one that kept her shrill and awake at night about matters she could do nothing about.

Already knowing how Woolf's story would end was as terrifying as having someone living in your household whom your deepest heart feared would someday step into the bay with her pockets full of stones. Yet Flossy could not disavow the fascination either of Mrs. Woolf's ability to describe a mind unravelling. That eloquence had broadened her understanding of Thomas's desperate world, corrected it perhaps as a ground lens placed before imperfect eyes, and taught her heart about her brother. She had a mere seventy pages left in the last of the diaries.

Who would she take on next, read from stem to stern? Would there be a next? Maybe the Bishop. Fifteen years after her death, a substantial biography had just emerged last year and a fat book of Elizabeth's correspondence released in January, though Flossy could have her qualms about poking among the letters of someone they'd actually known. Maybe it was too soon. Elizabeth's estate had released some papers to Vassar but no one knew if there were other writings to come or journals. Flossy dearly hoped there would be journals. A shy writer like Elizabeth Bishop could remain obscure behind her poetry, whereas someone like Woolf, Flossy felt certain, scattered her heart onto every page of those journals. They were entirely written for a public of the future. She'd ask Richard about this. Oh Richard, she remembered with a sigh.

"Wasn't she lesbian?" Ruth plunged on. The innocence of a question that would hover as briefly as a dragonfly in another generation's consciousness and so like the young now, all apparently casual about sex but with no more confidence than their grandmothers. The question nevertheless tore at Flossy as if she were St. Sebastian himself wounded by arrows intended to bleed the body slowly while withholding the mortal blow.

Was she lesbian? It sounded rather bald-faced put out there on the kitchen table with Mealie's breakfast scones, raspberry jam and Devon cream. Flossy didn't think Mrs. Woolf would have called herself a lesbian. She didn't entirely approve of the Sapphists, had said so in the letters. Nonetheless, when confronted with the ardour of a Vita Sackville-West, Woolf's inclination to approve or disapprove took flight out some window somewhere. Whatever she was, Virginia Woolf was not impervious to love. When Flossy compared the affair to the marriage with Leonard Woolf, she felt that, yes, the relationship with the aristocratic Vita was most assuredly an expression of love. Did that constitute a lesbian? Flossy preferred to think her more a hybrid of sorts.

What would she have thought, her dear Mrs. Woolf, of the four of them sitting around Flossy's kitchen table, discussing her intimate life, half a century after her death? Had there been an intimate life with Leonard or had he insisted on chastity for fear a pregnancy might unlatch Mrs. Woolf's fragile mental gate or, perhaps, for his own undocumented shortcomings? Flossy thought she wasn't a lesbian but how to ever weigh one gloriously irrational love affair against twenty-nine years of rational matrimony? Not possible from where they sat. And how to strain it all now for the shaveling's simple yes or no?

"Well, it seems she did have a brief relationship with a woman," Flossy said, "but for most of her adult life she was married, happily, so far as we know, and she never chose to leave her husband until she chose to leave her life."

What Flossy knew from that life, if she knew anything, was that there were riches beyond the curiosities, inside the life and psyche of Virginia Woolf. She wasn't a commodity to be sipped, tasted and passed around a circle, the mysteries of her heart lifted like worsted skirts and peered beneath. She was a bosom friend, the rich, long drink of a rushing stream in the remotest part of a dark forest to be entered at one's own risk and on the trembling wing of humility. With long study, the calluses Flossy formed from working those books would be the slow and laboured buildup of compassion on each of her hands.

The young were quite unlikely to enter such a forest for a good many years. Perhaps they did know of suffering, passion, sacrifice — no doubt they had their own anguish and disappointments to bear, their heartaches, fears and desperation — but Flossy felt sure they had not yet worked out the hollows in the same way, stepped into the darkness that has no end, believed in it, sat in the dusk of those despairs to see their solitary night flowering and let their spicy perfumes invade their every pore.

Of course, unlike Virginia, Thomas hadn't put stones in his pocket and walked into the bay. No doubt he'd wanted to, had possibly longed to with all his heart. It was as good as death, though, the way he chose or had chosen for him: The way of no sense, no desire or action. It was as good, if not worse, to feel fear and anxiety every moment but to have not the relief of oblivion, not the strength to smash his own hourglass and release the sand to the bottom of the ocean. He'd lost whole decades to that underworld. Flossy thought her brother knew more about suffering than did all the rest of them put together, even the ones who'd come back from the war and thrown themselves into hard work or whisky. He knew just how much could be born by the human spirit. He may have been a prisoner of war of his own mind, but he had been chained face to face with his misery each day of his life as surely as any member of a gulag could be.

There were spirits, Flossy believed, placed among the rest of them but never really intended for this world, like Thomas and Mrs. Woolf. Flossy herself was one of the plodding practicals, a Leonard Woolf, a wall to protect the others as they carried the burden of their psychic pain. That these spirits would not die in their beds at ninety, with children to surround them, didn't much matter. Mealie'd often said that length of time had nothing to do with a life well-lived and Flossy had to agree. Though her brother had never picked up a pen and written a poem, she would always consider him an artist like Woolf.

How jittery she was, this Sylph, Ruth Trotter-Schaeffer, sitting near, drifting in and out of conversation with two generations of elders, restless like the tide, wanting neither in with them nor left out. She had freckles still on her nose, cinnamon stubble like Colchester earth covering the perfect contours of her head, the way she rubbed at it, stroked it actually as Flossy might Mealie's old cat, without so much as a flicker of consciousness, her shyness all dressed up as chill indifference that met Flossy's eyes but briefly.

How fresh and innocent she was to the possibility that any sorrow might be out there lying in wait for her. Her very own, like a tumour, dark, foreboding and fertile, entwining itself and feeding on the landscape of her psyche, it might be as unique to her as her hairline or the bottoms of her feet. The young are never able to imagine the demon that will take them under, Flossy thought, and there's always one, at least one. There might even be one, she imagined, in the depths of this child right now whose name Ruth could not know, raising only one fierce eye above the waterline every now and again, barely breaking a ripple, that would someday snatch at her bare ankle and haul her under. It would behoove everyone who took her sanity lightly to acquaint herself with Virginia Woolf.

Mealie had deftly turned the subject to Vincent van Gogh, was telling Ruth of stunning pictures, breathtaking vision and colour — skies, sunflowers, wheat fields and starry nights — all painted within three years, and for a good third of it locked up in a French asylum. "The one who cut his ear off," Mealie added, no doubt before Ruth could. "He took his own life too, but I've always thought it didn't much matter how he died, or when," Mealie continued, with a voice that could saw through a small tree, "like Woolf, he'd already left us some of the finest work of his century."

"You know that little print I have, dear?" Marjory interjected cheerfully, while blowing her nose, "Of the sunflowers in the upstairs bathroom?" by way of explanation, "That's him." Her cold was worse today. She was puffy and pale, unable to breathe through her nose.

Flossy was grateful for Mealie in countless ways. She could see what her friend was doing. Mealie was nudging the conversation delicately, like one might turn an invalid patient too long in bed. She knew the Woolf talk would be rubbing at Flossy, rubbing her raw, and she wanted to give it a rest.

"He killed himself too?" Ruth asked. Mealie nodded. "That was kind of dumb if he was so good," the youngster continued.

"He *was* good. Exceptional, but you know something?" Ruth stared at Mealie as she spoke, "he never sold more than one of his pictures. He traded his paintings for more paints to paint some more. And some prefer, as do I, to call his death self-deliverance," she smiled, gently ignoring the rest.

The child's optimism was touching, striking in its artlessness. All the young ones thought they had too much going for them, were too shrewd to make the mistakes of their parents, to let go the opportunities this good life afforded, choose the wrong person to love. They were optimistic, yes — too green to burn, some would say — but too tender as well to see that everything was choice, even the not choosing, the missed opportunities, the dreams packed up, salted on both sides, put off or put away forever in bottom drawers.

Flossy had taught in Great Village all her life, most of the adults up and down the shore for twenty miles. Some of them sat in her classroom day in and day out for six years, from the time they cornered the multiplication tables, straight through gerunds and the thorns of puberty until they issued forth as young men and women. For three generations she'd taught them, knew their possibilities and probabilities. Nobody had to tell her how soundly people undermined their own dreams — fear of leaving, fear of reaching, fear of failure. She saw it every day. And how frantically they searched for some other feet at which to lay the blame. Oh yes, Flossy O'Reilly saw infidelity up and down those shores of Cobequid Bay again and again and again and ninety-nine per cent of it had not a thing to do with sex.

"*Bon courage*," she'd always said to them as they walked out of her classroom at the end of grade twelve. "*Bon courage.*" If she knew anything from her many years of teaching, she knew for certain it wasn't dying that people feared, it was living.

But how to school the young in compassion? School them early, cushion the blow for the time when they'd need spades of courage and compassion. Not for the others who would go down early but more importantly for themselves, for that endless, corrosive drip of self-disappointment. Flossy didn't know. She was a good teacher, but she knew teaching could only go so far, get a good student to the threshold.

"I don't like her," Ruth announced, tossing the book back onto the pile. "Woolf," she barked the name at the others.

Mealie, seated beside her, reached out and touched Ruth on the forearm, "Good. We'll leave it at that then."

Ignoring Mealie, she looked directly at Flossy and repeated herself. "I don't like her writing."

"Ruth," Marjory warned.

Flossy nodded her head. At her age, she often found listening much more tiring than walking from one end of the village to the other. "Well," she began, "I don't suppose the emergence of one more literary critic is going to matter all that much to Virginia Woolf's legacy." She smiled at Ruth. "When I was your age and read Will Shakespeare for the first time, I said the very same thing: 'What's all the fuss about?'" She passed the plate of Mealie's scones around the table once more. "But I've discovered over the years that the older I get," she paused as Ruth took one and set it on her plate, "the smarter he gets." Flossy next passed the butter dish. "If I'd given up reading these writers at your age, I suppose I'd have missed quite a lot."

Was it an art, compassion? A gift, like so many others? She'd always wondered. Was it a form of genius or predisposition, in some people from birth, just as the ear for perfect pitch or the capacity, like Mealie's, to catch an emotion in five splendid strokes? Perhaps it was only those who'd already foundered on rocks too barren or massive, who were able to offer it to others? Had her brother Thomas, in the end, unearthed this pearl of compassion for himself, the meagre grain of sorrow washed day in and day out with sea-water tears for twenty-four years? What exactly had moved him to sit up in his bed one morning and once again breathe into the farthest reaches of his lungs, reclaim some vestige of life?

He only had two or three more weeks after that but all he wanted to do was sit and watch the water. He never had strength to do anything more. He was Lazarus, the spirit blown back into him, a man given a brief reprieve from death, death in life.

"Flo?" Mealie called her.

"Umn?"

The others were looking towards the door and someone standing outside. Ruth, sitting nearest, stood and reached to open it.

"Hello," she said softly.

"Hi," Bobby McLellan said, a big smile and a blush spreading over his face. He had something in his left hand but was staring at Ruth. He swallowed hard. The right hand was grasping the elbow of the left. Tufts of hair jutted from his head as if he'd gone to bed with it wet.

"Hello there Bobby, come in," said Flossy, standing.

He looked over as if startled to see her. "Oh, hi there, Miss O'Reilly, Mrs. Marsh?" he said, taking in the entire room now. "These came in after you left the other day? I was telling my dad you were in?" He set a neat stack of three cans of Peruvian sardines on the table. "We got some more."

"So, the Peruvians didn't get them after all."

"No, ma'am," he replied, "these few got away." He grinned

at everyone in the room, scratching his nose.

"That's very nice of you. I'll get my purse," she said.

"Oh, that's okay," he said. "My dad says you can pay next time you come by. He says you're good for it and you've got a memory like an elephant," he smiled again, as if warming to his audience. At seventeen Bobby McLellan was gangling enough not to know what to do with two free hands. Flossy thought he'd probably take up smoking any day now. He shoved them deep into the pockets of his jeans. "We have more if you need 'em."

"This should do me for a day or two, but I'll send Ruth along to get some more if I do. Thank you, Bobby." She took a step towards him but realized that he wasn't ready to leave. "These are my guests," she said. "This is Ruth and her mom, Marjory. Bobby's one of our local musicians. His rock 'n' roll band is playing this week at the Economy Clam Festival, isn't that right?"

"Yeah," he said, looking at Ruth, "but I'm not like a musician who knows music or anything? I just play bass for our kind of stuff. You don't like need to know music." Mealie's eyebrows rising up over her glasses had a look of staggering incredulity; Flossy hoped Bobby wouldn't see. Mostly, he wasn't looking at anybody but Ruth. "You could like come, there's no admission," he said. "All of you, if you wanna." She smiled and he blushed again. "I gotta go now, bye," he said abruptly, turning towards the door.

Flossy opened it for him. "Thank your father for me. Maybe we'll see you at the festival."

"Hope so," he said, waving and jumping down the four steps. Bobby picked his bike up from the grass and raced off.

As Flossy closed the door, she glanced across the table at Mealie who winked and said, "I do believe our Bobby McLellan's had his first near-life experience."

IX

THE TWO ICE CUBES SNAPPED AS MEALIE DROPPED THEM into hot coffee.

Closing the freezer door with her elbow, she padded towards Flossy's kitchen table.

"My favourite is Macbeth's 'rump-fed ronyon,'" Flossy said, looking up at her, "nobody insults better than Shakespeare."

"Remember in Lear when the daughters are wheedling down his entourage?" Mealie offered, taking a quick hot sip of the coffee.

"Plucking the Old Lion's whiskers," Flossy put a knuckle against her nose.

"There's a line in there," Mealie rasped, grabbing the copy of Shakespeare's *King Lear* that she was returning, as she dropped into a chair and flipped through the pages, "every woman must know," she stuck her tongue out and licked her thumb, "especially in the face of opposition," she looked up briefly to be sure someone was listening, "to the purchase of new ... red ... shoes."

Leaning towards Ruth, Flossy asked, "Have you read *King Lear* in high school yet?"

"No," she answered, frowning and not looking up from the cereal bowl.

"Well, Old Lear has decided to divide his kingdom among his daughters, Goneril, Regan and Cordelia, according to how much they love him. The first two have never loved anyone more, nor *will* they ever love anyone more, than their father," Flossy said. "The last daughter, Cordelia, refuses to flatter the old coot and says she loves him with the love due a father, no more, no less ..."

"And she happens to be the only one of the three," said Mealie, still thumbing through pages, "who genuinely loves the silly old bugger."

"The condition of dividing up his kingdom is that he be able to keep a company of a hundred knights that will move with him between the two daughters' castles month by month. Cordelia has been disinherited and dismissed."

"Goneril in September, Regan in October, back to Goneril," Mealie explained.

"But, like most soldiers with nothing to do, Lear's boys have got a bit rowdy, so the daughters complain and eventually collude to get rid of them, which is, of course, the last remaining symbol of Lear's power." Flossy thought it wasn't unlike the time Marjory had to wrest her father's car from him, Frank Trotter was an atrocious driver, but Ruth wouldn't be interested in similes this morning.

"Here it is," Mealie announced. "Goneril has already demanded that he get rid of fifty of the knights. True to form, he picks up his hundred lads and huffs off to the other daughter, Regan, but he gets no better reception there. She adds insult to injury by suggesting a further cut of twenty-five. By this time Goneril has arrived." Mealie looked down and began to read, "She says, 'What need you five and twenty, ten, or five, to follow in a house where twice so many have a command to tend you?' and Regan says, 'What need one?' To which, an exasperated Lear replies, 'O, reason not the need.'" Mealie slapped her thigh and coughed out a starchy laugh that disappeared for a minute while she drew in air, to follow it with a second wave of defining cackle. "Keep that line, honey," she leaned towards Ruth, who squinted up at her, "it'll come in handy sometime."

Marjory had left for Sackville yesterday, not before Flossy slipped her Richard's telephone number on a Post-it with a last-warning look, and this morning Ruth was doing her best to ignore the others at the table, even as Flossy spilled the juice and burnt the toast.

She asked her which of Shakespeare's plays Ruth had studied and got a muttered "*Othello.*" In her house, Ruth said, no one talked to her for a good hour after she got up.

"Maybe I'll take *Measure for Measure* this time, Flo," Mealie said, picking up the newspaper.

As Flossy stepped into the parlour to return *King Lear* and retrieve *Measure for Measure*, Ruth leaned over to Mealie and asked, "Doesn't she have any, like, *living* friends to talk about?"

Flossy smiled to herself. Ruth made little effort to lower her voice. No doubt the youngster had been hearing more than she wanted to about Virginia Woolf, Will Shakespeare and the Bishop but, then again, this morning she seemed annoyed by the effrontery of other human life forms in her field of vision.

Flossy, replacing books on a shelf just inside the parlour door, peeked out and could see Mealie's newspaper and the back of Ruth's head from where she stood. Mealie was initially silent. Lifting one eyebrow up over the newspaper she was reading, like an alligator to the first plop of hoof in water, she replied, "A few." The paper went back up and Flossy thought Mealie must have resumed reading, when she began to speak again.

"Which did you want to hear about most, Emmy Blaikie's hip replacement, the arthritic knees keeping Truina Hill awake at night, or maybe Penny Corbett's irritable bowel syndrome? That one's particularly entertaining. You go ahead and ask her about her friends." Mealie smacked her tongue on the roof of her mouth as if a daub of peanut butter were stuck there. Just when Flossy thought it was safe to go back into the room again, Mealie continued. "They're just about as boring as dirt." Flossy sat down in the parlour rocker. She was enjoying this.

After another few minutes, Mealie resumed talking in a morning voice that scraped out like metal on metal, "She's not doing this for you, if that's what's on your mind," she said, turning a page and tapping the seam flat. "It's a bit of freelance income she gets testing a new form of torture for the Yanks. CIA. You heard what happened at the Allan in Montreal in the fifties, with sleep deprivation and such?"

"Not really," Ruth answered cautiously.

"Oh, no? It was bad, but this one's much better. Yup, LSI — Literary Saturation Induction's the technical term they use for it, I think. We all pretty much broke after a week." Flossy caught Mealie's eye peering out over the serrated edge of the newspaper. "You're holding up pretty well, but everybody caves in sooner or later. Matter of time." She tapped the centre crease of the paper. Ruth was silent.

"Just kidding, honey," she said, giving the younger woman an exaggerated wink. "This is just Flo. She's gone on like this all seventy of the years I've known her." She leaned towards Ruth and dropped her voice confidentially: "If a tree falls in the forest and you're not there? Flo's still gonna be talking about

Yeats," she said, crinkling her nose. "Might just as well relax."

Later that morning, after the kitchen door had closed behind Mealie, and Flossy was left alone with her Guest, Ruth asked, "Why doesn't she get her own paper?"

"Beg your pardon?" Flossy leaned towards her.

Ruth raised her voice. It made her sound annoyed. "Why doesn't she get her *own* paper?"

"Who?" Flossy asked.

"The Deputy-Warden," she replied, heaving her voice at Flossy.

"Her own *paper?*" Flossy looked puzzled, as if the thought had never crossed her mind.

"Yeah, *newspaper*. Buy her own?" Ruth was shouting and pointing to the *Chronicle Herald* left on the chair where Mealie had just been sitting, "*Why doesn't she buy her own?*" Flossy was sure Mealie could hear them as she walked back to her place, two houses away. She glanced outside and noticed the studio door swinging closed.

"Well, she does, dear," Flossy replied kindly. "She just has it delivered here."

X

THE COLLIE LEAPT INTO THE AIR AND CAUGHT THE FRISBEE in one mid-flight twist, then dropped, pranced and wagged its way proudly back to Ruth.

Jimmy and Flossy leaned on the windowsill watching them play in the lane. A fresh breeze was blowing the curtains in around them this morning, a welcome break from the humidity of past days.

Outside, beneath the bright sunlight, Ruth was unaware of them watching, unaware of anything but the little black and white sheepdog dancing around her. Flossy heard her giddy laughter and observed the young woman's athletic grace as she threw, ran and played with the young dog. Nothing like a puppy to turn a woman into a girl all over again.

Jimmy O'Reilly had pushed through the screen door earlier with two Sobeys bags splitting with too many tomatoes, cucumbers, beans and beets.

"This is Ruth," Flossy said as he made his way to the sink to deposit his cargo. Jimmy nodded to Ruth who gave an indifferent wave, scarcely lifting her head from the newspaper, until she heard a single yip from the truck. She was on her feet, then, asking if she could see the dog.

"Does he have a leash?" she asked.

"Don't need one," Jimmy said. "He's not going anywhere."

Flossy dragged her finger along a line of dust on the windowsill, but her gaze was drawn back to the activity outdoors. Any photographer would capture that blithe face and the springing dog in this brilliant morning light as a millisecond of perfect happiness. How innocent and easily-come-by, a youngster with a dog.

"You know, Jimmy, that's the happiest she's been since she arrived."

He nodded his head. "*Ain't she* a pretty little *thing*," he said. "No *bigger'n* a *wishbone*, so she is." He stepped over to the counter and poured himself a cup of coffee then came right back to the window and settled in beside her like a chicken on a nest.

"She *got* a *dog* at home?" he asked, sipping his coffee.

Flossy shook her head. "Jack has allergies and her mother has no time."

"Kid *needs* a *dog*," he said, scratching his temple.

"You wouldn't want to leave Logie for a couple of weeks," she said, looking slyly at him from the corner of her eye.

"Oh, heh, heh, that *ain't* to say an old *feller* don't *need one* too," he grinned.

Watching this radically altered youngster laughing and playing, Flossy thought of Virginia and the diary she was so close to finishing. When the Woolfs' house was bombed in London, it was the diaries Virginia and Leonard had gone back to dig out of the dust and debris. Blessedly, she thought, because *they* were Virginia, her personality much more so than the other writings. Keeping a journal, Virginia had said, made her comb through each day to find the encounter that allowed her to see things in an entirely different light. These transformative moments were, she claimed, her grasp of reality.

Flossy looked across at her brother. The lads would be waiting for him at the general store but he was in no rush to be on his way. Nor was he talking about all the sprains and indigestion to strike the village since Flossy saw him last Friday.

No, Jimmy's old blue eyes were crinkled. He rubbed the back of his hand over his cheeks and his chin as if he'd just finished shaving. She could see his grin, the chip on the edge of his front tooth, the white scar along the jaw that he'd come back with from the war and his cupful of contentment as he leaned on the window, perfectly happy to stand there all day watching a youngster vaulting about with his dog.

XI

FLOSSY O'REILLY LOOKED FROM RUTH TROTTER-SCHAEFFER to the calendar on the wall above the long kitchen table, as if a symbol of time alone might transport her to the distant past.

If she'd wanted to, from where she sat Flossy could stretch a hand out and touch the square for today, Monday the eighth of August. The date stroked a recollection of some kind for her, of sadness she thought, as if she'd placed a hand where an arm had recently lain and felt its warmth but with no memory of who had been there. All throughout the morning and into the afternoon, the winking significance of the day had tugged the edges of her consciousness like a dream she was trying to remember that lay tucked away in opaque sleep.

Was it somebody's birthday? She ran through the ones she tried to acknowledge: not Mealie's, nor Jimmy or Noreen, their girls. She tried to fix her mind on the usual suspects, things that could chase out her unholy ghosts at this time of year: the shorter days, a reminder of grey November looming; the beginning of school and with it the unsettling memory of standing in front of a new crop of students. Though she'd not had a class in twenty years, September still had its way of bubbling up in her cauldron — once a teacher, always a teacher. Some of the best of them, Flossy knew, didn't sleep at all the last two weeks of August.

She looked around: a Brown Betty teapot with a chip out of the top sat on a metal trivet in the shape of Newfoundland that Jimmy's grandson had brought her after a trip there a few summers back. An unmatched salt and pepper, their contents looking tired and dusty, sat quietly beside Noreen's ladybug serviette holder with three different sizes of napkin squeezed between the wings. The white paint on the windowsill was beginning to crack and chip. She should try to get it painted before it turned cold. Did it matter? Would she even be here when it turned cold?

She looked back around the kitchen. The sun streaming through the window showed every splatter and speck on the wall. This was where she fit now. It was the season of make-do, with chips and nicks and dust settling quietly over everything. Others thought she didn't see the dust anymore, no doubt wondered if maybe her eyes were going the way of her hearing, when in fact Flossy'd just stopped caring about it. If you only have a finite amount of time left, she figured who in her right mind would be worrying about a little dust.

"There'll be dust enough where we're headed," Mealie liked to say, as if anyone needed to be reminded.

Flossy didn't miss teaching any more than she missed dusting. She didn't miss bored and unhappy teenagers, like the Sylph across the table. She liked how age simplified things. Now she had everything she needed within the compass of her outstretched arm: the old *Funk & Wagnall*, a notebook, pencil, half a pink eraser, ruler, her books and the calendar. It was a pretty thing, Maritime views with houses, churches and seascapes put out by Stanfield's, though at that moment Flossy wasn't actually looking at the photo for August, the days or even the few scattered appointments pencilled in here and there throughout the month. She was merely perched on her yellow chair, thinking of the Sylph's question, posed only a moment before: "Didn't you take him to a doctor?"

Flossy took a small sip of strong tea. It was the question of a scientific age, perhaps even a psychological one, she thought, a generation sure that every action had a reaction, every question an answer, each dilemma a solution. *Was* there an answer to every question? Were questions, like matter and energy, never lost, only transformed? Was it possible to find, now, for example, answers to questions posed years ago, questions bent around the universe or buried under half a century of tides and shifting sands? Were they even the same questions that had drifted there in the first place? She lay one hand on top of the other on her lap.

"Oh, yes." The doctor, in fact, was the first one their mother had brought to see her brother Thomas when he took to his bed. She trusted Doctor Rushton. He, a son and grandson had been doctors this side of Truro for as long as Flossy could remember, though Rushton Senior may have cured more horses than people in his day. In their family, Doc Rushton was next to God, from the time their mother had been so sick after Jimmy was born.

The doctor had come around to see Thomas a week or so after he'd taken to his bed. Flossy could remember the commotion of his arrival. Dr. Rushton had a motor car — not so many did in those parts in the summer of '27 — and you could hear the gears grind as he whined and chugged up the grade from Great Village in a cloud of dust, thumping along the washboard road. Their mother hadn't told them he was coming, if she knew, so it was no small shock for Flossy and Jimmy, racing each other up from the bay and tumbling into the house to tell her Doc Rushton had gone by, to find him squat, square and spilling over a wooden chair in their own summer kitchen.

Dr. Rushton was chatting and laughing with their mother. He'd been telling her a funny story about a sister of his who'd kept a pet pig in the house, as Flossy recalled, before hoisting himself to his feet and asking her to take him to the patient. Their mother carried a chair up behind the big man as there wasn't normally one in Thomas's room.

The doctor had a jolly, booming voice that made you think he was always speaking over your shoulder to a crowd behind you. You'd hear his wheezy laughter outside after church service on Sunday, shaking hands with the other men as if he himself had delivered the sermon or was just uncommonly pleased with himself for being there. He was a man used to putting a lot of people at their ease. Their mother always said of Dr. Rushton, "he could talk to anyone." She valued it. Being a huge old man, though, the talker was winded by the time he'd got upstairs that day and it was a few good minutes before he could huff any more than two words at a time.

"Thomas, m'boy," he exclaimed, as though finding their brother in the bed had taken him entirely unawares. "How's th'boy?" he wrapped a foot around the chair leg, scraped it towards him and dropped heavily into the seat. He sat there beside Thomas like a fat old Rhode Island Red, his neck short in his shirt, and took a handkerchief out of his pocket, so as to mop the sweat beads that formed on his shining bald scalp. "Hot day." His bulk was imposing, half an inch of flesh spilled out over the tight collar he was wearing. Their mother smiled more than usual when he was around. "It is," he panted.

Dr. Rushton had never been upstairs before, hadn't even been in the house as far as Flossy could remember. It wasn't a small thing to have him there. His breadth, substantially larger than their father, who'd been no small man, his puffy hands resting on his knees, his thick-glasses gaze, the soft, wide face and massive, wiry eyebrows, all gave the impression of a man of importance who filled that room, the whole house in fact. He knew their mother and maybe they'd talked about Thomas, but he seemed to like to give you the idea that he knew something about you, inside you, the way you thought.

"Now, I know what you're thinking" was one of his favourite ways of tidying up a story. He would hook a thumb in one suspender and point a finger of the same hand at you, but he never really knew, only fancied he did.

Doc Rushton was used to people paying attention, nodding and asking no questions. If he told them to run up the nearest pin cherry, most people would hurry out the front door and shinny away. He expected it. You'd feel wrong for not obliging someone like him. If it had been Lillian up there in bed instead of Thomas, and he'd told her to get up, without hesitation she'd have got up and, quick, made him a pan of biscuits.

He listened to Thomas's chest, tapped his back and looked inside his mouth. He made him roll his eyes around and cough. Their mother motioned the two younger ones out of the room, but Flossy loitered on the top step.

Dr. Rushton asked Thomas if anything had happened to him the day it all started, if he'd had any sharp pains in the chest or head, if his eyes had blurred, if he'd passed out or had a sore throat or rash, any blood in anything he'd passed? Thomas said no. Was there any swelling in the feet? Sores on the fundament? No. Did he feel sick? No. "Any discomfort whatsoever, son?" he asked. No.

"What about defecation?"

"Wh-wh-what?"

"Can you use the thunderbox, the outhouse, do your business?"

"I've w-w-went most days."

"Any bloating?"

"N-n-no."

When Dr. Rushton didn't get the answer he was looking for, some straw he could sit and chew on, he let out a huge sigh and leaned back in his chair that creaked under the great man's weight. Flossy could see him through the open door: he removed his round wire-rimmed glasses, slowly unhooked one side then the other from behind each thick ear, scratched both bushy eyebrows with the thumb and forefinger of one hand, then he fixed those tiny chicken eyes straight on Thomas and set in on him in a low voice about letting their mother down when she was a widow woman and had suffered enough over the shock of their father.

Flossy had to hand it to him, the doc was good with words. He talked so earnestly and for such a long while that she was convinced by the end of it that Thomas was letting Dr. Rushton down too, his wife, all of Great Village and the entire Presbyterian Union. He was the eldest, he said, the man of the house now, and there wasn't anyone to fill his shoes. Thomas should act like a man. He said it wasn't right to just turn in like that, lie in bed while the womenfolk did the work that was properly his.

"God alone knows everyone feels like giving up some time or other," he said, "*everyone*, but it isn't the kind of thing a man does." Thomas must have felt those tiny eyes burning into him. "Every man must remain, always and in the presence of everyone," he said, pointing one stubby fat finger at him, "master of himself."

FOR A LONG WHILE AFTER that, Flossy thought about what Doc Rushton had said to her brother. She wondered if every man did have this some time in his life. Was it some initiation ritual that every other adult in Great Village had passed except Thomas? Was he not a man then because he'd taken to his bed? She didn't believe Doctor Rushton; couldn't believe that everyone had this the way Thomas did. It took him over like a ghost sickness with none of the usual signs of something being wrong. He couldn't act like a man, either, that was the problem. He couldn't act. Was Thomas the only one who couldn't? Had Doctor Rushton, along with her father and all the other men of the village, been just a troupe of better actors?

The doctor descended the stairs, weaving from side to side to see each step out over his belly, and told them he seemed healthy as a spring foal, couldn't figure what was keeping Tom up there: strong heart, perfectly sound in the chest, good reflexes. (They never called him Tom.) Said he was baffled, hadn't seen anything like it in the forty years he'd been practising medicine, a young buck taking to his bed for no apparent reason.

Doctor Rushton plodded through a dozen diseases they'd all heard of. He gave them the symptoms, complications and cures, then slowly argued his way back out of each one. He was stumped, couldn't come up with any illness known to modern medicine that could match what had got into Thomas. He wasn't sure he was sick.

Dr. Rushton said some people might come down with an illness that doesn't show up in the normal way for a time. The fatigue couldn't be explained all at once but eventually it would be clear what had got him, although he confessed he saw this more with old people. He told them to watch for rashes and a fever, especially the fever. It would tell him more. There could be seizures too. If he ever wet the bed they should let him know. His face crumpled in the centre as he hooked a thumb through his suspender and lost himself in his own thoughts while cleaning his thumbnail. "Then there're the melancholics ...," he said, letting his voice drift while glancing in Flossy's direction.

Her mother shook her head, "Flossy's been doing the work of a grown man around here, she deserves to know." Doc Rushton cleared his throat and proceeded in a low voice while those little eyes burned through his glasses into Lillian O'Reilly.

"The melancholics," he said, "go like this maybe once every few years or so, take straight to their beds and there's nothing can be done." It runs in families, mostly with women, he said, a species of nervousness. It was an inclination by nature, a hereditary taint, he cautioned, not to be confused with outright malingering. He had seen it often and no amount of talking seemed to do them any good. These ladies often had difficulty seeing the winter come on, filling up with dread and hopelessness as the fall advanced. It was possible Thomas had something like it.

Sometimes it was brought on by a shock or disappointment but often it grew from something entirely insignificant that's built out of proportion "up here," he said, tapping his temple just above the arm of his wire glasses that dug permanent grooves into each side of his wide head.

"On the other hand," he argued, "could be a spurt of growth, stumbling on depleted soil. Feed him up," he counselled, dropping his fist emphatically on the table. "Six eggs a day, meat with every meal, two cups of meat blood between meals and a regimen of strychnine, in prescribed doses until his energy returns." If they did this and avoided constipation at all cost, Dr. Rushton said it would only be a matter of time before he came around to himself again. He'd be a new man before the snow was flying.

Flossy peeked at her mother who shifted uncomfortably in her chair. She knew as well as Lillian O'Reilly there was no money to feed him up like that. All they had was one cow and a calf. If they killed the cow, Flossy calculated, they wouldn't have milk or butter for another two years until the heifer freshened. If they killed the calf, would it be enough meat and blood to cure him or would they then have to kill the cow too? Her mother was, no doubt, figuring the same cruel calculation.

Then there was Queen Esther to consider: if there was but a single vital thing left to the survival of this remnant of the O'Reillys, it surely had to be that cow. Yet Queenie was so much more than a cow; she was their friend, their rock, their brindle comfort, had provided richly for the house for years. She would have let the Grim Reaper milk her, would even stand patiently for Jimmy who tugged away at her and could no more milk a fly. They couldn't possibly repay such fidelity with a blow above the eyes. Who between them could have done so? Not their mother and not Flossy. Besides, they'd all perish without that cow. Just the thought of it quickened her pulse.

Their mother asked him if people recovered from the melancholy. While most did, he told her there was a certain small number of incurables. Usually, they ended up in Dartmouth, he said, the ones that were a danger to themselves.

There wasn't anybody who hadn't heard about Dartmouth or knew that only the most desperate of souls ended their days there behind barred windows and locked doors. Mount Hope they called it, though there'd be precious little hope to be found anywhere among those walls. Doctor Rushton warned their mother she mustn't worry about that happening to Thomas. Those cases were extreme and wouldn't apply here, like the Bulmers' daughter, Mrs. Bishop, who'd lost her mind after she'd been widowed so young with a brand new baby. The Bulmers had had to keep vigil on her day and night. He'd seen many of those committed and Tom was nothing like them.

Their brother wasn't mad and he was never dangerous to them or himself, as far as they knew. There would never be a question of sending him off to a place like that. He'd not last a month. He was like those eggs that get laid by the chickens when they haven't enough grit; the shell is soft and transparent and if you were to put your finger on them you'd leave a dent in their oval perfection. You couldn't send someone like Thomas to a place like that.

Doctor Rushton said he figured maybe Mah was being too soft on him, that she let him think too much about himself. He said this while buttering the second half of his biscuit as a piece of chewed food escaped from his mouth and lobbed out onto the table. He dabbed it up with his finger and licked it off.

"If his father were here," he said, his mouth full and waving the knife with a flag of butter on the end back and forth while he swallowed, "he'd have a birch rod behind that woodshed door and not be a particle afraid to give the lad something to brood about. He wouldn't be lying in bed for long." He scooped the last half of a biscuit into his mouth and blazed Lillian O'Reilly with those tiny beads of eyes to make sure she was listening. "The lad's a man in years," he explained to her, "but there's still some boy in him that's gotta be toughened up. Spare the rod," he warned, taking a bite off the end of another biscuit he was preparing to slice and dress, and shaking one of his immensely fat fingers. Fowler's tonic combined with arsenic was another consideration, but Dr. Rushton concluded the strychnine the superior cure.

These last notions were just dried leaves blowing in gusts of wind, thoughts tossed out before them as the doctor wound down his impressively unhelpful clock. They'd had their disappointment laid out by then. Neither Flossy nor her mother had a question left between them. They'd been desperate to hear something concrete from Dr. Rushton, so sure he'd offer something definite to pursue for their brother's cure that would, at a minimum, burn away the layer of fog that obscured the entire matter. They could barely get Thomas to eat the smallest helping of porridge or potatoes in a day. He was about as capable of eating meat, eggs and drinking cow's blood as a newborn.

"He saw a doctor, yes, Thomas did," Flossy replied to the curious, open young face seated across from her over afternoon tea. "They weren't then what they are today, at least some of them," she added.

And like all those everywhere up and down the shore awaiting word from the doctor, Flossy and her mother expected bad news, didn't even much hope for good. They just wanted it to be one or the other, not something in-between, neither tide-in nor tide-out. He didn't know. What was in between was indefinable. He couldn't really say.

So, after all the words and opinions of the great man, his arguing back and forth with himself, they were none the wiser. Dr. Rushton sniffed a great deal about this whole affair. He really didn't know anything more than all the rest of them but nonetheless he spoke with great authority. You sensed, though, among all the sniffling, that he didn't like being baffled by medical science. Perhaps his disappointment lay in this even more so than his inability to make Thomas better. The doctor took pleasure in knowing what was best for everyone and being taken to heart.

Bolstered by two cups of tea and four of their mother's warm biscuits with butter and crabapple jelly, Dr. Rushton said he felt certain he could reason Tom out of his gloom and would consider his approach in the coming days. He warned them never to give in to the bleakness: at every opportunity they should tell him how much stronger he looked and how much better he seemed. Dr. Rushton would do likewise and by virtue of his natural authority and the confidence Tom had in his skill, the symptoms would gradually disappear.

And so he proceeded to do just that. In another week, Dr. Rushton was back upstairs to spend an hour talking like a Presbyterian preacher about patience, hope and joy. The week after that, he argued the case of science, disputing with their brother, curled up and mute on the bed, his silly misconceptions of illness and turning his mind towards the light of the doctor's own healthy vision. On the next visit, he pursued his efforts to persuade Thomas to renew the attitude of good health, while emphasizing the value of exercise. This after three weeks of increasing doses of strychnine that would send Thomas into violent spasms of vomiting so that he seemed weaker each day. All the while he lay pale and fetal on his bed and the rest of them came to think they'd lose him if it went on much longer.

The next time they expected him, Dr. Rushton didn't appear; mercifully, Mrs. McLellan had delivered her fourth in the middle of the night and he'd been called out. Thomas's treatment, far from restoring him to robust health, was bringing the rest of them to despair. The dinner table had gone silent with the unspoken knowledge that someone was dying upstairs. It was little Jimmy who finally took that whole bottle of strychnine and dumped it down the outhouse. Neither Flossy nor her mother could scold him for it.

What became apparent was that Doctor Rushton could not bear mystery, could not accept that the mind alone might cripple a healthy young man as permanently as the infantile paralysis.

He could not abide that which was not quantifiable. Perhaps that's why his attitude towards Thomas ultimately hardened to the opinion that their brother suffered nothing but wilful malingering.

The visits troubled their mother for weeks afterward. Flossy knew this because Lillian admired Doctor Rushton and her faith in him was such that she would have made herself do whatever he'd said, all but this, bringing her son to the edge of death. As for the whipping, she would have much preferred to whip herself. She had to find her way of thanking him for his time and concern, while suggesting they'd care for Thomas the best they could themselves.

She was low for the longest while afterward and Flossy couldn't make her smile over anything, even when she brought her daisies that she'd picked near the creek, and there were times when she swore she saw her mother's eyes welling up over her sewing. To think that she should take a rod to Thomas, that it would be for his own good to beat her son, that she might even be failing him by not doing so, was hard for Lillian O'Reilly. She could be severe with them, the disciplinarian, but there was no cruelty in her; she could yell when she really had to — on a windless day you could hear her to the other side of the barn — but she wasn't one for striking anybody.

Now their father, he was another matter. Dr. Rushton was right; their father would have fleeced the hide off Thomas but Flossy thought it wouldn't have served a whit. Maybe that's just how their mother reasoned herself out of it; she knew exactly what William O'Reilly would have done and that nothing good ever came of it. He was never the one to call forth someone's better part. The rod was no way to call forth Thomas's, that was certain, but they were still left at such a loss to know precisely how to do that. It wasn't will they had to beat out of him, they knew that. It was something that needed restoring.

Their mother didn't say much after Dr. Rushton's treatments but she did talk to Flossy one night at the barn. Pushing her palm against Queen Esther's flank to move the cow over a step so she could get in to milk her and patting the warm wide side, she spoke to the plink-plink rhythm of her milking, "It'd be like … taking a birch rod …," plink, plink, "to this one …," plink, plink, "after she'd given …," plink, plink, "all the milk she had to give." Said she didn't see how poison and a whipping could cure what ailed him.

Flossy was relieved that her mother fell back on her own good sense. She couldn't have encouraged her in the other, didn't think it would have turned out any differently.

Some might have thought it couldn't have turned out worse, when you consider twenty-four years of it — the best part of a young man's life lying in a bed — but with all those years behind her now and all the tragedies she'd heard of in the village over the time, the desperate souls who'd run shrieking off into the bay in the middle of the night, the young and old swinging their disappointments from a sturdy barn beam, the hunting rifles too near at hand when hope dissolved — she'd have to say it really could have been worse, much worse.

The youngster sitting just then at Flossy's kitchen table licked raspberry jam from the palm of her hand that had dripped over the side of a banana muffin. She rubbed the hand on a napkin then leaned forward in the chair she was sitting on and confided in Flossy that her mother, too, "*loved* to stay in bed."

In fact Marjory Trotter, Flossy was to learn that afternoon from her daughter Ruth, kept three alarm clocks in her bedroom and the last, loudest and longest to ring was placed so far under the bed that she had to pull herself out, get down on her hands and knees to reach it and shut it off.

"Pretty good for a minister, eh?" As Ruth said it, she giggled like a girl half her age and pulled her shoulders up in anticipation of Flossy's amusement.

The tiny older woman looked from the youngster's mouth up to the twinkling eyes. With a small tilt of her chin towards her chest and a conspiratorial smile, Flossy O'Reilly had to agree.

XII

"RUTH TROTTER-HYPHEN-SCHAEFFER, UP AND AT 'EM PEANUT butter. We're hyphen outta here in something like fifteen minutes." Mealie Marsh stood at the bottom of the stairs, sharpening her voice like an axe on a whetstone. "Time waits for no man and precious few women."

It was Tuesday morning. Flossy and Mealie were already on their second cup of coffee. She came back to the table.

"She unpacked yet?" Mealie asked in a low voice.

Flossy shook her head.

Ruth shuffled into the kitchen a few minutes later, stretching and rubbing her eyes.

"Mornin'," she said.

"Sleep well?" Flossy asked.

"'Til now," she replied, glancing warily at Mealie. She reached down to rub Oscar Wilde's ears. "I'd prefer Dash," she said, nudging Mealie's foot with her bare toe.

"Unh?" Mealie turned one corner of the paper down, pulled her chin in and looked up at her over the top of her half-glasses.

"Trotter-Dash-Schaeffer," she said.

"Okay with me," said Mealie. "Then, we'll be dashing outta here in ...," she checked her watch, "eleven minutes."

"Why?"

From behind the newspaper, Mealie replied, "Why is not in question."

Ruth stood in the middle of the kitchen thinking about that. "Where, then?" she asked.

"My Life Studies class, at ten, with *the* most gorgeous body either side of Cobequid Bay." By now Ruth had seated herself at the table before an empty bowl and a glass of orange juice. She was shaking cereal into her dish when her eyes suddenly opened. She sat forward and looked at Mealie.

"Nuuuude!" Mealie crooned, one eyebrow reaching up.

Ruth's cereal dribbled over the side of the bowl. She picked up two Shreddies and put them into her mouth.

"These are for you." Mealie pushed a sketchpad and a set of charcoal pencils in a wooden case towards her.

"Really?" The young woman opened the pencils as she munched on the cereal. She looked from them to Mealie then Flossy. "But I can't draw."

"Who said?" Mealie scowled.

"Oh, you won't want to miss Peter, dear." Flossy leaned towards her confidentially, "He's ...," she paused for a moment, stretching for the right word, then, in a low voice, murmured, "*extraordinary.*"

"A *man*?" Ruth scratched her saffron crown, focussing now on Flossy. "Are you coming?" the words tumbled out.

"Oh, no, no, I'll wait to see your work." Noting the puzzlement drifting into the young woman's eyes, Flossy added from the perch of her yellow chair, "There are some appreciations, Ruth, that time doth not wither."

"One just gets over talking about 'em," Mealie added from behind the newsprint.

A suppressed smile drifted slowly across Ruth's face as she looked from Flossy to Mealie and down to her bowl of cereal.

XIII

FOR HER PART, FLOSSY O'REILLY DELIBERATED OVER HER writers and their lives that sweltering August as carefully as she might string a prized scarlet ibis for fishing along the bends and bows of the Great Village River.

The art with any student, she felt certain, was in the casting — wrist straight, pitch a fly out just beyond the reach, ravenous as they all were about life's flashy questions, and she could almost count on them to leap and snatch before it could scratch the water's skin. Flossy had spent the better part of a lifetime casting her morsels about, illuminating sweetmeats about the works and lives of the writers she so admired.

As Ruth, Mealie and Flossy sat quietly around the table early Wednesday morning, the rough rhythmic crunch of feet on gravel filtered into their consciousness. Ruth's head went up, the others followed, like birds detecting motion.

"Anybody ho-ome?" a low voice sang out. Flossy slipped from her chair and pulled the screen door for a young man clad in shorts with a cardboard carton of eggs in his hand.

"Hi, Flossy. Mom asked me to drop these off. The chickens

are laying their brains out. How's things?" A shaggy head of sun-bleached brown curls, wet along the hairline framed ale-coloured eyes. He was flushed; sweat dripped off his face and soaked through his T-shirt. A pair of wire glasses sat upon a sturdy nose.

"Manganiferous," she replied, "what about your chickens?"

"Laying," he said carefully, "can't stop 'em." He held the carton out to her.

"Come in, come in, don't let the flies out," she said, waving him in. "I'll get you some juice."

"Thanks. It's way too hot out there ..." Phil stepped to the threshold then abruptly stopped, noticing the others quietly watching from their places around the kitchen table. Balanced there, he filled nearly the entire screen door.

"Oh! Y'ra ...," he stammered, "a girl!" Then, somehow, one huge foot caught on the other and he stumbled into the room, mercifully catching the counter just short of Flossy's arms. The three women passed an amused glance that spared him outright laughter. Phil mumbled on. "I saw you leave the store yesterday," he said to Ruth. "Sorry, I thought you were a ... I only saw you from the ... We needed a ... shortstop," he finally blurted out.

Stepping entirely inside now, he nodded towards Mealie, "Hello, Mrs. Marsh." Turning back to Flossy he said, "I wanted to bring your books back too." He took the glass of orange juice, switching it between hands as he pulled a knapsack down each arm and retrieved three books from inside. "Thanks, Flossy. If you have any more of this guy's stuff," he said, tapping the book on top, "I'd be happy to see it." He spoke carefully and watched to be sure she caught his words. He pressed the cold glass against his forehead for a minute before drinking the juice.

She leaned over and glanced at the book. "By stuff, my Sesquipedalian, I gather you mean Mr. Rilke's writings, not shaving soap or cigarette papers he might have left behind?"

"I do," he grinned, glancing over at the other women. Ruth smiled back.

"Well then, I think there may just be some stuff around. How about the letters, the Rodin letters, have I ever given you those?" He shook his head. "Two volumes; I'll bring them by the store. Thank your mother for the kindness, Pumpernickel." As Flossy spoke she loaded a crust of fresh bread with butter and raspberry jam for Phil Spencer.

"This is Ruth Trotter-Schaeffer, Phil; she's here from Ontario and we're hoping she'll stay awhile. Ruth, Phillip Spencer."

"Good to meet you," he said, putting the glass on the counter and wiping his hand on his shorts before reaching it out to her. Phil had, by now, entirely collected himself and smiled confidently in her direction. In fact, the others noticed he'd barely taken his eyes off Ruth from the moment he saw her sitting there. Mealie winked at Flossy.

"Nice to meet you too," she said, sitting up and stretching a long hand out to him.

"Ruth plays ball," Flossy offered in a quiet voice.

"Oh, yeah?" shaking his mane and pushing the sweat-soaked curls back from his face. "This's hardball," he replied.

"That's all I play," Ruth said, flashing her brown eyes at him.

"Oh, yeah?" he smiled and shrugged. "This's only guys."

Other, different women might have jumped into the silence that followed to cluck and assure Ruth she'd not want to play with the Great Village Ironclads — too rough, too competitive. Flossy, arms now folded, stared at Phil too as if waiting for him to rise to some unyielding challenge.

"What?" he asked, looking at her. Nor was Ruth letting him

off. Mealie Marsh was getting interested. She closed the paper and set it aside.

"What do you play?" he asked, turning back to Ruth.

"First base. It's a mixed league."

"Oh." Phil Spencer's eyebrows jumped. He bobbed his head thoughtfully. (Even Flossy, who didn't follow baseball, knew first base had to be a good player.) It was a wedge and Mealie was the one to follow through.

"Just call her Dash," she said casually, her voice scratching out from the end of the table.

Phil shifted on sandal-clad feet that Flossy noted were fit for a young draft horse. She could see him thinking. He looked from Mealie to Flossy, who lifted her chin in an unspoken question, then to Ruth. He bit his lower lip and Flossy could see he was sizing up the fact that long, lean, Ruth Trotter-Shaeffer might well pass for a fine-boned boy, albeit a pretty one. He quickly shook his head.

"She's way too ...," he started, paused, looking at Flossy, "we'd never get away with it." He shook his head.

"I'm really good," she said.

"You ought to see her spit," Mealie interjected.

"Now then, my Boonfellow," Flossy began, taking him by the arm and drawing him a little closer to Ruth, "do you not suppose that if Will Shakespeare could put all those lads on stage at Stratford on Avon and convince everyone in the audience that they were women, that the four of us couldn't pass off one little woman as a shortstop on the significantly more short-sighted stage of a Great Village baseball field?"

Phil looked at Ruth again. "You have your glove with you, Dash?"

"No," she said with a wince. "I wasn't expecting to play."

"She'll have one," Flossy chirped.

"Needs a uniform," he said.

"Who's out?" Mealie asked.

"Jeff," Phil replied. "Broke his digit," he said, holding up a middle finger with a grin.

"Who, Jeff Moore?" Flossy asked. Phil nodded. "He's not much bigger than Dash." Not wanting to give him a chance to change his mind, she added, "You get the uniform; Dash'll be ready."

Phil grew serious, "Not a word to anyone; we'd get bounced from the league."

Ruth raised a two-finger Brownie salute. "I promise to do my best ..."

Mealie followed, two fingers in the air.

"Agreed," Flossy raised hers as well.

"I'll get you at quarter to six." He turned back to Flossy. "Thanks Flossy," taking the bread in his left hand and a bite from it. "Don't be late ... Dash," he said to Ruth with a huge grin, as if the idea had been his all along. She gave a little finger-wiggle of a wave in reply.

"Bye, Mrs. Marsh." She, too, gave a finger-wiggle wave, as Flossy shot a teacherly look in her direction. Turning back he reminded Flossy, "Don't forget the stuff."

"On your way, Stringbean," she said, "you'll be late for work," closing the door gently behind him and watching as he ambled away. Turning back towards the two others in her kitchen, the pleasure she saw on their faces as Mealie and Ruth hunched closer together, Flossy noted how delicious conspiracy could be. Mealie was already making a list of things they'd need for Ruth's disguise.

Flossy leaned for a moment against the door, her hands

behind her back, watching them. So, it hadn't taken long after all. Remarkable. She'd wondered if there might be a courageous local lad somewhere in Great Village to place himself in the sights of the fair maiden. She *was* pretty, the kind of woman who would attract admiring glances even with her hair shaved to the wood, perhaps because of it. Flossy thought the absence of hair made her eyes even more fetching. They hadn't come so far from the courtly days of Arthur's Round Table after all, when gallant knights all a-gleaming in mail, shield and helmet would enter tournaments to do fearless battle to win a lady's glance and possible affection.

This one looked considerably more vulnerable, Sir Phil the Awkward, in sweat-drenched T-shirt, summer shorts, big knees and long-boned, hairy legs. He may have stumbled into the arena but he'd made an endearing recovery and she was sure she'd detected something, a spark arc across her kitchen.

"You'll need a wad of gum," Mealie was making notes, "and I'll get you a cup at Kilmers when I'm in Truro this afternoon."

"A cup?" Ruth giggled, "I don't need a cup!"

"If you don't have something down there to adjust when you're up to bat, Honey," Mealie was saying, twiddling her pencil back and forth before pointing it at her, "they're *never* gonna think you're a *guy*." When Ruth grinned, she added, "In fact, I'm gonna get you a large. Might just as well create a stir for the village. What do you weigh?"

"Hundred and ten," Ruth said.

"I weighed that once," Mealie said, catching Flossy's eye, "for twenty-seven minutes when I was ten, I think." Ruth giggled.

Phil Spencer knew Flossy's routine better than she did herself. There wasn't much that missed his gaze at the general store. He could have run that shop with both hands tied behind his back and a wiggle of the ears if he'd wanted, but all Phil Spencer needed was a summer job to make a bit of money, play some baseball and catch up on his reading.

With his visit, Ruth Trotter-Schaeffer had come to as well. She'd swung 'round from the table, stroked what little hair she had and leaned towards the newcomer in their midst, poised on the edge of her chair like the charming Sylph she was, inhabitant of ancient forests, testing the winds. She'd noticed. And bright-eyed Mealie Marsh never missed a thing.

"Who was that?" Ruth asked with the usual cool indifference when the three women were again seated quietly at the table.

"Just now?" Flossy asked, "Phil Spencer? He's from here, home for the summer."

"What's he do?"

"Works at the general store," Mealie offered.

"With the other guy?" Ruth asked.

"Who's that?" Flossy looked up.

"The sardine guy?"

"No, no, Phil works for the competition, the other general store across from the church." It was the short answer. Ruth looked back and forth between the older women, who had each returned to her reading. Friends who went back as far as they did knew each other's mind with little more than a twitch or glance and right here in Flossy's kitchen they had wordlessly colluded to hold out, to keep young Phil Spencer in the shadows. Mystery, above all. Flossy stroked her hand along the seam of the page she wasn't actually reading. One had to cultivate mystery to awaken the heart's curiosity.

In another minute, she felt the gentle pressure of Ruth's hand on her arm. Ah well, she supposed mystery didn't have half a chance where hormones prevailed. She hadn't been a teacher all those years to forget there was no stopping an on-rushing train.

"I mean, the rest of the year," the young woman persisted.

"Oh, he's still a student." Again Flossy let her attention fall back to Virginia Woolf. Phil was a good boy. He'd be fine company for Ruth, a godsend. But they mustn't for a minute let her think this was anything but her own idea. In fact, better to outright discourage her interest wherever possible. "There's an old glove in the garage, hanging on the wall," Flossy said to Ruth. "If that one's had the biscuit, we'll drive down to Jimmy's later and borrow his grandson's."

When she had stepped outside to retrieve the glove, Mealie leaned towards Flossy with a twinkle in her eye. "Now, why didn't *you* think of that, Miss O'Reilly?"

"Because I'm not sixty anymore," Flossy replied, a knuckle concealing her smile. It was beginning to look as if she wasn't going to have to influence either side of this equation; she'd never been much of a matchmaker anyway. Mealie'd always said, "You couldn't see a match till it was blown out and the smoke drifting towards Glenholme." It wasn't entirely so; Flossy saw a lot more than she let on; heard a lot more too. She was just an exceptionally wise editor.

"Is her knapsack still packed?" Mealie inquired.

Flossy nodded, "I give it twenty-four hours."

Perhaps she might beg off the afternoon errands tomorrow after all, plead weariness, send the shopping list and Rilke books to the store with Ruth. She disappeared to her bookshelves in the parlour and returned a few minutes later with the two volumes of Rodin letters she'd promised Phil. She'd left the three books he'd just returned on the table near Ruth.

No sooner had she returned with the glove than Flossy saw

her pick up the copy of Rilke's *Letters to a Young Poet*. Ah, a perfect place to start.

"He studies books, literature, at Acadia in the Valley," Flossy said to her, "you can't hold that one back. Phil Spencer's been gobbling up my books since he was no higher than this table. Now he's reading them all over again. You watch, he'll have those two big volumes of Rilke letters back by next weekend."

"Day after tomorrow, now that he knows you're here," Mealie interjected without looking up.

"His family lives up the road from Jimmy, near the old farm, a couple of miles from here."

The three were quiet again. Ruth opened the Rilke book and Mealie's attention had returned to the *Chronicle Herald*. Just as Flossy was about to resume her reading and feeling a certain satisfied relief with this turn of events, she glanced at the youngster to her left.

A trick of sunlight, glossing the back of Ruth's head, instantly flooded her memory with Patricia Trotter Campbell. She nearly spoke the name. The fine details of the young woman's face were in shadow but it was a particular gesture of turning the head away then looking back as if from the corner of her eyes, that brought Patricia right back again.

Flossy closed her eyes. How capricious genetics could be, pinching the nose of long-tamed grief. Patricia, Patricia; Flossy had missed her. And here in her granddaughter an insignificant gesture had somersaulted a generation and landed four-square in her kitchen on a sweet summer's morning bringing her dear, dear friend back to her. Patricia Campbell, Ruth's grandmother, youth all restored, sitting right there beside her — they'd been closer than sisters — before Frank, before the babies, before leukemia, before the years of wasted wasting. How Flossy had missed her, missed how they'd talk and laugh till their ribs ached, missed growing old with her. How she'd longed for more time, a last word, glimpse, this very thing.

It was nothing short of remarkable how puckish genes could slumber like that — sleeping beauties — ready to turn inside-out in a generation thirty-years distant, the spirit breathed back in them, with all the power to pry up rusted memory and rend hearts anew. And those still living who'd once known that nose, the chin, and adored that hairline, those lashes, could only limp behind in wonder on stiff knees and gouty feet. My oh my, what is taken and what is given in a lifetime, in a lifetime. If Flossy lived to be a hundred she'd never cease to be humbled by all the things tidal life took away and when she least expected it, just as mysteriously, so graciously restored.

"You're so like your grandmother," said Flossy, "she would have loved you." Ruth smiled but said nothing. Mealie looked out over the paper.

It seemed to be just one more of the severed circles of Flossy's eighty-two years that had turned up unceremoniously healed and haired-over of these last few weeks. Inside her head these long-forgotten memories were returning and with them the many years of loss and longing stirred again, her mother, Thomas and, now, Patricia, the past mysteriously coexistent with the present. Was she, with this, reconciling the two, weaving the fine threads of her own end to her beginning? She felt well enough but Flossy knew lots of people over the years who'd gone to bed at night and never got up in the morning. She looked across at Ruth. She wouldn't want this youngster to find her, but then who would it be? Mealie or Jimmy? You had to admire old cats that just took themselves off to the woods one day and never returned.

Flossy was reminded of all the ties Ruth Trotter-Schaeffer had to Great Village yet how foreign it all must seem to her. She imagined the youngster's utter frustration: dumped there, cast off from her family and friends for three weeks — a teenage eternity — reluctantly backed into another century with an old woman she didn't even know. No wonder she hadn't unpacked, was asking sly questions about getting to Truro and where the bus station was located. And how unexpected this glimmer that she might emerge from the hostile mood she'd dragged behind her all week like a grubby old blanket.

Little did Ruth know that right there in the elbow of Great Village was a whole other universe that belonged to her. So many people she passed on the street, at the gas station and general store were distantly related. She'd commented on Great Village being so friendly, that everyone smiled or said hello. Mealie had raised an eyebrow to that one, "Oh yeah?" she'd said in her gravelly, noncommittal tone.

The two older women could have told this youngster a tale or two of feuds over diverted streams that went back a good two centuries and were still flammable among the descendants, long after the mill wheels for which those same waters had been shifted in the first place were set out as garden ornaments. It would have taken the bloom off the friendly rose but Flossy had lived a lot of years and was wise enough to know it was the story of every village everywhere, entirely out of place in this kitchen on a soft August morning. Every bride, after all, deserved her honeymoon.

Fortunately for all of them, word had not spread that Patricia Campbell's granddaughter was in town. Flossy had purposely withheld Ruth's connections from her brother because what Jimmy knew his wife Noreen knew, and she, a woman who cut

the hair of a good half of the village in a little shop they'd fash-
ioned in the front room, was a high-efficiency talking machine.
Flossy knew better than to tell Jimmy anything she didn't want
the rest of the village to find out. As yet, there hadn't been an
opportunity to talk to Ruth about her extended family.

"You wouldn't know this but I'm pretty sure he'd be a cousin
of yours," she offered quietly, anticipating the surprise that
quickly peeled across Ruth's bright face.

"He is?"

"Mmm."

"But how ... how can I have a cousin I don't even know?" She
was finishing a glass of milk.

"Oh we all have scads of those, you go back far enough,"
offered Mealie. "Problem out here is everyone goes back too far,
they never leave and get to be old as herpes."

"Now, let's see, he'd be the ...," Flossy glanced up to the right
for a moment as she pursed her lips and mentally counted off
the generations, "grandson ... no, that should be great grandson
of your grandmother's eldest sister. Now, of course this is on
your mother's side."

"Let's see." Ruth smoothed her hands along the tabletop
beside the orange and red poppy placemat as if she were looking
at a huge invisible map. "I've never really thought about that
grandmother. She had a sister?"

"Heavens, child, no one ever told you?" Mealie put the
paper down. "There was a whole slew of them; half a dozen
Campbell girls and they all married around these parts, hatched
about three, four kids apiece, and except for Millie and your
grandmother they're all living and smoking in metropolitan
Great Village."

"There are any number of Phil Spencers out there," said Flossy.

"Everywhere you look in these parts, you pretty much belong."

"I do?"

"Half that baseball team's gonna be related to the Campbells," Flossy said, "in some way or another."

"They're all first-rate players," said Mealie. "Must be in the bones."

Flossy watched Ruth's puzzled face gaze at the table as she traced a finger along the wood's grain. Placing a marker in the Woolf diary, Flossy closed the book. Mealie dug into her canvas bag and pulled out a drawing tablet. They cleared everything else from the table while Mealie began drawing a chart, writing in a fine, clean script: *The Descendants of Samuel and Martha Campbell.*

"Time you met your kin," she said, passing it across to Flossy. Picking up her own pencil and ruler, Flossy drew a long line beneath the Campbells, under which she wrote in the names of each of their six daughters, including Patricia, the youngest.

"Milly was the eldest — that's Phil's great grandmother — and she married Thomas Spencer. They had a son, Crawford, who married Lily Grue." Flossy wrote the names in as they went.

"And one of their four sons, Frank," offered Mealie, as Flossy wrote, "is Phil's dad."

"Terribly bossy; we were all a bit afraid of Milly," said Flossy. "But I'll tell you this, Ruth," she ran a finger over Milly Spencer's name printed on the page, "she sure did miss your grandmother. We all did." She shook her head. "*Then* there was Frances. Did you know her, Mealie?"

"To say hello."

"Frances Campbell," Flossy began, "spent six months in New York City in her twenties and *never* got over it. They couldn't get her to the barn. Franny, you see, was born a lady," she said, raising her brows. "Sally was the third of the sisters." Flossy wrote the name carefully.

"There's someone you've gotta meet," said Mealie. "Sally's jitterbug was the best along these shores. Get Phil to take you to meet her; she'd adore a visit from you and you won't get away from her without learning the hop-polka. She's a character."

"And the last two before your grandmother," said Flossy as she pencilled the names in, "were Nell and Pritchard."

"Why ever a fine pair of Presbyhooligans like Samuel and Martha Campbell would name a daughter Pritchard was beyond all of us," Mealie laughed. "She hated that name, so everyone's always called her Billie."

"Oh yes," interjected Flossy. "Now, Patricia, your grandmother, and our friend, was at the very end. She was someone absolutely without guile, Ruth."

"And hilarious," said Mealie.

The three huddled over Ruth's genealogy the better part of the morning, Flossy writing in each name, then she and Mealie clucking and telling all the variegated stories they could remember about the Campbell descendants: husbands and children of the six sisters, including Marjory and her brothers.

Beside Ruth's mother, Flossy printed the names of two husbands. Ruth looked up at her. She pointed beside Richard Archibald's name. "I go here," she said.

Mealie noticed right away. "Richard Archibald?" she croaked. "You've gotta be kidding." She looked across at Flossy, who nodded.

"I only found out myself, just before I got here," said Ruth, a little sadly. "My mom and dad didn't tell me before." She turned to Flossy, "I thought you knew."

Looking from Ruth to Mealie again, Flossy answered with a sigh, "I did."

"Mom always said she never made an important decision without talking to you."

"Pregnancy ain't always a decision," Mealie interjected in a much-softened voice.

"Do you know him?"

"Richard?" Flossy nodded. "Oh yes, yes, he's a good man."

"They don't come much better," Mealie joined in. "And you'll find an Archibald under every rock in Nova Scotia," she said, taking a sip from her coffee cup, sitting back in her chair and looking out the window.

"The Archibalds were some of the earliest settlers out here. They used to say they were the first men to have a squeak in their boots," said Flossy, "it meant they were wealthy, but Richard's people were the humbler cousins. Your mother and he would drop in regularly when they were travelling to Halifax." Flossy took a white handkerchief from the belt of her dress and wiped her nose. "He's a wonderful man," she swiped the handkerchief across the nose twice more then tucked it back up under her sleeve. "Gentle and kind and as honest as the day is long. He was good for your mother. I was so sorry when it didn't work out, for them both."

Stroking the top of her head thoughtfully, Ruth said, "I don't know where he is, but I thought I might be able to meet him."

"Did she tell you he'd be here?" Flossy asked.

"Yeah."

"So that's why you've hung around," Mealie chuckled.

"Kind of."

"Don't worry," Flossy said, "he'll be here, by the weekend for sure. We'll be hosting the very first meeting of the Elizabeth

Bishop Society over at the Legion. Your mother has promised to call him this week and, let me tell you something, you're going to be an even bigger surprise to Richard Archibald than he is to you."

XIV

FLOSSY NOTICED THE CAR AGAIN THIS MORNING, A DUSTY green Volkswagen parked beneath Lottie Fulton's sugar maple. She thought she'd seen it there for some of the evening yesterday too. No one parked on the street in Great Village.

As she hung her dishtowel on the clothesline at the side of the house, she could see there was someone inside. At first she hadn't paid much attention, nor would she have now if Jimmy hadn't mentioned he'd heard there was a guest at the bed and breakfast asking about Elizabeth Bishop. He'd heard it was some professor from down in the Valley. She stepped back inside the house and glanced at the telephone. She should cancel Atlantic-Tel; who needed it with a visit from Jimmy three mornings a week?

It was another hazy day, already warm by nine-thirty. Ruth had gone off with Jimmy and Logie earlier to check the weir. Flossy reached for her hat. Beyond the screen door, a huge crow caught her eye lighting on the corner fence post at the back of the garden, like a black cape dropped from the sky. It bobbed and bowed in the direction of the house as if it knew there was someone inside. She could see the cool blue mantle shimmering on the bird's shoulders and hear it's rattle and caw caw caw.

"Elijah?" she whispered. It hopped from foot to foot, flapping and calling. Flossy counted the decades off with her fingers. Seven. She looked again at the bird, dancing its antics. Had it really been seventy-five years since Thomas took her down to the spruce grove by the bay to see the crow chick that had fallen from its nest? It had no feathers at the time, just a dusting of grey lint over its scrawny body. Seventy-five years? Mighty Sakes they were all getting old. Stepping outside, Flossy watched the big bird. It stood its ground, watching her too. The bird flapped its wings, bowed and called twice — she could see the black head rear, the long yellow beak snap — as if introducing the last act of a play.

"Out, out, brief candle!" she replied, "Life's but a walking shadow, a poor player that struts and frets his hour upon the stage and then is heard no more." She, too, reached her arms out, bowed, and by the time she was upright again the bird was off. She watched its graceful retreat to the southeast.

She was not ready. "No no," she whispered, watching the big bird disappear. She looked around. They needed rain. The grass was parched. Even the leaves of the shadberry and red currant were mildewed and dull. She must remember to put a pan of water out for the birds and get some to the pots in the backyard. The farmers, she knew, would be snuffling and stomping over at the feed mill, spitting and growing anxious over their withering crops. Flossy wondered if this heat might last into September.

Every year they could count on the weather breaking by the middle of August, leaving the mornings to drift in cool enough to search out a woollen sweater. Morning rains would come, then set off down the shore by noon. Though it happened every year, every year just the same the change came as a shock, bringing them all back to the grim reality that golden summer was rushing headlong to its twilight. Though it was still hot, other things were already retracting, like the light. She was getting up in the dark now, and by the time she and Ruth were sitting down to supper the light was fast fading. Gone was the summer's abundance of endless hours of soft evening. Fall, the herald of winter, was tightening the noose. Apples and pears were dropping and birds were flocking. It could make you sad, if you were so inclined. She thought of Thomas.

Sitting in a car on such a warm day had to be unpleasant. She stepped back inside the house for a moment to fill the kettle and place it on the stove, then walked back outside, ignoring pots in want of water, and headed down her lane way towards the street.

But the dusty green Volkswagen and Richard Archibald were already gone.

XV

TWO FATHERS. FLOSSY TURNED THE THOUGHT OVER IN
her mind as she stood at the back of her garden in the
late afternoon snipping the pincushion heads off spent purple
coneflowers.

Mealie had mentioned that some people were leaving such
blackened knobs for the finches to eat or what was now being
referred to in gardening circles as winter-interest. She could see
their charming bronze glow in the heavy light of a late afternoon,
but Flossy didn't much like the idea of leaving them all winter.
She thought old used-up things ought to be allowed their peace
beneath the earth. It wasn't a stretch to imagine herself set out in
some cornfield for someone else's winter interest or crow feed.

She'd had her father thirteen years. Unlucky thirteen, she
thought. One man can do a lot of damage in thirteen years, and
a different one a lot of good. What if she, Flossy O'Reilly, had
learned one day that William wasn't really hers, that there
had been another? Any other. What would it have meant if someone outside the family, even maliciously, had planted that seed
of doubt?

A sudden stabbing pain in the chest that swiftly migrated to the round of her left shoulder and slowed as an ache up into her jaw forced Flossy to hunch forward and clutch the wire mesh of the fence. Her heart flopped to no recognizable beat. The scissors dropped from her hand. She got her head down. One-matchstick, two-matchsticks, she began to breathe shallowly, three-matchsticks. In a minute or so she could half straighten up again to reclaim some balance. She looked out over Hustler's Hill towards the church spire for something, a point, for her eyes to hold onto until the fluttering and pain eased. She was fine, fine, her vision returning, able to breathe again. The stars that were blinking throughout her whitened field of vision were disappearing one by one.

She looked over towards Mealie who was staring into a pot of marigolds near the house. Flossy knew that colour-gaze. A rust, orange perhaps, had caught Mealie's eye and she'd be absorbed in it for half an hour. She hadn't noticed. No need to alarm.

Feeling steady enough to carry on, Flossy bent over for the scissors and lifted the green watering can. The pain was not much more than a squeeze in her chest when she inhaled now. Moving gingerly around the garden she drenched wilted plants with water. The pain was retreating. That was better. Refilling her can halfway at the back of the house, she turned to the pots on the patio. Much better. Standing over them, she watched the soil darken and the liquid rise in each terracotta pot until a stream dribbled from beneath: staked cherry tomatoes, parsley, dill already gone to seed, sage and rosemary. The herbs could take a beating though the tomatoes wanted their water twice a day in these temperatures.

Twenty years ago, she'd think nothing of packing a lunch on a scorcher of a day like this and striking out for the Portaupique woods or the road to Five Houses to pick blueberries. Nowadays everything took so much more effort and she wilted about as quickly as those tomatoes. The pain was almost gone. She hadn't had one of those in awhile and how suddenly it overtook her. Flossy once visited someone in a nursing home in Truro where she noticed two ancient Italian ladies leaning towards each other saying their goodbyes, kissing each other on both cheeks and whispering, "Have a good death." At the time she couldn't believe her ears. Back then she thought it funny. So did Mealie but now Flossy was beginning to understand those old gals. Hers would be swift, she felt sure, like that pain. She thought of Jimmy telling everyone up and down the line "She got away from us of the heart," and Noreen chiming in that she never would go to a doctor. (Noreen wasn't likely to let you off, oh no, not even in death.) They were all, of course, terrified of having a stroke and lingering, or worse, losing their minds and having those old John Deere tickers their doctors took such good care of pump for another senseless decade. She'd prefer to go quickly but not so quickly she couldn't say the odd goodbye.

Bumping up against a tall urn of acidanthera gladiolus, the long necks of the delicate white triangular flowers bowed to her like a herd of miniature giraffes. A rough spot on the side of the pot had caught her leg just below the knee. Putting the watering can down, she fished a handkerchief out from beneath her belt to wipe the bubble of blood that was forming.

"Mealie, I think I've lost my epidermis."

"Maybe it's with my mouse, did y'uh check under the fridge?" she asked without looking up from the pot from which she'd begun snapping pungent dead marigold flowers. Flossy could smell their strong burnt scent from where she stood. Mealie was sitting forward in the lawn chair, a little snug across the beam. She squirmed from one hip to the other.

"Mealie?"

"Unh?" She looked across to Flossy who was holding a bunched handkerchief against her knee.

"I've wanted to tell you about Richard and Ruth," she looked down, "I've been stewing about it."

"I kinda figured that," Mealie replied.

"He was parked in front of the house this morning but by the time I got around there he was gone."

"Needs a bit of time, Pet."

"It was like Bubba all over again. I ... I didn't want to keep it from him, but somehow I felt caught between the two of them."

"I can see how you would."

Mealie understood. She always did. Flossy didn't know why it had been so hard to tell her. "You know, the terrible thing is I can't even remember if she asked me not to tell him or if I just kept it to myself, which seems so much worse, especially that he means a great deal to me."

Mealie sat back in the chair again and looked more closely at Flossy. "Awfully hard to know when to insert yourself into someone else's affair, Flo. It would have been kinder if Marjory had left you out of it," she said, "but she's not likely to do that in this lifetime and, with your luck, the next besides." After a few more minutes, she said, "I don't see how you could have told him before they'd told Ruth."

Flossy looked down. "Sometimes silence is golden," she said, "and sometimes it's just plain yellow." Mealie gave up a soft affirmative snort. Had it been so hard after all? Could she not have told Mealie months ago and saved all that fussing?

"He'll come around. He's got a big view when it comes down to it."

UNADULTERATED RELIEF IT WOULD have been if Flossy'd learned that William wasn't *her* father, though she knew things never worked out that way. Imagine, though, what they all would have been able to step away from if troubled William had been the late arrival like Jack Schaeffer — a senseless lifetime of guilt.

"Blessed relief," she muttered, but all that was fantasy, birthday-candle wishes, the future imperfect, and it didn't have a whole lot to do with the past imperfect or getting on with your living. And Thomas? How frequently her older brother crowded into her mind these days; she didn't even have to dredge him up. He was there, a benign presence, still lying upstairs in some mental attic, to be stopped-in-on and tended each day. What would it have meant to him if he'd heard that William was not his?

"Blessed relief," she said it again. Catching the words slipping out of her this time, Flossy looked up at Mealie, who was looking back.

Her eyebrows went up. "That for me or just you?"

Flossy shook her head. Her mind swung like a pendulum from Thomas to their father and back again. Once more it settled on a particular day in the barn that, to her mind, shifted everything that came before and after. Remarkable, how a single incident in one small day of a life could so alter the way she'd look at everything else.

Before that day, her father would have his usual little rages and they were in their petty way something you came to expect if you couldn't altogether get used to them: tantrums that Flossy thought would have been well served had her mother broken a

chair over his head in the early months of their marriage. It was
a bad habit he'd got away with. This other, though, had been
something else, something sinister that she'd never mentioned to
another soul.

"Mealie?"

"Unh."

"Do you think the younger generation's better off for telling
all its secrets?"

Mealie didn't answer right away. Dropping several dead
flowers into the bucket beside her then pulling her half-glasses
forward towards the end of her nose she replied with a shake of
the head, "I wouldn't say so."

"Was ours the worse off for having kept so many?"

Again she took her time answering. She closed her eyes and
rubbed her left earlobe thoughtfully for a minute or two, so
long that Flossy wondered if she were going to answer at all.
"I think so." Leaning her cheek against the hand and looking
aslant towards Flossy she added, "Any you can think of now
that deserved to be kept?"

Flossy smiled.

Mealie nudged the glasses back in place with her knuckle and
let her gaze fall to the flowers again.

It would have been a flat-out lie to say William O'Reilly was
any kind of man to grow up around. He had a dark Irish rage
always on low boil, the visitation of which was a privilege he
bestowed upon his family almost exclusively. Their mother called
him their Gate Angel. Beyond the gate, he was the charming
angel to everyone he met. Inside the gate, his fury would strike as
unpredictably as lightning from a cloudless sky.

Flossy could recall him in the barn leaning against one of the
pens, relating some Irish yarn one minute when a shadow would

fall across him the next, something he'd remember or maybe didn't like in the way you were standing. His face would twist up red, the eyebrows huddle, his bottom jaw shift to the right and there'd slither out a vicious blast in the same choked breath. He might of a sudden lose patience about a knot he couldn't untie or a pail of water the cow had kicked, Thomas standing before him sputtering over a hard consonant that struck a burl on his tongue. In an instant their father's voice would screech an octave higher.

"Outta the goddamned way," he'd roar at him through clenched teeth in that squealing voice that issued like dragon's fire straight from the bowels of hell. He had a way of making his mood everyone else's in the household, broadcasting it before him like grain to the chickens.

Thomas bore the brunt of the fury from sheer proximity. Their father never hit any of the rest of them in such a mood but he thought nothing of skelping Thomas. Poor Thomas, he always thought he deserved it somehow or other, when all along it was just the temper.

"We always tried to keep things from Thomas, secrets or news of any kind." Flossy had emptied the watering can and was standing motionless in front of Mealie with it pressed against her stomach.

Looking up again over the glasses, Mealie nodded understandingly, "Oh yeah?"

"But that man could hear bad news drop on the other side of Burntcoat Head," Flossy said. "Always knew when something was up." This last she uttered turning away.

Dropping another handful of spent flower heads into the bucket at her feet Mealie took a long look at Flossy. "Is he hanging 'round you these days?" she asked.

"Umh?"

"Thomas. Is he hanging around?"

"Oh," she smiled, "considerably."

A pout of Mealie's lower lip told Flossy she understood. She went back to her task, turning the pot around to get at the plants at the back. She was a big woman, Mealie Marsh; capable, dependable, solidly kind, could hold a lot inside her. Flossy admired these things about Mealie. She kept her own counsel. Never one to pass on gossip, yet she was also the most directly honest person Flossy knew, would always say exactly what she thought, even if it might not land so sweetly on the ear. You could put money on it and she, Flossy O'Reilly, was no betting woman.

They'd known each other since grade school. Yet there were things Flossy didn't know about Mealie too. She didn't know all that much about the years in Montreal, the two husbands she'd loved and left behind, why she ever decided to move back to Nova Scotia.

"I sold a picture yesterday," Mealie said, collecting her things and pulling herself out of the chair. "What do you say we go over to the Palazar, get some lobster, tomorrow noon? We'll take Dash."

"If Dash can work us in," Flossy replied softly.

Ruth was at a baseball practice, getting ready for another game tonight, her second in two days. Flossy checked her watch. In an hour or so they would make their way over to the field to watch her play. Mealie had done a credible job of fitting her out with a sparse boyish moustache and tiny red sideburns from a makeup artist in the Drama Department at the Teachers College. Between the two of them, Flossy and Mealie had coached her to swagger some when she walked, jut the jaw out and lower her voice, though they thought she could get away with the occasional grunt. They filled her pockets with gum before sending her off, cautioning her to use the men's washroom, spit frequently and always pat herself southward before stepping up to the plate. Ruth could only giggle.

"Mighty sakes, Child, never *ever* giggle," Mealie shook a finger at her, looking sternly out over her glasses, to which Ruth giggled all the more.

The genius of the disguise, though, couldn't compete with Ruth's own ability to play baseball. She flew at that hardball and no matter how she clutched and tumbled to a halt, always delivered a steady, reliable throw. The few who came regularly to the games stopped mid-sentence to watch her. "Did you see ...?" echoed across the bleachers. At bat, she wasn't likely to drive anything out of the park but she frequently got a base hit or two. In fact, no one on the team was driving anything out of the park, so a base hit was entirely respectable. This late in the summer, the Great Village Ironclads wouldn't be changing their fortunes at the bottom of the league, so no doubt the occasional blind eye was being turned in order to play some baseball. And with a Major League Baseball strike all but a certainty, a few in the village were already suffering withdrawal.

Flossy and Mealie had gone to the game last night, setting their lawn chairs out behind the bench and quietly watching, which surprised and pleased Ruth. Neither of her parents, she told them later, had made it to any of her games in over two years.

The two women had huddled at the window earlier watching Ruth and Phil go off together with baseball gloves tucked snug beneath their arms for the second night. As they walked down the Station Road towards the baseball field, they kicked a rock along in front of them, completely absorbed in each other and

beaming enough to fairly eliminate all need of street lamps in
Great Village. Such beautiful, young, carefree lives.

"Mealie?" Flossy sighed.

"Unh."

"Were we ever so young?" she asked, turning to watch Mealie
as she spoke.

The big woman shook her head thoughtfully, "Not that young,
Pet."

WHAT IF THEIR GENERATION had grown up as carefree as
those two? What if there'd been no drowning, no war, illness
or Depression? What a difference two generations could make.
There they were, Ruth and Phil going off to a baseball game,
money in their pockets, hundred-dollar running shoes on their
feet, with nothing more to fret over than a pimple on the chin.

Pointless thinking that way. Why did she even cast about in
those murky waters after so many years? It was like some desperate compulsion to pick at a scab. The past was. Period. Flossy's
parents had had a hard life and they'd lifted their burden like
gunpowder high above the water, kept it dry and intact, to deftly
pass onto the shoulders of the next generation. There was not a
thing carefree about their living.

It was Thomas, as the eldest, who bore the brunt of that burden.
Except for the hours that he slept each night, he had an uncanny
awareness of everything that was going on in the house, like an
animal sleeping behind the stove whose ear lifts when a forearm
is scratched on the other side of the room. From the moment he
heard William's boots strike the floor or the door slam each day,
Thomas tried to divine his father's mood. If William was broody
and silent, Thomas retracted; if he was sunny, Thomas too was
cheerful and open.

Their mother saw all of this and either from reaction or compassion or both looked indulgently on Thomas, which only fuelled their father's contempt. It wasn't something you could finger directly with concrete examples from around the house or at the dinner table, that she gave Thomas the preferred portion of a Sunday chicken or the hen's heart tucked beneath his dumplings, which he loved best of all. She was straight-up fair about things given to each of them. It was, rather, a bend to her branches, a gentling lent to Thomas that wasn't there with the rest.

He was close to her, too, but you could see that as he grew older he longed to be under his father's wing. Thomas fawned for William's approval, though he was unlikely to have got it, Flossy was convinced, if they'd both had eight more lives to live.

If her mother cleaned Thomas's boots Saturday night for Sunday church, he'd be anxious his father would find out. William always said he had nothing but respect for a man at church Sunday morning with polished shoes, though the ones who had them you could be sure were unlikely to have done the shining themselves. Thomas would buff his tattered old boots Saturday night until the last of the kerosene sputtered from the lamp.

Unlike Jimmy, who had the same bull neck and even walked like the O'Reillys, Thomas hadn't inherited a single feature from their father, not eyes, ears, the set of jaw, the length of bone or shape of feet. He, instead, bore a striking resemblance to their mother, even in temperament. You might have thought he'd sprung from her rib. Perhaps some men don't need to see themselves in their sons but someone like William O'Reilly surely didn't want to see a Davison every time he turned around. Though he wouldn't have Thomas close to him, even less did he want the boy close to his mother. He was determined to toughen up his boys, both of them. Flossy'd overheard him once saying to

Jimmy, who couldn't have been more than four at the time, "I want you to remember this son, you can pick a snake up by the tail but you can't trust a woman."

Winter and summer, Thomas was the one who got up at five every morning without complaint to go to the barn with William before school or church and he was the last one in after him at night. From the time he was ten, their father said he was old enough to do the work of a hired man. If Thomas had been a mongrel that strayed to their door, Flossy was certain her father would have boasted to everyone for six miles up and down the shore that he was the best dog he'd ever had. But he was a son and their father never did say such a good thing about him. Besides, no dog ever stuttered.

"Were you around when the crow was here?" Flossy asked as she cut a cluster of late-summer roses for the kitchen table and placed them in a jar with water.

"Crowe? From Portaupique?"

"No, no, Elijah."

"I went to school with Peter. Didn't know Elijah."

"No, no, Mealie, a crow, a bird."

"Mighty sakes, Flo, between your hearing and my misunderstanding, it's a wonder we get anything across."

"Beg-pardon?"

"No, a bird? No," she raised her voice a bit.

"Thomas found a chick, had fallen from a nest in the woods. He kept it down by the spruce trees so father wouldn't find out. Called it Elijah and, when it got big enough, it followed him everywhere. If he went down to the far field to get the cows, it would lumber along, hopping from fence post to fence post. William didn't like it. Then one day it vanished. Thomas thought father had caught the bird or shot it."

Mealie looked up.

"Elijah was smarter than that," she continued. "After father died, the bird was back."

"Just followed nature?"

"I suppose." She looked down the hill towards the centre of town. The fire truck was pulling out of the station, lights flashing. "The Merson boys killed it," she said.

"No!"

"Elijah followed Thomas to school a couple of times and they got it. You remember how they tormented Thomas. Then they sang a little ditty for him. 'You da da da didn't cry when your old man died, but you cried when the old crow died.'"

"Brutes."

"Schoolboys," she corrected, looking off again. "For years, though, there'd be one crow that would perch on the same post at the back of the house where Elijah used to wait, making a ruckus until someone would go outside. They're terribly clever."

Mealie made a soft noise in her throat that said she was listening and thinking too.

"This morning, when I was going out to get Richard," Flossy pointed to the back of the property, "there was a huge old crow, sat on that post right over there for a good ten minutes. Cawed and cawed until I came outside. Mealie, I know it's crazy, but I always think it's Thomas when I see something like that. Do you think that's too silly for words?"

"Nope."

How good it was to have Mealie near, though one could get used to her, take her for granted like you took for granted a good liver working quietly away inside the body, straining everything you so carelessly threw at it. Mealie was the one person Flossy could always say things to, soft-in-the-head things, just like that about Thomas and the crow, and she'd listen patiently. You'd never say such things to Jimmy and, God-forbid, Noreen.

Of course the crow wasn't Thomas, they both knew that. It was just that sometimes things could call so convincingly from the past that it was nice to tell someone else without danger of committal.

THE DAY IT ALL changed for young Flossy O'Reilly started out as a seasonal gift, the unexpectedly sweet fall day or two that's lodged between chill incursions of winter. A flush of Indian Summer had settled in along the bay and brought with it a remnant of fair weather to Colchester County. Flossy's interior eye could still rove the barnyard of that unusual day, the leaves twirling like giddy little girls on windless warmth; Jimmy feeding the horses fallen apples through the fence. They were all out in short sleeves when their father took Thomas aside and said they'd be going to the barn after dinner to butcher the pig.

All three children gathered to watch: Thomas, a long willow switch of a boy at thirteen; Flossy, tiny, just short of a full year younger; even Jimmy, barely five, stood and waited as their father heaved and dragged that fat old pig to the centre of the upstairs barn floor that had been swept clean for the killing. Thomas had carried that pig, the runt of the litter, up there in his arms five months earlier to fatten him for this very end and now, almost two hundred pounds bigger, they could barely budge the beast.

Killing was the one uncommon chore of the year that required the house and barn to work hand in glove. As the children watched a safe distance from their father scuffling with the pig, their mother would be in the house stoking the fire to boil pots of water, one to scald the coarse white hairs off the butchered animal, another to prepare a brine to preserve the hams and shoulders and the last for the slow rendering of the animal's head. A barrel, half-filled with coarse salt, would cure fat pork and bacon that was cooked with Saturday baked beans or used for frying throughout the year. The feet would be boiled for soup the next day. Today, though, was a day of happy abundance; there'd be pork chops for supper.

A large hook dangled at the end of a rope over top of William's head. It had been threaded through a pulley as big as a man's hand that was screwed into a low beam three-times Flossy's height off the ground. They'd all seen animals killed each fall; no one could be shielded from the coarse grain of farm life. The mechanism would haul the pig aloft by its back feet to allow the cutting of the throat and blood to drain, then expose the long pink belly to be sliced clear up to the back legs for the entrails to tumble out.

Oblivious to the threat of these new surroundings, the dumb pig blinked its beady eyes and snorted twice in the direction of the children, a faulty hesitation. Front legs spread, its stumpy snout snuffling and rooting the air, the pig swung its head in William's direction as he lifted the sledgehammer with both hands. The chuck of metal on flesh was traced by a thud as the beast crumpled to the floor, making the little ones jump. The animal lay unmoving, eyes open.

William, thick like the pig, grunting and clearing his throat, grabbed at the rope Thomas held and knotted it tightly around the animal's hind feet. He clutched at another overhead, whose slack Thomas had freed, and clawed a thick iron hook between the pig's bound hind ankles. With his left hand outstretched he motioned Thomas to pull.

Still tottering on boyhood, with so little muscle, Thomas heaved until his face reddened and his arms shook without getting the pig's rump more than half-lifted off the ground. William clamoured over to help as they hoisted it into the air and tied it securely.

Catching at one of the beast's numbed ears and twirling it like a dance partner a yard off the ground, William passed the butcher knife to Thomas, who guarded it carefully, knowing how clumsiness enraged his father. Standing behind the pig, holding the animal by both ears and stilling its free-floating whirl, William turned its neck towards his son.

"Come on, come on, and from the side," he said impatiently, "otherwise you'll be cleanin' blood off you into next week." Thomas stepped gingerly to his right and held the newly sharpened knife out for his father again, the shaft turned towards him.

"You," he said bluntly.

From Thomas's open mouth, words tangled then jammed altogether. Flossy held her breath. In the engorged minute between command and answer that refused to budge, she counted: one-matchstick, two-matchsticks, three-matchsticks ... She could see his shoulders shake, his head jerk, the eyes gripped tight. The knife drooped then fell from Thomas's hands. She stiffened, squeezing her eyes and praying her father would ignore him just this once.

"Damn, you bloody piss-tail," their father scowled, "he'll not be staying like this 'til supper." Still, the boy didn't move; he stopped gulping words. Fifteen-matchsticks ...

"*Pick* up the knife!" William snarled. He took a threatening step towards his son. Seeing the menace in their father's eyes, a rage on the rise, Thomas bolted for the door but William leapt after him quicker than Flossy had ever seen her father move.

He yanked Thomas back with both arms around his chest. The two staggered then collapsed on the floor in a delirious jumble of panting, squirming, twisted bodies. Flossy remembered Thomas looking straight at her, terror in his eyes as he fell back into that dreadful embrace. Limbs flailing like a deer in a cougar's jaws, he scuffled with his father, the knife somewhere beneath them. Someone's foot caught two stacked pails that skidded along the floor and separated as they rolled in different directions, another struck the blank-eyed pig suspended above them that spun like a tethered top. Though up against an opponent twice his size, Thomas put up a stubborn fight, not even a fight so much as a frenzy to escape.

William by now was a blue-faced, snorting, spitting fiend, slamming a tight fist into Thomas whenever he could. At least five hard blows struck the boy's head and face. Blood was pulsing from his nose, running down his chin and smearing the floor beneath them. Thomas made little effort to shield himself and, unlike many a lad thrown into similar stew, gave not one punch back.

Flossy at twelve, small for her age, moved a few steps closer, instinctively fearful of William finding that knife. Jimmy had already scampered off like a spooked fox. She was shaking, her heart pounding, and just as she stepped into the scuffle's circle, her arms stretched out and reaching for the steel she could see beneath them, her brother slipped free, rolled to his feet and skittered off like a wildcat as their grunting father lay curled and winded on the ground. Flossy stepped back into the shadows and vanished before he had time to recover his breath and find his feet.

All three children scattered like a puff of smoke to their most secret places throughout the farm that afternoon. Seeing such fury in her father chastened Flossy, and something she sensed more than understood, did not have words for, hardly did now, would be altogether different from then on.

It wasn't a scuffle on the barn floor and a cracked nose that broke Thomas's spirit back in those troubled years with William. This was more of the same treatment her brother had come to expect from his father, only a degree more in severity.

It was *she* who'd been trampled underfoot that day; Flossy who could never look at her father the same. She knew he'd hurt Thomas and there was not a doubt in her twelve-year-old mind that he'd meant to.

That sweet autumn day, William would take a place among all the other males she'd learned to be wary of around a farm — the ram, the billy goat, the rooster, Chisholm's bull — animals you crossed a field to avoid, animals you never, never turned your back on.

BLOOD DIDN'T BOTHER THOMAS. Killing one animal or another was something they did every fall and each year he was the one to wash the killing floor, carry the pail of organs — the steaming heart, liver and kidneys — back to the house for their mother to clean or cook up for supper. It was the killing of something he'd named that Thomas couldn't bear. He could gut a fish, kill a rat or take the head off a chicken but not an animal like Runty Pig, who he'd been feeding up on corn meal and turnips, whose dull head he'd scratched each morning and night for a full five months.

Thomas had an extraordinary tenderness for any lame or weakened animal around the farm. The orphaned or sickly young he brought to the house and bottle-fed, as he had that pig for its first two weeks. Even as a child he was always putting birds' eggs and chicks back into nests, however futile.

Flossy, who had been standing with one hand braced against the white clapboard of her house, suddenly realized water was pooling at her feet, flowing over the top of the watering can and from its spout. She scurried to close the tap below her. Mealie was watching.

"You okay today, Pet?" the big woman asked. Flossy nodded.

Had Jimmy any memory of it? Or had he been too young to understand and therefore see? Did any piece of that cruel afternoon float back at him, as it had Flossy unguarded this afternoon, as he crossed the part of the barn again where they'd once slaughtered animals, as he walked the lonely mudflats to his weir each day or drove the familiar roads to and from Great Village? Or had it merely sifted like silt to the ocean floor of his deepest dreams? The episode in the barn that no one ever talked about cured young Jimmy of wanting to spend time with his father. Maybe Jimmy had just seen too much more in that war he'd gone off to fight in Europe, had too much else he was working hard to forget. Mealie'd often said, "You wouldn't be the first brother and sister who grew up in apparently different families."

Thomas was string: sinew, long bone and little meat. He had their mother's dark hair and cowlick. For a week that fall, he looked out through two slits in the middle of swollen, blackened eyes. The broken nose set his breathing apart from then on as something you'd always notice in a room.

"What do you suppose Thomas would have done, Mealie?" For so many years Amelia Marsh had been near, a friend, who knew the family well enough to see to the seam of Flossy's question.

"Thomas?"

"Mmm. If he were Ruth's age, now, what do you suppose he'd have ended up doing, his work?"

"Oh." Thoughts flickered back and forth in Mealie's intelligent eyes a couple of minutes before she answered. Flossy waited. She liked this about Mealie, that she was capable of picking up any random thought that tumbled out. "Oh, something precise," she said. "I'd imagine him working in a museum, Boston maybe, New York, cleaning the bones of reptiles or birds no bigger than the palm of your hand. Cataloguing their parts. That, or maybe fixing clocks, old clocks, works-of-art clocks, worth standing back and admiring."

"I think of him working over something fiddling, too," said Flossy, "with big thick glasses."

"You kidding me? Spiked hair, pierced ear and *Silhouette* designer frames."

"*Silhouette?*" she asked.

"Only the best. Born into the wrong century," said Mealie. "That's all that happened to Thomas."

Flossy thought about it for a minute. Maybe she was right; a century might have made a difference. "Mealie?"

"Unh?"

"I can't tell you how good it is to have an old head to talk to."

Mealie wrinkled her nose, "You tell me that just about every week."

"Do I?" she asked. "Huh. Must be the memory's enfeebling some."

"Convenient."

A century. Thomas never found the tool or instrument to fit perfectly into the curve of his long hand tight against the lifeline, not a burin for delicate engraving nor the finest set of callipers to measure the distance between himself and the rest of humankind. He'd never had the time or luxury. Of course, no one in the family would have known how to help him find his calling even if there'd been more time, not with their father gone.

In those days the family had a need as big as a Fundy tide pressing in on it every day of their lives: it was survival, and you filled it with whatever means you had at your disposal. You didn't for a minute forget that. Like so many others around there, they had nothing but the land and strong backs and the only way to make a living — avoid starvation, actually — was by farming. They weren't unusual that way. Once the Great Depression settled in upon them like a winter that wouldn't end, most everyone in every direction was frantic to stay three steps ahead of the County Home. By then it would all be so much worse than any of them could have imagined.

You never considered what someone might have done; luxury again. They'd known fishermen from those parts who'd had the first joints frozen off three fingers on each hand. You'd never have asked them if they liked fishing. They wouldn't have known what you were talking about: it was what they did, bald-faced survival.

If William O'Reilly hadn't drowned, things might have been different. In the unholy marriage of loss and necessity that follows such tragedies, Thomas became a farmer. It was the one thing they all were sure he wasn't cut out for.

He had a natural timidity far more deeply rooted than an undermining tongue. Thomas was afraid of the big animals, especially the gelding, and even as he and the horse matured he never overcame it. If anyone was going to be stepped on, kicked or bitten by that horse you could be sure it was Thomas. Their father had always chided him about his carelessness near the animal: "The bay mare you can walk beneath in a thunderstorm; the colt, never, never turn your back on him." If William said it once, he said it a thousand times. Even Jimmy knew as much. Horses, like people, their father would always say, were to be trusted or not; it was that simple.

After William died, the beast was no better than it had ever been, four years older and gelded, hooves the size of stovepipes, the horse was a brooding soot-black demon that never held still and was no better in the harness than the first time they put him there. How often had that beast tormented Thomas? How often had he seen its massive black hull backing towards him in a stall set to ram him into a corner?

No, Thomas's work should have been quiet, dry work. He might have been good with fine wood, cherry or bird's eye maple, something he could carve, sand and polish. It should have preserved the sensitivity of his hands, the ability to see and inquire with those delicate fingertips, never something like smithing that required brute strength and sweat, the taming and pounding of iron with fire and hammer. That's perhaps why their mother's work had seemed so natural to him.

He loved textures, the feathers, satins, felts, ruchings and quillings of the hats their mother made. Grandmother Davison had taught all her daughters the art of hat-making. It was in the family's little shop in Truro that Lillian and William had met. For that first year after William died, when Lillian had to take up her millinery trade again to bring in some needed cash, Thomas would sit beside her at night and read from the almanac or just be quiet. He stayed while she stitched her grief away into bone weariness. It comforted her, no doubt, to have him there and calmed him besides. He'd sift through her basket of scraps: velvets, furs and tweeds.

You'd see him take these remnants out and place them on the table, side by side, moving this one over by that one, in some order that made sense to Thomas alone. Sometimes he'd rub them against his cheek, sitting beside Lillian watching her work, humming softly to himself. He never stuttered then, though such shilly-shallying of fabric bits and bobs was something he'd never have done if his father were alive.

A couple of times early on, when they'd be sitting like that around the kerosene lamp and he'd be sorting Lillian's scrap box, she'd of a sudden think of something she'd forgotten to do that had to be done urgently, stoke the fire, save the potato water for bread-making next morning or address a letter ready for the post. She'd gather up the hat, needle and thimble and dump them onto Thomas's lap, saying, "Just finish that stitching right to the end, like I've done. Mind you do it neatly, now." He was an obedient boy and, unlike the work he did on his feet, which always courted mishap, Thomas's fingers up close were capable of infinite, even artistic, precision. Mother always said he could sew a seam to put his grandmother to shame, and Grandmother Davison was ever the standard of perfection in the household.

Sometimes, instead of sewing a seam to the end exactly as she'd instructed, he'd make a small loop in the fabric, maybe cross one end of a seam over another. Eventually, it was Thomas who was making the odd suggestion here and there about colour or ribbing to their mother, a tuck along the side or flair at the back, a remnant of fur or feather perfectly placed, the more defined sweep, and, oh my, she could see just like that that he had a rather extraordinary knack for improving the design. Over those years, their mother began to feel that his suggestions were giving her a small edge over the Great Village hat market. They were the calling detail, the leap in design, that drove the eye over the rack of so-so hats to the distinctive Reilly Hat.

It caused no little stir in the village as one of the clerks at McLellan's general store, was brother-in-law to the town's other hat-maker. A couple of times over the course of the twenty-five years their mother was making hats and selling them to McLellan's, he tried to have the Reilly line discontinued, supposing that if the villagers had only his sister-in-law's hats to choose among they'd

no doubt still walk away with a hat. He was successful only once
and briefly until their mother went to the store herself and spoke
to Mr. Walter McLellan, the owner.

"May I remind you, Mr. McLellan, a woman's hat," she said
with the dignity due her creations, "is an emotion." Fortunately,
all the McLellans from those parts were good businessmen who
fully appreciated the virtues of market competition. They were
also married men, to discriminating women who adored those
hats.

That kind of work, though, would never do for a man. People
from there wouldn't accept that a man could be more suited to
the setting of perfect stitches or know the subtle possibilities of
dimension and texture, the juxtaposition of fabric and colour;
that he might have a flair for symmetry and proportion, an eye
for drawing out every woman's beauty in a simple accessory,
or prefer these occupations over what went on outdoors in the
lumber woods, the mines, at sea or the barnyard. It was a family
secret. It would never be easy to be a man of uncommon delicacy
in Great Village.

In another century, he might have become a student of the
shoreline creatures, or charted the pathways of the brain,
painted landscapes or even like Mendel studied the genetics of
the common pea. He was the kind of boy you felt had a unique
possibility in him, a gentle and gifted sensitivity with the promise
of doing something lasting. Sadly, he was born to a place too
small for him, a creature without carapace and the world into
which he was thrust was one where strength was all.

The village, now, was its own matter. Of course people
talked. Talked in a hybrid way that dusts a pollen of curiosity
over feebler concern. People outside a situation have their standard ways of understanding things of this nature that come over

someone. Some said Thomas had a case of nerves and if you didn't subscribe to that, then it was laziness.

Any Thursday in the nice weather you could walk by the Liar's Bench, set out for the old timers to gather and gossip in front of the general store, and hear them talking about some old codger who'd lost an eye from a pitchfork. Half would say it was his own fault, always left his tools underfoot; the others, a bad-luck accident. If you passed that bench ten years later and remarked on that same glass eye, they'd no doubt drag out those same petrified opinions. People around there never much pulled the thread of a notion back through the eye of a needle for a new understanding.

Back in those days, you didn't get many people defending anyone who didn't fit in, like the old Faulkner twins, a pair of spinsters who'd been living back on Portaupique Mountain. They farmed on their own up among the woodlots and some said they picked mushrooms and cured with herbs and roots. People didn't like that they farmed without a man. Even some of the local women joined that full-throated chorus.

"It's indecent," they chided, "women dressing like men, asking old Adam Chisholm to bring his bull over to cover their cow." Chisholm didn't mind; the sisters paid him for his trouble and money was money to him.

The rest thought the Faulkners queer and shunned them when they came into town wearing their trousers and smelling of the barn. You might have thought it a crime they hadn't married or had a brother to live with them and make them the more respectable. You might have thought, too, that the women around there who truly held farms together over the years, while their husbands sat company with a whisky bottle from breakfast to last light, might have nursed a larger view.

You might have thought, after all, in a village like ours, a little sympathy cost anybody money.

XVI

H ER FIRST IMPULSE WAS TO FIND A BLANKET, THOUGH IT was far too warm for that. As she stepped into the parlour for a copy of Woolf's *Between the Acts*, Flossy was startled at the sight of Ruth asleep on the chesterfield.

For some moments, like this, of some days she could forget the youngster was even in the house with her. She glanced at the clock, nearly seven-thirty. She must have been there all night. In the morning's half-light, with one hand fallen to the floor, a book at the end of it, not a frown, wrinkle or flaw, she looked more like twelve than her awakened sixteen. A gloss of fine perspiration gathered on the creases of her eyelids as they twitched in dreamful sleep. The morning's red sunrise cast pink highlights along one half of her hair, cheekbone and nose. Sweat glistened at the crook of her elbow. She was girlishly curved, the skimpy camisole she wore scarcely concealing the rounds of delicate breasts. The ridge of collarbone extended from the middle of her throat out to a tiny bump at each shoulder dusted in cinnamon freckles. Feminine hips and slim tanned legs down to narrow feet showed her lithe and firm. She wore white athletic shorts that revealed soft blond down visible on her thighs and a massive blue-red bruise just above the right knee in the shape of a baseball, of which she was most proud. She'd taken a searing drive at the baseball game last night, recovered the ball, tagged the runner at third and thrown another out at second — a heroic finish at the bottom of the ninth.

Defenseless in sleep, Ruth's face held all the radiance of youth. It was the sheer flawlessness of the breaking bud or unfolding flower that has met none of the brutality of a noonday sun, beauty at its purest that might in no time be all past, some small bone not fully formed slips from proportion's ideal, the nose a fraction longer, the jaw more pronounced. Such youthful perfection Flossy had seen last but a season in some women. It too was fugitive, just as Mealie had said of light and colour; perfect beauty was fleeting.

As she stood there, wondering whether to risk awakening her by covering her or lifting the arm to the couch, a fragrance reached Flossy's nose. She hadn't noticed it before. Was it perfume? Not our Ruth. Maybe shampoo. The nose was getting more sensitive as everything else was fading. The synthetic odour seemed jarringly out of place here. Flossy might have expected, instead, the scent of an armload of clothesline-dried laundry. She would much sooner have put her nose near the flesh at the top of that youngster's arm, her slender wrist, to smell sweet sleep on her skin, each finger to catch the air of peanut butter lingering from a late-night snack, the knee for hints of grass lifted from baseball to punished flesh.

She longed to put a hand over the sleeping brow, to smooth the tender young mind inside. "So little matters, Child. Shhh, there now, so very, very little. In half a year, this summer'll be so far behind you." An endless succession of such summers had vanished entirely from Flossy's old memory.

Ruth hadn't wanted to come to Great Village and somewhere over the last weeks or months, Flossy imagined, this lovely young creature had let sadness settle inside her. Perhaps even getting ready for Nova Scotia, she'd invited it in for a day. No doubt it would sit quietly, well-behaved, while Ruth felt slightly detached from everybody else's energy and activity. When no one noticed — her friends, her mother, maybe her father didn't call when he said he would — she would let it stay for another day or two, a pout gone unseen or unmentioned that wedged a toe in the sadness door.

Eventually, what started as low-grade moodiness would persist. Flossy had seen it with her students over the years like dejected little paper boats that no one could reach drifting farther away from shore. She'd seen quite a lot of it by Ruth's age, sixteen, then younger and younger, as early as ten by the time she'd finished teaching. Sadness took up residence in them, a strange, troubled roommate with no boundaries that they were unable to turn out, until it became something they were merely observing as someone outside of their humourless selves. And sadness was demanding. Its own kind of grief, it drained the colour from everything in every direction. Things that normally made them happy could not. Music they once loved no longer moved. Nothing gave pleasure. They found nothing to amuse or console them and nothing to look forward to. It took over with no drama, no fury, just slow-rising grey water that left them ever so tired.

Yet somewhere along that dark way Ruth Trotter-Schaeffer had pulled herself back. Flossy didn't know why or how but she could see a difference in just a week. Here in this unlikely village that all the young people fled just about as fast as they could, here in Flossy's little house — a worn, dusty old place with lace curtains and crocheted doilies, books piled on every step of the stairs, windows that hoisted and clanked on pulleys that didn't work and a bathtub with no shower and a leaky tap — here where Ruth had discovered a world turning lazily on its axis, where the business of each day was set out against the look of the morning sky or cobwebs on the grass and could be put off with impunity until tomorrow, she had somehow found colour again.

Of course they'd all merrily missed the train. Flossy knew that and knew how unfair it was to dump Ruth here. She must have thought the entire village had been left on the platform. Here was a youngster accustomed to activity, to doing and being and going and preparing. There were agendas for lessons and sports, for friends and movies, not an unscheduled minute in her normal life. In the village, by contrast, there was no driving force in their midst, nothing to catch, to hurry for, nothing that couldn't be set aside for a good cup of strong tea, nothing the world revolved around except the long-ago written word. They ambled through their days like an aimless flock of guinea fowl turning this way or that according to whim, wind, scratchings or nothing much at all.

Ruth had dreaded coming and, that first weekend in the village, would discover the place to be far worse than anything she could have imagined. Flossy could still see the look on her face, some desperate fusion of disbelief and terror, when she broke the news that she had no television. Ruth had mumbled something unintelligible. Of course, there were no movies in town either, not even a local library to find a computer. Ruth sat down and Flossy fully expected tears. There she was, imprisoned in a one-horse town with an old woman and nothing but walls and walls of books. She did not envy her.

That first weekend Ruth had written her father, Jack, having just learned of another father. She didn't have stamps to mail it and would not ask for any, so Flossy waited. Each time the young woman thought of taking it to the post office, something got in the way. Then Mealie happened to mention the post office had been closed a good dozen years anyway, though everyone still called it the post office and there it sat, boarded up in the centre of town. Ruth could only shake her head. When she finally did get some stamps at McLellan's, she'd lost the urgency to send the letter and there it lay on her dresser, forgiven trespasses, beneath the baseball glove.

As Flossy lifted her outstretched arm to the chesterfield and pulled a cotton sheet up to her shoulders, Ruth emerged just enough into consciousness to blink twice, smile up at her and sink soundly back to sleep.

Now, when she cast her thoughts back over the few days Ruth had been there, Flossy couldn't say how or where it had changed, or if there had been a particular moment when she'd first heard her young laughter mingle with her own over something outrageous Mealie had read from the paper. She felt as if Ruth had come up for air after being too long underwater.

"Listen to this." Mealie flipped a corner of the paper down to be sure Ruth and Flossy were paying attention. "Bluey, a long-tailed macaw, was thrown out of a parrot show on the Isle of Wight for unbecoming language. It says here they even got him an elocution teacher — that could be a second career for you there, Flossy — but Bluey told his teacher to 'take a sexual hike too.'"

Mealie had knees the size of Ruth's thigh and from just about every perspective she was unavoidable in Flossy's kitchen. Ruth didn't take to her right away, did her level best to ignore her too, but couldn't escape the heavy scrape of Mealie's voice — audible, she complained, through two pillows stuffed against the ears.

Seated at the back of Mealie's Life Studies class on Tuesday, though, it seemed Ruth had taken another look. Flossy was sure she'd only gone to get directions to the Truro bus terminal. At the class, Mealie set her up beside one of the lone wolves. He'd stumbled in behind all the rest, unshaven and yawning from a short night, but she knew him to be of robust talent and uncompromising about his art, so much so that even Mealie found him inspiring. Of course, she was taking a chance that Ruth would get her map to the buses, but she also knew the enthusiasm of the artist sitting beside her was infectious. Mealie was absolutely certain he'd notice that new face in the class and if anyone could move Ruth along the path of her own small peeve, it was this one. She left them entirely alone.

"Some knots've just gotta work themselves out, Pet," she'd said later.

Mealie was easier-going than Flossy in that regard. It was the artist's eye that saw everything on a bit of a slant. Walking back to the van after class, she'd talked to Ruth about complementary colours, pulling a colour wheel out of her grimy canvas bag and stopping in front of a dress shop display window to show her how certain colours were used together — that blue with orange, chartreuse and purple — and explaining to her which colours would go best with her terracotta hair and complexion: avocado, chocolate, aqua and soft blues. They went inside to try some dresses on so Ruth could see it was true.

As they drove back to Great Village, Mealie even said she'd much prefer to drive Ruth to the train or bus station if she were determined to go, rather than have her try to find her own way, would buy the ticket if she needed money. Her back door, Mealie said, was always open and she should just come by when she thought it was time.

As they talked about it later, Flossy had to agree it would be much better than having her disappear in the middle of the night. Once Ruth was offered that clear and easy way to leave, she promptly and mysteriously settled in. Much against her will, she'd taken to Mealie, had asked if she might go back to the class the following week.

"Horror-scopes," Mealie announced that morning at the breakfast table. "What's your birthday, Peapod?" She leaned towards Ruth.

"June 24."

Mealie looked down the columns. "Cancer. Let's see. Spotlight on creativity, prosperity, marital status." She turned a corner of the paper down to plant an eye on Ruth, who giggled, before continuing, "Follow your heart as Venus rules. Virgo plays a role."

The eye again, "Who's Virgo?" she asked coyly.

Ruth shook her head. "What's Flossy?"

"Capricorn: 'Big changes ahead. Focus on long-term goals. Surprise in store." She looked up from the paper and croaked, "That's no doubt the party we haven't told you about."

"Yours, Mealie," Ruth urged her on.

She read, "Scorpio: Don't confuse wishful thinking with facts. New love on horizon, if you are ready," she peered over the paper again, "and you thought Mr. Third Baseman was hanging around here because of *your* braided little tail." Ruth put her hand to her mouth and giggled. "Money picture bright. Taurus figures prominently. Who's Taurus?"

"Phil's Taurus," Ruth chirped.

A huge smile peeled across Mealie's face. "What'd I tell ya?"

Flossy stayed out of it.

RUTH HAD SETTLED IN TO Flossy O'Reilly's world, nearly a century in reverse, like a dry-rock wall settles in to a slope it's meant to lean against for the better part of a lifetime. It was the last thing anybody expected, but no one more so than Ruth Trotter-Schaeffer.

It may have helped that Flossy passed her the keys to Falstaff that first weekend in the village, and told her just to hold on to them, which pleased the youngster enormously. She washed that old tank on Sunday and cleaned it inside-out as if it were her own first car. Flossy and Mealie watched from the kitchen window. When Ruth finished, Mealie said Falstaff probably wouldn't start with all that primping, but it did.

Each morning after Mealie went back to the studio to paint and Jimmy set off on his rounds, regardless of the tasks at hand, Flossy and Ruth would jump into the old Valiant and head for the shoreline.

"There's tangible weather out there," Flossy'd say from the kitchen door, gusts of wind blowing every piece of clothing away from her small frame, "Get your shirt on." The harder it blew, the more determined she was to be out in it. Sometimes they'd take their shoes off and stroll a mile along the beach, as far as the O'Reilly homestead. If the sky were low and broody, they'd sit and watch birds, pick rocks or examine filmy creatures caught in tidal pools. Ruth loved collecting rocks, would fill her pockets with a vast array of shapes and colours. Flossy showed her geographical points of interest, where the old Spencer lighthouse had stood at the Point, where cottages squatting along the edge of the bay had to be hauled back three feet each year, where an entire sports field and the Chisholm farm, farther out beyond those cottages, had been sheared away by the tides, lest Ruth think there wasn't much power in the calm lapping at the water's edge.

They would talk, sometimes Flossy would take out her own small booklet of copied-out poems, those she was determined to learn by heart. She would read these softly when they stopped, as Ruth picked rocks. "Like as the waves make towards the pebbled shore, so do our minutes hasten to their end ..."

Staring out into the bay, Ruth asked, "How do you tell if the tide's going out or coming in? It always looks like it's coming in."

"Doesn't it? They never stop rolling in," Flossy explained, "they just roll in less and less when it's going out." She pointed to a rock in the distance. "Look at that big rock about four hundred yards out there ... now bring your eye down to some other rock or landmark at the water's edge ... and back to the big rock." She paused for two or three minutes. "Now look down again to the water's edge. See a change?"

Ruth said, "I'm not sure ... maybe."

"Well, you could check the newspaper like everyone else."

"Does it always come back in the same way?" Ruth asked.

"Twice a day, about a half-hour later each time: it'll come in, go out and be back to do it all again in twelve and a half hours. In the old days, a gang from the other side of the bay, in Noel, would get on a boat in an evening sail across with the high tide to Portaupique where there used to be a dance hall. As soon as the dances were over, everybody would pile back onto the boat and ride the tide home again by six the next morning. A fair few romances straddled those shores over the years." She closed her book and they strolled on.

As Ruth poked for rocks up ahead, Flossy let her mind drift back to Roger Fry. She'd been thinking about him all morning, the influential British art critic who'd become a lifeline to Mrs. Woolf. Shortly after his untimely death in 1934, Virginia Woolf was persuaded to work on his biography, which she finished the year before she died. Virginia seemed to have poured her grief into that labour and, when she'd finished articulating his vision, she likened it to a child, their child, hers and Roger's. Once the biography was born, however, Flossy could see Mrs. Woolf beginning to slip and it seemed as if no one was noticing. She could also see, in that final year of Mrs. Woolf's life, how vital Roger's encouragement had been to her throughout her writing career, a form of intellectual wall around her: as long as Roger liked her books, Virginia could rest assured they were good. Unlike so many of her Bloomsbury friends — or perhaps Virginia's perception of them — Roger was not the slightest bit withholding. As one of her most ardent critics, he always understood what she was trying to achieve in literature — so similar to what he and others were attempting in painting — and gave unstinting encouragement. With him gone, it seemed as if Virginia Woolf had lost her moorings. In that last winter, she described a "vast sorrow at the back of life," an emptiness, owing in part to Vita's drift to another lover and Roger's death. Of her work, she'd declared, "no echo comes back." Roger Fry had been her echo and with him gone, Mrs. Woolf had begun the long descent that would end in suicide.

Throughout his life, Roger Fry had himself survived his share of ridicule for trying something new. After curating exhibitions of some of the European Post-Impressionists, including works by Manet, Cezanne, Matisse, Gauguin and Van Gogh, he was denounced by Britain's art establishment, incensed that such rubbish paintings should have any claim on art.

Fry always said everyone needed two lifetimes: one to find

out what to do and another to do it. He was determined to go back and look at the painting Masters every ten years or so — Michelangelo, da Vinci, Renoir — not to see how they had changed, but to see how he had with ten more years of living. Flossy loved this tidal notion. She couldn't think of one area of her life where it couldn't apply. There was always a need to look into the distance, up close, beyond again and back. So much could be lost, she knew, by the look that never looked again.

"See that sandbar way out there, up out of the water with grass growing on it?" Flossy held a hand up to shade her eyes from the sun's glare as she spoke, "was never there when we were children. There's change out here but so incremental you can't see it until it's behind you and then you can't imagine how it ever came to be."

They walked along a little farther and Flossy stopped again. "It's always been instructive to me," she said, "how each day's small wearing away can change a coastline, can change a person too."

Apart from their walks by the shore, Flossy and Ruth had found quite a lot to do in Great Village and beyond, things the young woman had never done before. They'd dug clams and made chowder together; Flossy showed her how to make pastry for a raspberry pie and on Sunday after her mother had gone they'd driven to Parrsboro to watch summer stock in an old ship converted into a theatre. There were blueberries to be picked and the Economy Clam festival with Bobby McLellan's band, Badd (the band formerly known as Horridd, according to Mealie). After a trip to the weir, Jimmy was bringing Ruth as wide a variety of fish as he could find and showing her how to cook them with herbs and garlic on Flossy's barbecue, but gradually, apart from the trip to the shore each day and baseball, the young woman seemed just as happy to be at home. More often than not, Flossy would find her stretched out on the parlour chesterfield, an oh-so-charmed Oscar Wilde curled beside her, reading one of the books left in piles throughout the house.

"Queen Mab?"

"Lady Partridge."

The two older women could hoist entire conversations with Ruth perched on a fulcrum waiting to see if they were being serious or silly.

"You could have been like Amy Lowell, if you'd aspired a little higher, and be driving around Great Village as we speak in a mauve Rolls-Royce with a cigar clenched in your teeth."

Flossy said, "I'll ponder it."

"Hmn." Mealie turned a page.

Ruth began picking up the biographies Flossy left at the edge of the table, then reading the writings that also appeared, marked with strips of white paper. Flossy talked of the times, too, who else was writing, the uniqueness of each artist's contribution to the literary canon.

AS THE TWO OF THEM walked along the shore picking rocks that day and watching the tide, Flossy turned to Ruth.

"I used to bring your mother down here when she was little."

It was a windy day. The youngster turned as if she hadn't heard, then she did and shrugged.

"See that tree?" She pointed up to one loaded with apples above them that was leaning over the cliff at a right angle to the shore on its slow tumble to the rocks ten feet below where Flossy and Ruth were walking now at low tide. The tips of the branches were growing straight up towards the sun. Half of the tree's tangle of root was exposed, washed clean of soil and bleached white as whale bone set out against the red cliff. The other half was buried in the bank. In spite of the inevitable destruction ahead, the tree was loaded with one final harvest. "It gave us the best baking apples in this whole area. Let's get some."

Flossy picked up a long stick and teased each apple free. Ruth easily caught them and stuffed them into the plastic bags Flossy carried in her pockets.

"I'd never have believed it when your mother was up there so many years ago." They looked up at the tree. "It'll be gone in no time ... another storm, maybe two. I tried to get Jimmy to graft this one onto one of his trees once but he was never so fond of apple pie that he did it with much heart. Now, maybe if *you'd* asked him ..."

Ruth grinned. "He just likes me 'cause I love his dog."

They all noticed Jimmy's attentiveness. He'd even come out to the baseball game last night with Logie. In fact, a good number of the villagers were strolling over to the baseball field, now that the Ironclads were making a modest showing and to see the new shortstop everyone was talking about. Flossy noticed a few winks exchanged among the fans when Ruth was up at bat. There hadn't been so much excitement in Great Village since the smelts were running in May.

"Is it hard to do, grafting?" Ruth asked.

"Nah, your grandfather showed me. All you need is a good clean paring knife, some rooting powder and something to hold the two pieces of branch together, wax or elastic, snug bark to bark, until this apple twig heals itself to a branch of your tree. That grandfather of yours could put knitting needles into the ground and make them grow."

Flossy looked out towards the water and watched the waves roll in, her small head high. "You have to get to my age to see how the unresolved ache can erode a life, Ruth. And I'm not sure just what's worse: the slow erosion, like my brother Thomas, or the rug pulled from beneath you, like your mother." Ruth was quiet, watching the ground. She bent over and picked up a green and purple stone.

They walked quietly back along the roadway uphill towards the car with their bags of apples. It wound its way through the woods and eventually levelled off at the old Spencer orchard. Flossy stopped to catch her breath and bent to pick up a yellow transparent apple that had rolled onto the road.

"Why is my mother," Ruth paused for a moment, "like that?"

"Like what?"

"She messes everything up. She promises to do things then she doesn't have time and sometimes she doesn't even tell the truth." Flossy stepped away from the road and headed towards an ancient tree that had been split down through the trunk with one half tumbled to the ground. She turned and sat down on it and patted a spot beside her where Ruth joined her. They were both perspiring and the small cast of shade from the half of the tree that was still alive provided relief on a day so hot the grass crackled beneath each footstep. In the meadow not far from them they watched for a minute as a flock of starlings dipped and dove like a black sheet being shaken up into the air before settling into an old maple close to the woods.

"Elizabeth Bishop, our Bishop of the step-cows, wasn't born here but, like you, her people were from Great Village and she belonged. She has a poem about a sandpiper, an exceptional poem. I'll let you read it when we get back. It'll remind you of your mother, though I suspect the poet was probably seeing herself in the feverish running of those birds along the shoreline, the frantic scurrying at the water's edge, searching for something but not seeing anything but what's on the ground immediately in front of them."

Ruth waited.

The wind blew up for a minute and when it passed, Flossy continued. "You know, they all disappoint, one way or another. They can't help it. It's in the nature of parenting and if you have a child someday you will too, but differently than your mother has disappointed you. You'll correct *your* disappointment but you'll likely end up correcting something that doesn't mean a lot to your child." She looked out across the dry land. They needed rain badly; one careless cigarette could send this whole field up in flames. "There's an infinite number of places where we can miss each other." She thought of William and Lillian dragging their conflict into the midst of the children. "Parents have another generation's concerns they're brooding over; they're out there somewhere fishing their hearts out for something you've never even heard of, something that wouldn't interest you in a hundred years. My generation never got over the wars, the Depression, a feeling that the bottom could fall out of everything at any time, that nothing would hold. You never quite get over that kind of fear," she patted her tummy, "in here. We've all got closets stuffed to the gills with plastic bags and aluminum pie plates in case we'll need them someday." A cicada was whining in the hot afternoon.

Ruth rolled one running shoe back and forth over an apple on the ground.

Flossy took a small bite from the transparent apple she'd been polishing with her handkerchief and promptly spat it out. "They always look so much better than they taste," she said, tossing it away. She removed her hat and wiped her forehead. "Your mother was a lovely bright child, so like you, but she was bumped around, first by her mother's illness, which went on, honestly, what seemed forever so that we all got used to it. You can actually get used to someone dying, Ruth." She stopped and stared into the distance, remembering Patricia's last days. They were quiet for some moments. "We got used to waiting and seeing what would come next with your grandmother's illness. She was so good-natured about it. Funny, actually. It was remarkable when I think of it. Then all of a sudden she got sicker and died within days and, as incomprehensible as it may seem, we weren't ready."

Flossy always believed that Patricia just got fed up with being sick, with the body's daily rebellions, the peeling off of something else that wasn't going to recover, like an unwelcome guest who's had enough of sleeping on a lumpy couch and finally leaves. Within days she'd folded up and died.

"You might have thought we'd had time to prepare because your grandfather and I knew it was coming. You could get lost in the day-to-day there too, watching the small changes at the water's edge, like Bishop's sandpiper, and missing what's happening in a larger way out on the bay. And if the adults weren't ready to lose her, well you can just imagine how badly we'd prepared little Marjory and the boys. It was a hard loss. Then he whisked them away from everything they knew, off to Ontario within a week of their mother's death." She went quiet remembering them setting off in the old brown station wagon that day, all three children crying, Marjory inconsolably. "So many goodbyes," she murmured. "He was obstinate, your grandfather, couldn't talk to him. Your mother had all her bearings taken away," she said gently, "so she's always looked outside herself for them. And, you know, they're never there."

"Sometimes she doesn't even tell the truth."

"I'd say she's got a *gambling* problem," Flossy leaned into Ruth affectionately. "I think your mother's torn in so many directions, so many people needing her, that she gambles on who she can disappoint most and least. Every day she juggles all the things she has to do with what she can put off." Flossy reached down and picked up three small apples, tossing them into the air until one dropped. "Oops." She threw the others away too. "It doesn't mean, therefore, she thinks you count least and that's why she changes her plans with you all the time," she spoke deliberately. "It means she's counting most on your forgiveness." She looked at the young woman beside her who didn't say a word in reply. "It's an easy mistake to make." They got up then and made their way back along the dusty road towards the car.

Flossy slowed. "What seems like dishonesty to you, well, we all indulge it a bit, don't you think? Most of us don't resort to outright lies. They're like a hole in the pocket: you've always got to remember they're there or important things fall through, but it's so terribly hard to be truthful, entirely truthful and kind at the same time. Try it yourself; try to be conscious of it for a day even, then a week. We all stretch that fabric for convenience, or ego, sometimes privacy or the plain old burlap of getting along, not wishing to hurt or offend. Some days, I'll tell you Ruth, I'd dearly love it if Jimmy would forget I ever ate fish. I don't have the heart to tell him, though, to drop me off his route for a week. It would be just like him to take it personally and then I wouldn't see another fresh fish until Mealie dumps my ashes out here in the bay," she gestured over her shoulder. "You'd think it would be a small thing to put out there and have accepted, but he'd see ingratitude, and there'd be voices around his dinner table, let me tell you, to keep that chorus humming. We're all full of nettles and nobody knows quite how to handle anybody else."

Ruth had become a hard listener and was learning how to wait.

"What I don't understand is why did my mother go and tell me about that other guy?"

"Well, you were coming and he was going to be here too. Richard has always been a dear friend to Mealie and me. She had to tell you both or change her plans." She stopped and looked up into Ruth's eyes. "It's my fault. I insisted. You needed to know about your father and he needed to know about you. It was the right thing to do. I hope you'll understand that more as you look back on this summer. Of course, your mother wouldn't be the first parent to do the right thing for the wrong reason." They continued walking. The car was hot inside. The two women climbed in, opened all the windows and drove slowly back to the main road.

Flossy raised her voice to be heard. "What do you say we turn left at the stop sign and drive down shore for some fried clams."

"Sure." Ruth could eat endlessly without showing an ounce and she loved food, would devour anything that was put in front of her. They stopped at the main intersection of Highway 2 and Flossy continued.

"I've discovered that there's nothing so capable as the human mind to rationalize a shameful decision," she said. "Sometimes we get so entangled in fear and justification that we'll do almost anything to avoid the truth, what's right."

Ruth looked across at her.

"I'm talking about myself here." Flossy smiled at her and looked out to the countryside. "From your end of a lifetime, you think adults give a lot of thought to the things they do, that they reason everything through. From all I've seen in eighty-two years, there's a fierce lot of muddle out there and what isn't muddle is most often fear. Seldom, seldom are people doing their level best." The sky was filled with fluffy clouds today. "She's not a bad person, your mother. She's lost her compass. To my mind, there's always a lot to learn from context and history; it's true that you assess a work based on the work, but there's surely some clarity to be gained by understanding context. I thought I knew a lot about Mrs. Woolf until I crawled into her skin with those diaries and the letters alongside the novels and other writings. They made me realize what an emotionally crippling early life she'd lived and how insatiable was her need for affection later."

Ruth was a careful driver, hands always on the wheel unless she was changing gears, seldom letting her eyes leave the road, observing the speed limit and heeding all the stop signs that all the rest of them ignored.

"You and your mother don't have a lot of time left together. You could be gone from home in another year. If you leave her too far behind, by the time you're ready to take that second look," she reached across and patted her arm, "and you will be some day," she said, nodding, "she may not be around."

"Do you think my mom will talk to me?"

"I think she probably longs for nothing more. None of us talks about the things that hurt, Ruth, voluntarily, the things nearest our hearts. You've got to be patient. Go find your uncles, Richard, your father, ask them about their lives, your mother, all of it, then decide whether or not she deserves your compassion, but don't write the essay before you've done the research."

Ruth nodded.

The old woman nodded too. "And don't forget," she said, "if you don't make a few good mistakes when you're young, you won't have a thing to talk about when you're old."

XVII

"HOW LONG WOULD YOU SAY IT'S BEEN SINCE WE'VE BEEN TO church?"

Flossy was leaning her back against the counter with a tea towel in one hand that she wound around the inside edge of the blue mug.

Mealie raised an eyebrow. "Bazaars count?"

Flossy gave it some consideration. "I don't suppose so."

Dropping the corner of the *Chronicle Herald* to give the older woman her full attention, Mealie Marsh puckered her face up in thoughtfulness.

"Well, we went to a bunch of funerals. Reverend Mumford's, then Thomas and your mother ... It must be going on a lot of years, Flo."

"Going on a lot of years," she murmured, turning back to the counter. "You're right, Mealie, a lot of years." She put the mug down and picked up a plate. "I spent half my life busting my tail to get to church every Sunday and the other half doing my darnedest to stay away."

"So it seems." Mealie turned the newspaper page.

Flossy was trying to remember when it was that Mealie stopped going to church. Was it before she went off to Montreal? She couldn't be sure. It was as if the two of them had ended up in the same room through different doors. Mealie'd gone away and Flossy'd stayed in the village, though losing David, Thomas and her mother, three pearls dropped from the same broken string, all within two years, might have constituted the same degree of rupture. She'd tried to go back to church after a new minister had been appointed but it just wasn't the same.

In that building where David Mumford had so kindly presided for so many years, Flossy could smell her grief as keenly as if she were lying in his bed with her face in his pillow. Before they started locking the doors, she'd occasionally step into the church after school when she could be sure no one else would be around, sit there in the dark, close her eyes and wrap herself in his memory. She could almost feel him at her fingertips, as if he were there, behind some dimension she didn't yet understand, trying to reach her too.

She looked down at the front cover of the *Chronicle Herald* that Mealie was reading. It was a photo of a perfectly ordinary matron holding a photo of herself at Woodstock twenty-five years earlier.

Flossy lifted her glasses and looked closer. "Did you see that? Woodstock turns twenty-five."

Mealie glanced at the front cover again. "Yeah," she said, "quarter of a century can scare the hell out of you, can't it?" She turned back to what she'd been reading. "I myself am waiting for the tattooed generation to turn up in nursing homes. 'We're ready for your bath, Simon.' Won't they look like the wreck of the Hesperus?"

Flossy could hear the water running upstairs. Ruth must have gone back to her bed from the chesterfield. She and Phil were leaving early for Five Islands today to hike and hunt for amethyst.

"Ever miss it, Mealie?" she asked.

Mealie pulled the paper down, doubling it over against her bosom. "Miss what, *Woodstock*?"

"No, no, church?"

"You kidding me?" She peered at Flossy over the top of her glasses, amusement wrinkling her eyes, "I think I miss Woodstock more." When she saw she was serious, Mealie pulled the glasses down to her chest and was, at once, thoughtful. "No, Flo, can't say I ever missed it." She sat up. "Maybe a few people, but no one I wasn't likely to bump into at McLellan's on a Saturday anyway, and not enough to ever go back." She turned her face and stretched to see out the window but this was a thinking pose more than a looking, while she chewed it over a bit more. "Always had the feeling they were doing their best to hold things the same, like some tethered mule going around the same circle every year. I'd be looking for something that leans out a bit more ..."

"Jesus not do that?" Flossy asked. She and Mealie didn't usually talk about these things and though she herself didn't want the bother of going back to church, and explaining to all the curious, she could have a guilty pang every now and again about ignoring all of that Christian upbringing, as if she'd walked out on a husband and four children over in Bridgewater.

Mealie's thoughtful eyes narrowed. "Oh well, I'd have no quibble with that one, Pet," she smiled, "but for me, there's always been more searching among artists than in churchgoers." She folded the newspaper neatly, by feel. "That urge to make something, burn it right down to the wick, I've always thought these things showed much more gratitude and appreciation for creation than just taking a number and standing in line behind

the Rule Book Boys. Never seemed as if Jesus had all that much
to do with church, any of the ones I ever attended."

NATURALLY THEY COULDN'T GET Thomas to go. It wasn't unusual
for some of the local men to vanish from church a few years after
they'd tied the knot. Lillian O'Reilly wasn't the kind of woman
to allow any son of hers to stop attending but they couldn't even
get Thomas as far as the outhouse, let alone St. James United
Church on a Sunday morning.

To make matters worse, he wouldn't talk to the minister when
he came right to the house and Reverend Mumford had had no
end of troubles since coming to Great Village. Regardless, he still
faithfully came by for a visit every two weeks, snow, hail, rain
or shine. Not many would have done twenty or more years of
that.

"A rare soul, wasn't he? Reverend Mumford?" Flossy murmured wistfully. She'd stopped what she was doing, plate and
tea towel held against her breast, looking off and recalling an
early memory of him as a carefree young man, in bare feet, his
pant legs rolled up his white shins, sitting down by the shore on
a picnic blanket beside his pretty wife, Sarah, before everything
had come entirely unravelled. You didn't often see your minister
in bare feet. It made her smile to think of him.

"Lovely man," Mealie replied, as if completing some prayerful
invocation.

In he'd come every two weeks. Even now, decades after
David Mumford's death, Flossy couldn't resist the comfort of
the memory. He'd remove his black jacket, worn at the cuffs,
and place it over a chair in the kitchen, his hat on the seat,
greet Lillian and Flossy, have a word with Jimmy about fishing
or school, then plod upstairs to sit by Thomas. Every second

Wednesday, sometimes he'd read to him from the Bible or speak softly. For hours they might just sit there in silence. At the end of each visit, he'd put a gentle hand on Thomas's brow and briefly bow his own in prayer.

After a few of those visits, the others left them alone. It was always an occasion to have the minister to the house — special visitors were rare — and they all wanted to be around but their mother would shoo the youngsters away. She told them Reverend Mumford needed time alone with Thomas.

In those first weeks that slid into months then ground into years, Flossy wished with all her heart that Thomas would acknowledge the minister, say something, anything, that would make him believe his coming was in some small way helpful. Thomas was impenetrable. He rarely lifted his head from his pillow. There wasn't malice or hatred in his eyes, like someone who resented the minister. It was indifference, which made it all that much worse for such a devout man of God. It made no difference to Thomas whether their minister prayed for his soul or played tic-tac-toe on the wall.

Possibly the best thing about Reverend Mumford's coming was what it meant to all the rest of them. He would ask how they were getting on at the barn or with the harvest, the lady's hats, the churning, and he'd listen carefully as they rattled and sawed away on the same sad log about how hard it was and how tired they were. He'd offer help. Of all the people they knew, of neighbours and family alike (with the exception of Uncle James, who just showed up to sow the grain, and the old Faulkner sisters who put in the garden every single year until they were no longer able), Reverend Mumford had the imagination to realize there was still a farm to run and with their two men gone the adjustment was hard. There were four more hours of work to fit into a day already too short and overburdened. Flossy and Lillian couldn't be called prissy and they weren't afraid of work, but they were small women and the care of cows, horses and pigs took strength they didn't have.

Then, at the end of each evening, when they were cold, dirty and exhausted from milking, hauling water, cleaning pens and lifting hay at the barn, there was no one in the house with the fire lit and supper on the table. Flossy thought it was no wonder widowers remarried before they could turn around three times.

Even Jimmy, who was only nine, knew things were different without being told as much and took to the small fetch-and-chase chores of the young, keeping the kindling box full without being reminded, bringing Queen Esther up from the pasture to be milked, feeding the chickens and collecting eggs, keeping the potatoes from boiling dry, most of the things Flossy herself once did.

For their mother too, Reverend Mumford's visits eased her conscience about refusing to whip Thomas. Flossy remembered how he'd hung his head and shook it sadly as her mother related Dr. Rushton's advice and confessed how guilty she'd been for not whipping him as the doctor instructed. She thought she might be letting Thomas down by neglecting her duty as his mother Reverend Mumford patted her hand.

"Whatever has hold of Thomas," he said in a voice not much above a whisper while looking towards the top of the stairs, "will never be beaten out of him. The spirit doesn't need to be broken, Mrs. O'Reilly; anyone can see something's already done that," he said, bringing his gaze back to her. "The only thing for him is kindness, prayer and patience." Stopping for a moment and clasping his hands together, as he often did when getting ready to say just a bit more, the minister added, "forgiveness, quite a lot of forgiveness." He nodded his head and smiled, "I haven't met a soul yet who couldn't use a second helping of that."

He was a gentle man, David Mumford, not the stern kind of minister the O'Reillys were used to as Presbyterians, though by then their church had gone with the newly formed United Church. Reverend Mumford was more suited to the United Church anyway. He sat before the assembly of parishioners each Sunday with his head bowed and hands crossed, not at the wrists, but just enough up the forearm to bring his shoulders in and make it look as if there were a naked sorrow at the heart of him that needed protection. Few in the congregation thought him much good and though a sizeable contingent complained it was no easy task to find a replacement as amenable to poverty as was David Mumford.

Lillian O'Reilly wasn't like the rest. She was partial to him, motherly, though there wasn't a vast difference in their ages. She would sew a button on his jacket or make an effort to mend those hopelessly frayed sleeves as he sat upstairs with Thomas. They all liked him. A good many churchgoers thought a minister had to put the fear of God into people to be any good. "Doesn't he know," old Mrs. Starritt would list towards their mother on their way out of church, speaking from behind her glove, "people need to have the dickens scared out of them to behave?" Lillian would smile, uttering not a word. The value of well-placed silence was something they'd all come to learn from Thomas.

My but David Mumford could put a shine on a Wednesday, all adrift as it was in the middle of the week. Even now, so long after, Flossy could get up in a morning, look at the calendar and feel that Wednesday-glow all over again, as tangible as a long-forgotten smell that could bring him back in an instant. The Wednesday in between his visits to the O'Reillys, it was said that

Reverend Mumford went off with the early mail run to Halifax to visit his wife, who'd been committed to Mount Hope after a nervous breakdown from which she would never come home. Wednesday was also the day Lillian baked bread. The comforting smell of fresh bread in the oven would fill the house by afternoon and he was always given a loaf to take back with him to the manse. Being on his own, their mother worried Reverend Mumford wasn't eating all that well. Flossy came to associate the smell of fresh-baked bread, the coziness of the kitchen kept warm and still for the dough to rise, with David Mumford, and perhaps a pinch of loving yeast had its first sweet stirrings right there.

The more familiar Reverend Mumford became to the O'Reillys with those visits, the more his face seemed the incarnation of Job, a soul steeped in suffering. For years he came and sat in the ashes with Thomas, in silence, trying to understand where he'd gone and hidden himself. No doubt the good minister did the same on alternate Wednesdays on the other side of the province with a woman who, they say, no longer even recognized him as her husband.

In spite of what Thomas was going through, it was clear to Flossy that it must have pained her brother twice over to have David Mumford, of all people, sitting patiently beside him. To have to look at that one face of all faces every two weeks would have felt like salt water in open wounds. Flossy was sure Thomas dreaded the smell of freshly baked bread drifting up into his room as much as she adored walking into the house and being greeted by it, that inescapable reminder the minister was coming.

Since that night by the bay when they said Thomas and Reverend Mumford wept in each other's arms, there hadn't been anything said between them, but seeing the black circles beneath those gentle dark eyes, the lines carved into their minister's face — he wasn't but in his mid-thirties — shoulders stooped, all alone as he was and knowing the O'Reillys were married to his tragedy, to all its sad consequences, made those visits the more terrible for everyone but especially Thomas. Nobody ever said you shouldn't talk about things that made you weak in the hollow hours of the night. You just never did.

Yet there he was, like clockwork, stamping his feet at the cookhouse door as he came into the house smelling of fresh air, nodding at each of them, removing his hat and revealing a perfect little dome of shiny flesh fringed with a halo of hair at the top of his head, David Mumford, the soul of kindness. Not much taller than Lillian, but slighter, ears stuck out a little too far, he was a giant in heart and mind. No recrimination, not a hint or trace of bitterness, nothing but tender encouragement for every last one of them.

A rare sympathy would grow up between Reverend Mumford and Thomas over nearly two decades, entirely organic like vine on trellis. He took neither her brother's indifference nor agnosticism to heart, if that was what it was. He came, sat by him, talked softly and sometimes prayed. It might have been like sitting by his silent, inscrutable God at the end of each newly unfathomable day. The minister's constancy seemed to have its own wearing effect on Thomas too. The silence that lay between them would become a place of compassion, as of two old men of different languages content to sit beside each other on the same sunny bench every day for a dozen years only observing sights before them. They might have no words in common but they would come to count on each other and if the one were confined to his home with an illness or a broken foot, the other would have felt considerably smaller out there.

Flossy became aware of Mealie beside her, the coffee pot in her hand tipped towards the mug in front of her.

"Anybody home?" she asked.

"Sorry, Mealie, I was asleep."

Mealie began to pour. "They also serve," she said, "who only sit and stare." Flossy motioned *enough*.

Stirring a little milk into her cup, she said, "Mealie, if I were to go ..."

"What, you hiking off to Oakville next?" She replaced the coffee pot on the stove.

"No, no. Away," Flossy said.

"Away?" Mealie stopped.

"Away, yes." Flossy was watching her.

Seating herself back down at the table, Mealie took her own coffee cup into her hands and looked at Flossy over the top of her half glasses. "Ahh," she said, "you'd be referring to The Big Away."

Flossy nodded.

"You feelin' all right these days, Flo?"

"Yes, yes, oh yes, but if I were to go away, Mealie, I'd want you to be sure ... to know ..." She stirred her own coffee absently, working her mouth to find words that had turned tail of a sudden. "You've been, to me, you've been ..." They could hear Ruth coming down the creaky stairs.

"Yes, yes, Pet, I know, I know. Me too, me too."

Ruth greeted the others and they all cooed over her remarkable bruise. Settled back into her newspaper, Mealie suddenly sat forward. "Well, I'll be ..."

Flossy looked up from her coffee. Ruth stopped what she was doing.

"The Barnes is on the move. Never thought I'd see the ..."

"Old Barns?" Flossy asked.

"The Bishop's step-cousin's barns?" Ruth added, getting the orange juice from the fridge and a piece of apple pie.

"Albert Barnes," Mealie exclaimed.

Flossy and Ruth looked at each other.

"An eccentric old bugger," Mealie continued. "He managed to collect Picassos, Renoirs, Matisses and Van Goghs all his life. He died a while back but specified in his will that the paintings should never leave his home. Well, the place has been falling down around them for years and a judge has finally agreed to send eighty of the pictures on tour to raise money for the house. They're going to Toronto. You've gotta go see them, Dash," she looked up at her. "Part of your aesthetic education," she grinned. "Go for all of us."

"Why don't you and Flossy come too," she said as she finished a last bite of pie. "You can stay at our place."

Flossy smiled as she and Mealie exchanged a dubious look.

"That's an idea," Mealie said. She was just about to return to the newspaper when Ruth went back to the counter for a second piece of apple pie. As she sat back down at the table, Mealie raised her eyebrows.

"O, reason not the need," the young woman said with flourish.

UPSTAIRS, A PRISONER TO his bed, Thomas's world shrank to nothing. A fly could torment him for hours, unable as he was to get up and swat it. Up there he had only the slow path of the sun to watch on his walls during the day and the lights of an occasional automobile heading down shore by night, the rain chucking against the window, the clatter and voices of the downstairs world, food they brought him to eat, footsteps, doors closing. Flossy used to wonder if Thomas listened to them, if he followed their movements or heard what they all said to each other or just themselves, forgetting he was there and loosening their interior thoughts as they mumbled through the housework. Did he parse sounds with the family's customs to figure out what they were doing? It must have been as if he were blind, some things easy to follow from a distant room, the scraping of ashes, building the morning fire, the first sharp crackles of ignited kindling, the clatter of an armful of wood dropped into the box, a steaming kettle, kneading bread on the kitchen table. Others harder still, grudges and withholding, overt and covert anger. It was spare.

Reverend Mumford wasn't a reformer by nature, a man who put a lot of stock in dramatic conversions. No doubt he'd seen far too many people slide back to their old ways who felt the more disheartened about themselves for having done so. David Mumford was a believer in increments, or perhaps a man who hoped in hope. After all the usual religious talk was so apparently wasted on Thomas and made him turn towards the wall, Reverend Mumford began to talk to him from somewhere else. He spoke of his own doubts, disappointments and loneliness. He sought to be truthful, said he even admired that Thomas lived so honestly. Some days, when she would be putting the linens away and could catch a few phrases, Flossy thought David Mumford sounded sadder, far closer to despair than ever her brother did. It was, she imagined, something Thomas knew something about even if he didn't talk all that much.

Could a minister lose his faith? She'd often wondered about that. Did he ever lose confidence in those bits of hope he cast about here and there among his flock? Whatever happened to them when they did? What was there beyond faith and hope? Did they ever come up short on compassion when they heard the tawdry failings of those in their care? Was the assurance of God's continued love anything more than the hopeless return of the weak back into the world that would certainly overcome them again next week as it had last week and would the following week and all those to come? For Reverend Mumford, alone as he was, it must have been like crossing into Cumberland County and finding another hermit monk to confide in. Over the years Thomas turned out all the dogged patience and compassion, whatever he could find left in that husk, to give back to the other man and after the first decade or so, he did talk some and shook the Reverend's hand each time he left. It may have been the essence of friendship because those two men, despite the losses of a lifetime, had become just that to each other: the taker and the restorer.

Of course you could never discount what happened the summer before he took to his bed. It affected all of the O'Reillys, but none more than Thomas.

Living along the edge of the bay, those restless waters and sweeping tides became the symbol of unchanging change to them. As farmers, the bay was a god they could turn their backs to and, for the most part, get away with it. Fishermen may have faced the sea and taken its blows head-on, but farmers faced the road. The land was the angel they'd wrestled over the years, doing battle with fecundity, hacking back alder, spruce and birch.

That the land butted up against the bay was pure coincidence now, an earlier century's necessity when water was the sole means of transportation in an inhospitable land where trees squared off to shore.

Every few years, however, the unfathomable god demanded a sacrifice. It wasn't so often a fisherman — they knew what they were up against. Nowadays it was more than likely a tourist confusing a sandbar for the water's edge or some such innocent to spectacularly misjudge the tides and come to grief. You had to know your way through the bay's channels to navigate in a place where tens of thousands of tonnes of water rush back and forth twice a day. And back then, when Flossy and Thomas were children, no one knew how to swim, none of the farmers and precious few who were fishermen.

The sea, though, the bounty of its tides, the mystery of its delicacies, its ever-changing moods, colours and rhythms, the beauty of sunlight on wet rock, barnacles, lichens and marsh greens, held a solemn and incomparable attraction nonetheless, especially for the very young, the unseasoned who understood less of the dangers.

Every couple of months following the death of the O'Reillys' father, Reverend Mumford and his wife Sarah would come by their place on a Sunday afternoon with their boys. Flossy could only remember it as a time when other friends and neighbours stayed away. Those visits, with the children in tow, tugged the O'Reillys away from their clenched sadness. Lillian liked Mrs. Mumford who was naturally more lighthearted than her husband though easily frightened. She was delicate looking, with fine sandy hair and white skin. She dressed in plain long skirts and white blouses with the smallest bit of finery on her collar and cuffs, as if they'd been dipped into a vat of lace. There seemed always a soft transparency about Sarah Mumford, as of a filmy, respiring creature you might find caught in a tidal pool.

The Mumford boys were just enough older than Jimmy, nine and ten, to look towards Thomas for adventure, at least the older one was and the younger had rather cling to his brother than forge his own friendships. On those Sundays, Thomas obliged and would take them beyond the watchful eye of their mother to explore the barn and see the newborn animals. Living in the heart of the village, these were not farm boys and so they adored the kittens, ducklings and calves that were less interesting to Jimmy from familiarity. When the weather got warmer, the women would sometimes pack a picnic lunch and the two families spend an afternoon by the bay.

On the last Sunday in May of '26, an unusually warm day, the two families were to meet by Spencer's Point. After they had their picnic, with the tide well on its way out and the bay looking like a drained, barren mudflat, Thomas proposed taking the boys on an adventure to see some nests of gulls' eggs on the old Chisholm chimney beyond the point. Lillian cautioned him, Sarah fluttered, but Thomas and Reverend Mumford brushed off the women's concern. They rolled up their pant legs and struck off, Pied Pipers with three little boys in tow, Jimmy having decided to tag along. Like a good many of the men around, Thomas was familiar with the channels, deep crevices in those mudflats that quickly become fast flowing rivers and by which the tides rush back in to fill the bay.

It was nearly a full week later when, on a sunny Saturday afternoon, Jimmy was trout fishing in the stream beyond the edge of the farm when he met up with the Mumford lads again who were out fishing too. Charles, the elder, hadn't had a nibble all morning and, losing patience with fishing, got the idea to go see if the gulls' eggs had hatched. His little brother, John Calvin, threatened to tell their mother if he weren't allowed to go too. Jimmy shied away from the adventure and headed home with his catch of two fine rainbow trout.

The Mumfords struck out on their own. It being a week later meant the tide, which always gains an hour each day, had exactly reversed from where it had been on the previous excursion and was already on its way back as the boys set out. Normally they

weren't permitted to play down by the flats but here it was fine
weather and no one bothered much about the comings and goings
of idle boys on a Saturday afternoon.

By land it would have taken a man with a brisk walk half an
hour or so each way to get there. Along the mudflats, though,
it's always farther and much harder to drag through the thick
muck, over the sandbars and stones, and there is so much to catch
the attention along the way, that before they knew it, the little
one was weary and they weren't but heading back before the
water was flowing in around them. By mid-afternoon, the tide
was filling the channels and, like fingers it would surround the
boys and close off another route along each sandbar and it seemed
as if they were having to go farther out in order to find a way
back in.

It was just about three o'clock when Reverend Mumford
dropped by the house asking if anyone had seen them. Flossy
hadn't, nor her mother, and Thomas was just getting in from
the barn. In the commotion of everyone talking at once nobody
caught what Jimmy'd said. Reverend Mumford was already
thanking them and turning to go when Jimmy tugged at mother's
apron and said it again, louder, about the "gulls' eggs." This time
the words fell into a pocket of silence. As swiftly as they hit their
mark, as if one seismic shudder passed through all the adults at
once, Reverend Mumford and Thomas rushed from the house
and down towards the shore. Flossy was sent to the Simmons
farm to alert the men while their mother and Jimmy headed off
to Uncle James to get a ride into the village. They would stay
with Sarah Mumford while James returned by the Geddes farm
calling up the men along the way.

Sure enough those little boys were stranded on a sandbar not
five hundred yards from the shore. Charles was calling and waving,

when the men spotted them, and John Calvin began to cry. The water had risen to their waists and there wasn't any way they could get across the channel in front of them.

They found an old boat nearby that Thomas and Reverend Mumford hoisted into the bay but the minister hadn't paddled twenty yards from shore before it was half full of water and sinking.

Men began to arrive from every direction, on foot, horseback, carrying whatever their minds grasped might be of some help, rope or an axe, until a good group had gathered. Not one of them could swim. To a man they worked frantically to lash together a makeshift raft, pulling down and stripping the branches from trees leaning over the cliff or already fallen. One of the men who lived closest took off on his horse for hammer and nails. Others pulled boards off the boat to nail along the spruce trunks.

By the time the nails arrived, little Charles Mumford was holding his young brother in his arms, the water having risen to their shoulders. The men quickly secured the boards to the branches and then harnessed the minister's horse to pull the raft into the water. They whipped and shouted at that animal, while David Mumford paced back and forth along the shore, watching those boys, calling to them, "Be brave, my little ones." The boys called back, "Pappy! Hurry Pappy! Hurry!"

One horse and six strong men heaving and straining stretched every ounce of fibre and might to drag that wretched raft inch by inch into the water. Over their own shouts they could hear two little lads screaming.

Then just one.

Then ... as the raft sat like stone beneath long lapping waves there was no sound other than panting, moaning men. They looked out onto the bay and there was nothing to be seen but calm, dreadful water and David Mumford crumpled in a heap on the shore.

Of all those six big, broken-hearted farmers gathered there that night with the minister, it was Thomas, a fifteen-year-old scrap of a kid, who would go to David Mumford and put his arms around him.

Death can leave a bitter taste on the tongue, any death, but this kind of a tragedy, in a place as small as Great Village, leaves its trace forever. And it was their tragedy; it belonged to the O'Reillys too. Those little boys had been as familiar in their home as their own Jimmy. Thomas thought too much about them, naturally took it all on himself and no one could console him. Within six months, of course, no one would have asked the question of why the lads were out there in the first place. Thomas's name would have drifted away from the dark core of the tragedy — two little boys drowned — but he wore the blame like a twenty-pound albatross around his neck and never could forgive himself. Some people can't get over thinking there's got to be a reason for everything.

They all thought too much about it, imagining the lightness of setting out for a child's adventure and then how it turned out so horribly, the loss of the minister's two little lads. Some losses are inconsolable — there isn't any satisfactory way you can work even a Christian mind around them.

Sarah Mumford still took her place in the second pew on the right side each Sunday morning but everyone was aware the poor woman was in a bad way and no one knew what to do for her. She frequently wore her sweater wrong-side out and her once-pretty hair was seldom tidy beneath her hat. Someone always had to go back in to the church to tell her that the service was finished. "Best be coming home," David would say to her gently. Uncle

James would drive Lillian over there now and again to spend an afternoon with her but she knew it wasn't any help, maybe even made things worse, given they still had Jimmy safe and sound, and Thomas had taken the boys out there in the first place.

The fragile little woman took to walking the shoreline whenever she could slip away by herself. How many times had Reverend Mumford found her down there climbing over the rocks, no matter the weather, searching for her John Calvin, the little one whose body they'd never found. In the middle of the night, in bare feet, knees bruised and bloodied, her nightclothes billowing, he'd find her there.

"My baby's out here," she'd wail, pounding her fists into her husband's chest, as he struggled to take her home. He was terrified of losing her too.

After a couple of months of it, Doctor Rushton proposed taking Mrs. Mumford to Dartmouth "for a rest cure." Within a year they all knew she'd not be coming back. It wasn't so long after that Thomas took to his bed.

It was hard for every last one of them and they each bore their sorrow in a haze of silence. From that optic, the loss of those little boys, Flossy O'Reilly could understand what happened to her brother Thomas: the mystery wasn't that he awakened one morning and saw nothing around him, nothing of meaning and no reason to keep going. The mystery was that so many days and years of their lives all the rest of them awakened, saw the sky brighten, the sun push slowly up over the horizon, and found in that most distant, impersonal, mechanical event some meaning, a veiled promise, that allowed the trace of courage they needed to set out into the day with determination and lightness in their hearts.

XVIII

PICKING UP SOME LETTERS TO BE MAILED, FLOSSY O'REILLY slipped a heel down the back of each canvas shoe, stepped outside her kitchen door and set off walking in the direction of the postal box down by the general store.

Along the edge of the road, where grass and gravel meet, the evening's heat lifted the scent of sweet chamomile to her nose. The light was rich at the end of the day, casting copper warmth over the faces of houses on the far side of the street. With the heat's edge past, it was entirely pleasant outdoors.

Two cardinals dipped past her, lilting off towards Mr. McNutt's orchard. She turned to follow their path but caught, instead, the glare of the sun full on her face as it peered out like some fierce ancient eye from between the McNutt and Marsh houses. Here it was, halfway through August, and the huge crimson ball shivered on the horizon as if it were the first of July. Even the leaves on trees were beginning to curl and drop. This time last year, she was sure she'd been covering the tomatoes at night. Though her left hip had ached all day, a sure sign of rain, there wasn't a cloud in the sky.

She ambled on though her eyes were drawn back to the setting sun. Was it a perspective to love a day folding down tidily on itself, another one finished? Perhaps it was a late-life infatuation, some aging resonance with the dying of the light.

A family of crows passed between her and the sun. Seven silent black spirits beating southward, she felt their shadows pass through her. "The air is delicate," she whispered, "light thickens, and the crow makes wing to the rooky wood." How did he know so much? How did Will Shakespeare know about crows and everything else, cram so much learning into one short lifetime? It always seemed that whenever Flossy learned something new in her life, all she had to do was circle back around Shakespeare again, and she'd find him already there, that clever sorcerer, perched on a rock up ahead, thumb on his nose wiggling fingers at her. And what was it that drove such big birds to fly a hundred miles every evening to roost together by the thousand in a valley up the Shubenacadie River, then tomorrow strike off again in their family clusters for another day of scavenging and racket?

A little walk in a day, down by the shore, or like this along the road to McLellan's, could put things in perspective for her, restore a balance of sorts. Like Elizabeth Bishop, nature had always been Flossy's best comfort even when she most detested living on the farm. Oh, and she'd hated the chores all right, despised getting up on a winter's morning and pulling on chill trousers to go to the barn, the days so dark and cold her nostrils froze together with every icy breath as she carried steaming pails of water from the house over squeaky snow to thaw the pump and prime it to get more pails of burning cold water to haul to the animals, her fingers aching, knuckles bleeding from merciless winter.

Detested it all until she got down there among the shaggy hides, the animal calm and dungy warmth of the stable. Then the predictability of the animals, their pitiful contentment with a handful of grain, hay and water placed before them, salt licks and molasses, a scratch behind the ears, in turn gave her uncommon comfort. Flossy could still feel her forehead pressed against Queen Esther's warm flank, the sweet smell of milk rising from twin streams pinging rhythmically against the empty pail. She recalled the last steps of the nightly routine with the chickens roosting and animals settled, their cud-chewing tranquility restored. She'd blow out the kerosene lamp, its puff of acrid smoke curling into the air, pick up the pail of milk and collected eggs, latch the barn door and walk back to the house with the immense milky way twinkling so close up there in the infinite above. No warrior, prince or knight-victorious throughout the ages had a more welcoming return than to step back into the house, the old kitchen stove lashing out heat, her mother taking the milk and eggs, rubbing her stinging hands with a towel, Flossy could look back on those dreadful days with no small measure of affection. Curious how kind the revisionist mind could be, sixty-some years distant.

She surveyed the road in front of her. When the sun's long rays slipped between the houses like that and caught her figure, the shadow stretched all the way across the street and curled up into Mrs. Bill Curtis's front window as if Flossy were a giant, thirty feet tall, walking along the shoulder of the Londonderry Road, not her usual four feet ten inches that, with time, had settled like sediment to something more in the order of four foot eight. How does a woman lose two inches? Two teeth, yes — she'd stepped out of the car once at Sobeys and noticed a perfect molar on the ground — but two inches? They vanished about as mysteriously as whole decades in the middle of one's life. She didn't honestly mind the years flying by; it was the decades she most resented.

In fact, there had been at least one decade of unending physical drudgery for the O'Reillys' on that farm — she and her mother at the barn day in and day out while Jimmy was growing up — the horror of the Depression years of scrimping and scraping, living on turnips, potatoes and Jimmy's fishing, anxious they wouldn't survive.

Nothing had changed specifically, by the close of that first dismal decade after Thomas went to bed, but you could say it eased considerably. One could always see these things more clearly in other families: the crisis that lost all its sting with five years behind it. In fact, there weren't many troubles that could hold their shape at five or ten years' distance, those that thought the sky was falling with a daughter pregnant on the wrong side of the altar. People stretched a lot more than they ever imagined they could.

The single biggest change in that decade, of course, had to be Jimmy. By the end of it, he was nearing twenty and big enough to handle the farm, relieving his mother and sister of the morning and evening chores. Their little Jimmy would stretch into a round and sturdy six foot two and turn out to be as uncomplicated as he was big, the kind that have so little to prove. As a boy he ran, ate, fought, fell asleep and got up the next morning bearing no grudge for the previous day's disputes. Nor did he change all that much as he grew older. For Jimmy, each day brought its own reasons for grief and gratitude and he sought to borrow none from the morrow. He was content to do what had to be done in a day, do all a person could, whether it be work or play, and just as happy to surrender it all to a cup of tea by a warm kitchen stove and follow it with a good night's sleep.

That boy was made for farming: loved rising with the sun, setting out to the shore with his dog to check the weir, was patient with growing crops and animals. He took pride in solitary hard work, was not beaten down by poor weather or indiscriminate death visiting his herd. He'd found a woman to marry who could work right angles to him and bear him children whose children they'd watch into their old age.

Flossy glanced at the lime-green envelope in her hand among the bills she was on her way to mail. Little Jimmy would be turning seventy-six in another few weeks on Labour Day. She still hadn't found a private moment for a word with him. She mustn't let it drift. Seventy-six, she could hardly believe it. Jimmy could still pack in the day of a much younger man even with some arthritis and the daily undoing of the aging body. In another month he'd be out until dark harvesting corn with his son-in-law. Noreen was always so fond of saying, "Jimmy'll be the happiest man alive if he drops dead sitting up there in his big old John Deere." Her sister-in-law was another of the reasons Flossy was more than a bit complacent about losing some hearing.

Once they'd got through the worst of the Dirty Thirties, Lillian O'Reilly's millinery sales began to pick up and by the middle of the Second World War, Reilly hats were being worn across the province. It hadn't always been so. When the Great Depression hit there wasn't money for bare necessities let alone hats and the McLellan brothers initially said they'd have to decline her work, but Walter McLellan, the younger of the two, had a bit of a soft spot for the Widow O'Reilly's talent. He was also a sufficiently good businessman to know the lean years wouldn't last forever, especially for quality hats, and so agreed to take Lillian's merchandise and pay her in kind as he could: sugar, tea, kerosene, salt, seed, sewing supplies, the few things they couldn't grow or preserve themselves. It was more than the O'Reillys could have expected. He sent the extra hats to a son of his who ran a woman's clothing store in Halifax. By the late forties, custom orders were coming in as fast as Lillian could turn them out.

Flossy in her own right by then was the longest-serving teacher at the Great Village Public School. For a small woman she had built a reputation for being able to manage boys twice her size in any class and giving them the basics of a solid education. She didn't think all that much about it back then. If she'd dared take a long, critical look at teaching, saw how little she was accomplishing after the first four years, or could measure how hard some of them worked against what she was trying to do with them, she'd probably have walked away and started growing mushrooms at the other end of the province. For the most part, she figured school was children's work, keeping them occupied so as not to have packs of ten-year-olds roaming the countryside and shooting each other with rubber bands.

Would Mealie think that too harsh? She looked across and could see the lights on in the studio. It pleased her to see them, Mealie's lighthouse. It meant she was in a creative fog, burning her wick. It reminded Flossy of times when Mrs. Woolf was writing a dozen finished pages a day, pushing the work forward. Flossy would have to get herself to Halifax for Mealie's show in October. She hoped she'd be around for that, for Mealie.

THROUGHOUT THAT FIRST HARD decade without their father and Thomas, Flossy had been overwhelmed by the unfairness of it all. Not a little bit or even now and again. Her anger ran deep. She'd find herself awake at night, pacing the floor, obsessing over the day's transgressions, a pressure building inside of her. Back in those days, an egg not boiled to her liking could ignite her rage, then the fury would fly in every direction as she reminded the rest of them of all their shortcomings since the last eruption.

If anyone had asked her way back then, the source of that irritation, she might have pointed to Thomas. Not only did he not do a lick of work, he lay up there in that bed and wouldn't even come down for meals. Stuck in her brain and nagging like the chip off a back tooth, was a seemingly insignificant detail about the day he took to his bed. It was the horses' harness hung in its usual place inside the barn door. Going in and out of there every morning and night, Flossy's hand brushed against the leather as she reached for the door latch, a daily reminder of the mystery of that day. Whatever happened to Thomas out there in the hay-field, if anything happened at all, he'd had enough will to bring the mower back to the barn, remove the harness from the horses, water them and put them out to pasture. If he'd only left the animals in the field and walked straight to his bed, Flossy might have understood it more, thought there was not an ounce of will in any of it, but he hauled the harness off them — no small task — hung it behind the door and pumped them pails of water. Thomas wasn't an enormous clock that stopped working, rather he'd mysteriously wound down. If that was so, in her young mind, maybe it was a matter of will to wind him up again.

She often wondered if there was a month or year or maybe ten times in a day when the notion might have floated into his mind that he could get up, some shriek or whoop outside his window tug his curiosity just enough to scrabble those legs to the edge of the bed and slowly drop them out from beneath his blanket, feel the bottoms of his feet on the cool floor once more. But he never did. His body'd become stone. If there'd been a cup beside the bed filled with a magical potion that would restore his life, he could no more have reached out for it than a stone rolled itself into the bay.

His absence drew an awkward hush over the others in the household that separated the wish to ask from the wisdom to abstain as surely as cream rising from milk. It was as when they were expecting a long-awaited visit from someone they'd all been dying to see, like their mother's sister Margaret, who only made it back from Boston but once in three years. The hour for the arrival would pass, maybe another. They'd each grow quiet with the realization that something had come up, as so often did in the country, and all would be explained in a letter through the mail in a day or so. All the same, they'd ached for that sweet arrival, and the sadness would throb in the throat. They'd change back into their everyday clothes but couldn't resist the waiting and watching, taking one more futile look up the road.

Thomas had become a study in senseless worry. He was afraid of something, everything, but, like motes dancing in a shaft of sunlight, nothing you could ever put a finger on. He was beset by all the penny worries a healthy mind might pick up in a day, look at, and set right back down again.

For twenty-four years they had to wait on him as if he were a small, wilful prince upstairs to pamper day in and day out. In those many years of getting up at four-thirty in the morning with so much to do, emptying Thomas's slop pail or dragging his dinner up those stairs at night was just another chore among too many to fit edgewise into a day, and he was never so grateful as Queen Esther to get her meagre handful of grain or the horses their hay. And if Flossy wasn't provoked by Thomas, it was Jimmy or her students. There seemed always to be someone gnawing away in the attic of her nerves.

It came to a head with David Mumford in the summer of '36, the year of the Moose River Gold Mine Disaster, when Flossy was in her mid-twenties and Thomas was nearing a full decade in bed. Reverend Mumford had come by that summer day on his usual visit but instead of going straight up to see her brother, he sat down beside her on the porch steps where she was shucking peas. Flossy was in a dark mood having just had a row with her mother in the kitchen over something she couldn't even recall. The two women were at each other frequently and Lillian, throwing her hands in the air, had muttered, "You're every bit your father."

Still steaming outside on the porch, Flossy wasn't at all happy to see David Mumford ambling up the lane and the peas were flying in just about every direction but the bowl they were meant for. An angry blush ran right up her neck to her cheeks and ears. In the minister's presence, she struggled for composure. She talked about what was on everyone's mind, the mine disaster.

They'd all been caught up by that event. Each night Jimmy would go up the road to the Johnsons to sit around their parlour with a few others to listen to the wireless before bringing the news home to Flossy and Lillian waiting up for him. The CBC carried the first nonstop reports of the rescuers' efforts. People who had them were fixed to their radios, so much so that crops weren't getting in. Like everyone else, the O'Reillys followed the events as if those three trapped men, a hundred and forty feet underground, were their own brothers. Rescue teams from every part of the province worked around the clock and finally reached them eleven days later. Two had survived. For months, they followed the ups and downs of the survivors, even quite a lot about the rescuers. People in town talked of nothing else.

That day, Reverend Mumford sat beside her with two handfuls of peas from Flossy's basket and began quietly splitting them into the bowl with her, not saying anything at all. She talked about those poor trapped men, Mr. Scadding, Dr. Robertson and Mr. Madill, and what it must have been like underground, in the darkness all that time. She told Reverend Mumford all the details she knew about the latest news of a machine being

flown out from Toronto to save Mr. Scadding's feet. She related,
too, quite a lot that amounted to pure speculation on the part of
their neighbour, Spurgeon Johnson, who'd become an authority
on such disasters by virtue of being the sole owner of a wireless
along their section of Highway 2, with all the time in the world
to listen to it, though he'd never actually been within ten miles
of a mine shaft.

They were almost finished the peas. Flossy asked David Mumford if he'd heard that one of the rescuers had gone back to
Stellarton and died in a mining accident back home. He had.

"Lotta waste," he said.

She looked at him.

"Peas," he said.

"Un-huh," she nodded. Flossy wasn't used to sitting near the
minister. She liked Reverend Mumford. Normally she liked stealing
a peak at his long eyelashes as he closed his eyes in prayer or
seeing the smile that would shift across his face unexpectedly,
loved listening to his eloquent phrases at Sunday service, but that
day she was feeling affection for no one at all.

He picked up one of the pods and ran his thumb through the
empty waxy chamber again, turning it over. "I find it curious,"
he began, "that people talk so much about the bad things that
happen to others."

She felt a bead of sweat roll down the inside of her arm. A climbing rose beside the front door that always began flowering on her
mother's birthday was still covered in clusters of white blossoms
and she had an urge to point this out to him. Flossy hurried to
finish her task but he dallied with those peas as if this were the
only chore he had left to do before delivering his Sunday sermon.

He was seated one step above her, his elbows resting on his
knees to speak near her ear. "I've watched a lot of people with a

lot of troubles over the years, Flossy." He didn't look at her when he spoke; David Mumford knew she'd be listening. "I've walked a long while myself with anger, fear and sadness. I can tell you they've been my sole companions in the middle of many nights." He spoke with a different voice from the one in church. It was the voice he used by Thomas's bed and it soothed like trickling water.

A car came along the road and they watched in silence as it drove past, a trail of dust behind it lasting longer than the sound of the motor in the distance. "Sometimes I think they'll take me over too, be the end of me. On those days, I believe Thomas is a more truthful me, lying up there in his bed. And Sarah's a more honest me, rocking all day in a chair, staring at a wall. He's too sad to live and she's too wounded." He tossed the empty pod to the pail but missed. He reached over to pick it up. Flossy did not speak.

· "Anger's a little unique from the others; it's got eyes and looks for someone else to blame," he said catching her glance before tossing the pod into the waste bucket, "but it's never them."

Reverend Mumford carefully set the bowl of peas in the pail on top of the empty pods, stood up and offered Flossy a hand. As he turned towards the door he said, "Too much has happened that you're not responsible for," they both paused, "nor is your mother, Jimmy; nor is Thomas. Terrible things …" He stood close to her, his soft eyes looking down into hers, speaking quickly.

Flossy's heart pounded; she could feel her cheeks flush. When he saw her embarrassment, he added in a gentle voice, "No one can change what's happened." He motioned towards the house. "We can only prevent it from changing us. And anger's the one thing I've seen that ends up changing us," he tapped his chest, "in here." His hand rested there a minute. "We all can take a lot of hardship," he reached for the handle of the door and pulled

it towards them, "suffering, disappointment." He moved behind
to let her go ahead. "No one gets through this life without their
share sooner or later, Flossy."

She looked down.

"I know of what I speak," he reached for her chin and turned
it towards him, so that she looked into his eyes, "You're quite a
lot like me, you know."

"You're never mad at anyone."

"No?" He smiled at her.

They stood together quietly, not a sound came from within
the house. Flossy thought they should go. She turned towards the
kitchen but felt a gentle hand on her arm.

"Something's broken in Thomas and he's not capable of putting it back together. You're different. You're strong, you'll never
give up and go to bed like him. But that strength that keeps
you going can as easily burn you up. If you don't find your way
to struggle against anger, you'll push everyone away who wants
to be close." He hesitated, looking down. "All of us," he whispered. David Mumford met her eyes. He ran his hand over her
cheek and through her sandy hair. "It would be more than my
heart could bear," he said softly and deliberately, "to see anger
have any part of you." She reached for him, he took her into his
arms and pressed his lips against the top of her head then as
quickly released her.

David Mumford. Flossy, feeling weary this evening on her walk
to the store, looked over at the lights already on at the church.
That summer day, David had found his mark, all right. When
she looked back on that first brief encounter with him, as she so
often did, she couldn't honestly say that they were specifically
healing words he'd spoken that day but David Mumford had
done something more, he'd reached through the walls of silence

that tragedy upon tragedy had forced around them. There were so many things the O'Reillys dared not speak of, could hardly think of rationally. All he'd had to say was, "I see, I know." He was the only man who'd ever done that for her and it was a far deeper knowing than anything else offered her by any other man in her long life. There was nothing worse than people knowing of your sorrow and never talking about it.

After that encounter, she felt older, a woman more in possession of herself. Her life didn't change overnight, those things never do, but it continued with an ounce more courage that summer. She might have prolonged that tenderness with David Mumford, and she thought she saw in his sad brown eyes that he'd have yielded to it, but you didn't do those things to your married minister.

Over those years, Flossy would have to say that David had been the one to show them all how to live. He was a humble man, a man of tidal suffering who nevertheless found a way to love life and encourage others at just the right place in their own dark woods. However old or young, feeble, vulnerable or discarded a person might be, he always found a unique possibility in them, a small fidelity to honestly acknowledge and appreciate. He was forever encouraging the sad, lonely or bereaved to hold on, till tomorrow, the harvest, a new season, another year, as long as it took for the black wave of grieving to wash itself back out to sea. He'd known it. No one knew it more.

In the breadth of this confidence Flossy promised herself she'd be mindful of her temper and try to be patient with what wouldn't matter the next day, in ten days, a year. She tried and she failed. She tried harder and failed miserably, a dozen times in a week, but when she did she made her way back to tell the others she was sorry, something she'd never done before. They noticed and eventually even Flossy would have said it got better. For one thing, Jimmy and her mother were spending more time around her now and the work always went faster when they did it together.

It was about that time that she decided, as well, to go up to see Thomas for a few minutes each day, not simply to drop his tea in the morning or grab his tray from supper, but to sit at the end of his bed and talk to him. Flossy might take him the first ripened plum or a dozen baking apples for pies that she'd peel beside him, gooseberries they'd taste together. She might tell him of a classroom romance, mark papers and talk about the students or begin reading a book that had come from their uncle in the States. If you were ever going to get a thought from him, it would come just as the day was closing, as the sun cast those long bars of gold into his room, as he sat there obscured by the nodding, winking day. Flossy noticed her mother also learned to mine that sweet sunset hour, bringing in her latest hat to show him. He couldn't offer much. Sometimes the best he could do was to choose between the ribbon or piping that she held out to him.

"Which?" she'd ask.

"Better," he'd say, motioning to one with a nod. He was still always right.

Even Jimmy began taking his tea and cigarette up to sit with his brother at the end of the day, reading to him from the newspaper or telling him about this or that around the farm.

"He feels things ten times more deeply than the rest of us, Flossy," David said to her once. "He's taught me so much ... more than anyone in my entire ministry. Thomas and I are bound together in this life; we have a responsibility to each other. He doesn't need forgiveness for what he can't do, for what he never was to you and Jimmy and your mother, he needs to know you won't be held back." And in a whisper, he'd added, "It's the closest I've come to an understanding of God."

She wasn't sure she always understood what David Mumford meant. Flossy had come to think of her brother as someone virtually without feeling, like a blowfly banging endlessly against the same closed window, so absent was he from anything that went on beyond those walls, so seemingly remote from what distressed the rest of them, but somewhere towards the end of that horrible decade and the beginning of the next, a winnowing of wheat from chaff would take place regarding her elder brother. She no longer thought of him as their burden. She began to feel for him again, tender white-green sprouts of compassion, as when they were young and their father would berate him for stuttering. This paralyzing inertia that had overtaken him, just like that faulty tongue, she could see, was just as much beyond anyone's control.

THREE LITTLE GIRLS WALKED by in a cluster, huddled together and looking shyly at Flossy. She thought one was Gordie Faulkner's girl. The others she couldn't be sure. She smiled at them. New families had been moving into Great Village and communities like it all along the shore, some folks driving to work each day to Truro, others all the way to Halifax. There was a time when Flossy knew every child and her pedigree in Great Village, but she'd been out of the classroom far too long for that now.

So few details remained after fifty years. She shook her head: half a century; it hardly felt like that. She could remember where they'd ended up on some things but not always how they'd got there. Her life seemed not unlike that huge sandbar that had built itself up so gradually over the decades out in the middle of Cobequid Bay and now had marsh greens growing on it in the springtime.

That's how it had been for her and David Mumford. Never was there a particular day in the year that they could claim as their own, a day when they once declared their love to each other and marked forever after, a day that might still make her stop at eighty-two and miss him all over again. So much less intrusive was their love and so easeful, the waiting and watching for the other, week after week, month after month, the gentle advance, the shy retreat, tidal deposits of reliance and affection. Flossy did not awaken one morning in love with him; she only knew that this was where her heart rested, with an unfathomably holy man, a good and married man whose wife had imprisoned him, too, and would outlive him by three years, eating plaster off the walls of an asylum for the insane down Dartmouth way.

David was seventeen years Flossy's senior. He was her minister, and could not divorce Sarah under the circumstances — they both knew this — no matter how deeply he would come to rely on Flossy's love and she his. There was no room for scandal of that nature in Great Village. He would never have held her back, would have dutifully performed her marriage to any man of her choosing from Colchester County or beyond but Flossy's heart was never in it. There were men who'd come around, good men, farmers mostly, who would have given her children, but none of them was David Mumford. Who of them could have made her weep for Job's lost children, collected and aged those tears in a flask, filled her head with Hopkins and Donne or taken her to the heart of sad old Lear? What was it that they'd had over all those years? It would sound feeble to anyone out there — Flossy looked around at all the quiet village houses and over to the church — a walk to the water's edge every other Wednesday night where they might open their hearts to each other and share a tender moment, the exchange of books, thoughts to carry for another week, until the next glance. Not much, yet everything, everything she'd ever wanted and no one she'd wanted more.

Stepping out to cross the main street of the village, her eyes on the church tower, a huge lumber truck roared up from behind loaded with dozens of massive logs. The horn blared at her followed by a blast of dirt and wind that thrust her back from the roadway. She'd been lost in her thoughts, heard nothing — only felt a rumble through her feet. For a few minutes, waiting for the traffic to pass, Flossy felt as much embarrassed as shaken by how close she'd come to having a load of logs roll onto her four-feet-eight inches.

Was that what she'd been waiting for? Her brush with death? She needed rocks in her pockets, that's what she needed. Rocks in her pockets and to pay considerably more attention to what she was doing. Was that it? She laughed out loud, elated. She'd cheated death. Was that all? The transport was followed by a stream of cars and smaller trucks with impatient drivers unable to pass on the winding village roads. She waved at them. When all was clear, she crossed the street, relieved to be alive.

XIX

How busy people were, racing through town, rushing to work, rushing home, rushing back to work again. Nobody walked anymore in Great Village, other than the children, who dragged themselves back and forth to school, too young yet to drive. And Flossy knew they were only putting in time until they turned sixteen.

The steel bridge framed her view of the main street. She was half watching for her young people, imagined them making their way back from Five Islands about now. She checked her watch. It was early and they'd be in no rush. Ruth and Phil would be stretching out the time together, stopping for fried clams and chips at Bunchy's Canteen with sun-burned noses and shoulders and excited eyes from a day of hunting amethyst along the shore.

Flossy was relieved to have Phil around. He'd turned out to be a courtly companion for Ruth. The two of them were becoming close. They sought the other's eyes when things amused them. Phil was spending more and more time at Flossy's house. This was harmless, she thought, the circumscribed affection of cousins, a gentle initiation.

She wished these young ones kind loving, tender and careful loving; the first one was a path to be laid straight and clean, that was so full of consequence for all that might come after. In the small hours of disquiet before the robins stirred, Flossy found herself thinking about them, worried that hearts would hurt. Naturally, it made her remember David. Theirs was not the whirlwind she was witnessing in her little house these days but attraction was no doubt attraction no matter how lightly or heavily it overtook one.

She wondered how Marjory was feeling about the possibility of sharing Ruth with Richard. Was there still a little irritation from the Richard days, a little unresolved rash flaring up but not so much that Marjory'd ever had to figure it out? Flossy and Richard had found common ground right from the start in the Bishop. She'd given him a copy of her first book of poetry, *North & South*, when the two married. He'd done a thesis on Elizabeth Bishop's work, written articles and become a kind of local authority on her life, dedicated to the cause of broadening an awareness of her poetry among the wider Canadian academic community. Richard and a handful of others were determined to keep her poetry alive to new generations of readers. Flossy was proud of them.

No doubt Marjory had entirely forgotten that Flossy and Richard could talk about Elizabeth Bishop's poetry for hours on end. They would get their volumes out late at night, read and talk about the work as Marjory slept on that same parlour chesterfield. Maybe Marjory always thought she was vital to their attachment, that after she dropped Richard, Flossy would too.

Now Ruth had also taken to the Bishop, with no encouragement from Flossy. She'd only pulled the books out in preparation for the coming meeting of the Society, but Ruth had turned out to be a voracious reader. These days Flossy nearly had to hide a book under her pillow to keep it from her. A couple of times she'd found her napping on that same chesterfield with Bishop's *Complete Works* open on her chest. It wasn't easy poetry for a young person, and yet here she, Phil and Richard would be attending the founding of the Elizabeth Bishop Society with Flossy tomorrow. It was an encounter that might well have occurred with or without Marjory's intervention.

She wondered what would have happened if Ruth hadn't been told about Richard. Would father and daughter have recognized each other? Flossy imagined all of them ending up at that meeting and some stranger putting it together: "You two must be related." That would have caught everyone's attention. You never know what people are going to see in a face. Everyone had always said she and Jimmy looked alike. They still did. Heavens, they could fit six of her in a Jimmy.

Flossy thought of all those couples she knew of that all but vaguely looked alike, might Richard and Ruth have been even a little attracted to the Electra-mirror they'd have seen in the other? Ruth had some of her grandmother's likeness in the striking red hair and certain gestures, enough to astonish her great-aunts. Up close, though, at the expressive heart of her face she was entirely Archibald: brown eyes twinkling, eyebrows flaring when she was pleased about something, her nose crinkled at the top of the bridge, and she drew a deep breath in through that huge, gorgeous Archibald smile when she was about to say something she thought would enchant you, as it always did because when she brightened, so too did any room.

Walking back up the hill, Flossy slowed her pace. She placed a fist hard against her chest as if it might settle the uneven thumping inside. The ache was echoed by her weather hip as she limped along. Surely they'd be getting rain soon.

AS SHE STARTED UP the steps to the door, she could hear her telephone ringing.

"Hello," she said, a little breathless.

"Hello Flossy, it's Marjory."

"Oh, hello dear."

"Did I interrupt you? You sound winded."

"No, no, I was just out mailing a few letters. Where are you?"

"In Sackville. How are things going?"

"Splendiferous. And you?"

"Fine, just fine. I've been thinking a lot about things over the week, Flossy, and more and more I'm inclined to just come down there tomorrow and get Ruth. It probably wasn't a good idea to leave her there in such a mood in the first place."

"Oh, I see." Flossy hesitated. "Well, you'll probably want to talk to her about it and she's not here just now. She's been down shore all day hiking and hunting for amethyst at Five Islands."

"She's been what?" Marjory had to hear it again.

"Do you remember your Aunt Milly? Ruth's with her great grandson, Phil, her cousin, your cousin," Flossy said. "They'll be home sometime later."

"Later?" Marjory asked.

"Yes, sometime later."

"Do you know when?"

"No. Soon I expect."

"Did you not give her a time to be home, Flossy?" Marjory asked.

"No, no," she answered calmly. "They don't seem to need that."

"I thought she'd be there ..."

Flossy hesitated. "All the time?"

"Well, no," Marjory said, "but yes."

"Well, since she isn't, why don't you tell me how the conference is going?"

She sighed. "Oh Flossy, I realized this wasn't a good idea," she began. "The conference was a mistake. This has all been a terrible mistake."

Flossy shook her head, thinking of all the feathers Marjory had ruffled in order to get into that conference in the first place. David and Goliath, phah. Maybe she'd even have the nerve to ask for a refund. "Can't be all that bad. What's the trouble?"

"Oh, it's all very New Age here, Flossy, not my kind of thing, so I thought I'd just come and get Ruth and take her back to Oakville. We might do some shopping before she goes back to school. Has she been horrid?"

"Well no," Flossy chuckled. "Quite the contrary. I'm thinking of keeping her."

"Oh," she said, "that's nice." There was silence for a minute. "I called Richard."

"I thought so," Flossy pulled her chair over to the phone. "He was here."

"Richard was there?" she said it in a half hush as if he might overhear.

"Yes, of course. What did you expect, dear?"

"Did Ruth…?"

"No, no — she was with Jimmy. She's been a busy lass. Tomorrow morning, she'll be meeting Richard just before the Elizabeth Bishop Conference."

"Well, maybe I should just come and we'll go tonight," she said. "It'll only take me an hour or so to get there. I thought she'd want to go back. Home."

"To *Oakville*?" Flossy asked, hearing incredulity slip into her own voice.

"Yes, Oakville."

"Oh, I don't think she'll be wanting to go just yet." Flossy tried to betray no annoyance. "She has a lot on her plate: baseball twice next week, she's going back to the weir with Jimmy in the morning, the Bishop Society at ten — she's been reading her poetry and asked to come along, she and Phil — and the Campbells are having a reunion Sunday after the conference is finished, just to meet her, and she's got Mealie's Life Studies on Tuesday," Flossy glanced at the calendar beside the phone. "She's taken over my calendar. Let's see, fishing down to Parrsboro next weekend. I think she'd be disappointed to be missing all that, wouldn't you?"

"She could finish the games with her own team, in Oakville," she countered.

"Marjory, it wouldn't make things better to take her back just now," Flossy said in a low voice. "From what I can tell, she's quite ... fond of this cousin and having a reasonably good time."

"Oh." Marjory said. "She's not even there a week."

"A week, yes. Sometimes a week's a long time," she said. Flossy looked outside, across the way to the light on in Mealie's studio. She sighed. This was so like Marjory: she was bored with the picnic and thought nothing of pulling the cloth out from beneath everybody else's good time. Flossy had an idea. "You don't suppose you might just be worrying about Ruth meeting Richard?"

"I haven't really thought about it," she said, a bit too quickly.

Flossy lowered her voice again. "Marjory, you can't whisk her away now, before they meet. You can't do that to Ruth or Richard, now that you've told them, surely you wouldn't think of interfering with their meeting, would you?"

"Noo," she said defensively. "Well, yes," she was getting impatient too. "Flossy, it wasn't *my* idea to tell them!" she snapped.

As quickly as she let her anger bubble up, she became contrite. "Oh, what a mess. What a mess I've made. I've done everything wrong," she said. "What have I done with my life? Everything I promised I wouldn't do. I wasn't a good wife, mother, minister, a good anything. All I've been good at is taking a place in a line that never goes anywhere, sitting around every day eating and using up resources — scarce resources that future generations won't have because of *me*."

"Now, now, dear," Flossy said softly, "there's no reason to single-handedly claim the undoing of future generations. I dare say you've done a little better than that."

"What'll I do?"

"Well," she began, "there are any number of things you can *do*. You could think about this another day or two, see if the conference picks up. You could go back to Oakville on your own and we'll send Ruth home by bus before school. You might finish your holidays here, go to Halifax for a few days or up to the Cabot Trail. What else? You could take Richard out for a nice dinner after the conference, become acquainted again. You may wish to make a little adjustment for him in your life now, and you know what?"

"What?"

"You'll find he's the same wonderful man you once married," Flossy said.

"That's exactly what I'm worried about, Flossy," Marjory replied.

XX

SIFTING THROUGH A STACK OF PHOTOGRAPHS TWO INCHES thick on her lap, Flossy O'Reilly let a dozen or more fall against her stomach. She was awake early this morning and enough wound up to finally just get a start on the day. It was high time she sorted through some of these things.

"Ah, there you are," she whispered, removing one and tapping the rest on the table to straighten them. She replaced the tidy stack in the tartan shortbread tin. There were pictures from almost every year that she'd been in the classroom. It was a record of sorts of her life's work, forty-nine years of mostly black and whites with a few colour photos in the later years, but Flossy wasn't the least bit interested in them anymore.

One of these days, somebody would throw them all out. She should save them the trouble. She picked up one or two of the oldest black and whites and scanned the rows of faces. Day in and day out she had watched those children. She followed their learning, their spurts, acne and heartaches, the ebb and flow of their confidence, yet a few of those faces were as unfamiliar to her now as the population of Prince Rupert.

Men and women from Mealie's age on down were still coming up to her, as she picked up her prescription at MacQuarrie's or over the leeks at Sobeys, speaking solicitously about their years in her classroom. As soon as she heard that sing-song volley, "Hel-lo Miss O'Rei-lly," she knew she was in trouble. For years she'd taken great pride in remembering all their names. By eighty-two, she just couldn't be bothered.

Tattered on three corners, a crack in the gloss along one side, but otherwise intact, the photograph she had selected was Thomas's primer class. There he was. His face leapt out at her from among the twenty children sitting and standing in rows beside their teacher. She smiled to see him. Miss Chisholm had been Flossy's first teacher too, though she'd only taught those two years before getting married. Once a woman married in those days, her teaching career was over. Wouldn't Ruth think that quaint?

She looked back at the photograph. Thomas standing in the back row, an unremarkable boy, smiling shyly with his shoulders pulled up to his ears, arms at his sides. Among the others in the photo she searched for Elizabeth Bishop, who'd been in Thomas's class. She was seated in the front row, short and plump, as small and square as Thomas was long. Elizabeth held some of her baby looks into adulthood too, the round face and pouty chin. Her thick, curly hair had been bobbed with some gathered up in a fashionable big black bow. She'd always said you could pack dishes in that hair.

Flossy tucked the photo into an envelope. Today was a great day, a day for the history books, and she was gathering together all the Bishop memorabilia she had for the first meeting of the Elizabeth Bishop Society beginning that morning in the Legion, across from the United Church, at the heart of Great Village. It was her own small archive of a story long-neglected: each mention of the poet from local and regional papers, the Pulitzer, the Honorary Doctorate from Dalhousie — there hadn't been all that much — Flossy had carefully clipped, dated and folded. The yellowing stack had been set out the night before on her kitchen table. Ruth and Phil had combed through it all, asking questions, curious about Bishop's life. There were a couple of letters Flossy had saved, kind condolences from Elizabeth on the death of Thomas and her mother, and two photos of the adult poet back home with her Aunt Grace in Great Village in the forties sporting their new Reilly hats.

All of these things Flossy would entrust to Richard Archibald. He would know what to do with them and this might be her last chance to hand them to him herself. She must do more of this divesting. There was a whole house full of things she needed to pass on before she passed herself on.

Should she take the books too? Maybe the poems, at least those. Retrieving *The Complete Poems* from the parlour to add to the other few items she intended to take along, the anthology slipped out of Flossy's hands, as things often did now. Bending to pick it up, she noticed it had fallen open at "One Art," what she'd always considered a Bishop masterpiece. She wondered if Ruth had been looking it over. Flossy almost had this sad beauty by heart but couldn't resist sitting down on the arm of the chesterfield and reading its melancholy lines one more time. The poem always seemed uncharacteristically biographical for a woman as private as Elizabeth. There is an art to losing, it cheerfully suggests, that can be mastered with some little practice, beginning with the small things we're all familiar with losing in a day, the wasted hour, keys, things that don't bring disaster, to irreplaceable things, like homes, continents, even the one to whom the poem was addressed. It was Elizabeth's catalogue of loss, Flossy thought, and that was, in large part, her life. But losing was every life's lesson, she'd have said. By the time you got to Flossy's age, there wasn't much else. "The sad realities," Mealie called them. They couldn't turn around these days without hearing that another old friend was gone or well on the way. If you lived long enough, you lost them all, the odds were against you — for you and against you, in that lucky-unlucky way. And just what would constitute reality, she pondered? Outside the front window she could see that a fierce storm had blown through last night, entirely missed by the weather reports. Tree limbs were down, another edge of cliff would be torn from the shore; maybe the little apple tree gone. They still had two pieces of pie sitting on the counter. Ruth and Phil would probably finish those off for breakfast. It was astonishing what they could eat.

Was that reality or was it the much-needed rain for fields after weeks of drought? Jimmy would have wakened to thunder and rain on his roof in the middle of the night and rolled over a happier man. Was reality the maples and lindens storing their sugars in a few weeks and giving up a leafy flourish of gold, saffron and crimson to burn themselves up, drop copper and decay? Or was it the buds, already emerging behind each leaf scar, the promise of beyond, of return next spring?

Was there anything much more than losing in this life? By one method of calculation she'd have to declare a definite no. She was an old woman and the longer she lived the less she came away with at the end of each year: teeth, hair, hearing, stature, patience. Yet that wasn't entirely the sum of it either. There had been more, much, much more. You couldn't say that each loss had been balanced by something that drifted back in with the next tide, but there had been comforts, unexpected ones, when she most needed them that Flossy might never have anticipated.

Closing the book of poems, she stretched towards the front window and pulled the curtain back to get a good look up and down the road. This morning the house was creaking with the blowing wind. The street was quiet except for an empty ginger ale can that rolled twenty feet up the hill with a gust of wind, that caught it again, spun it around and rolled it off in the other direction, pattering beyond where Flossy could see. She imagined it taking itself back to McLellan's for a refund. The front lawn was strewn with branches from the silver maple next door, twelve-foot limbs blown thirty yards her way, still writhing with the morning's rain and restless winds. "Fear not, till Birnam wood do come to Dunsinane," she echoed Macbeth's bravado. A chill went through her as she looked down the road. Maybe she should put a fire on for the young people.

ELIZABETH BISHOP HAD MASTERED the art of losing because, in the end, she too had precious little left. There were few lives that could make Flossy as sad as Elizabeth's. (It was no small mercy they knew so little about Shakespeare.)

At the time the class photo was taken, young Elizabeth was quite happily settled in and, no doubt, doted upon by her Bulmer grandparents, a couple of aunts and an uncle. She and her mother had returned to Nova Scotia from Massachusetts following her father's death when Elizabeth was only eight months old. Her mother, who was both a nurse and a teacher, had begun to suffer mental breakdowns that would see her committed to Dartmouth when Elizabeth was only five. Though she would be in her twenties when her mother died, Elizabeth would never see Gertrude Bishop again. Mrs. Bishop died after eighteen unbroken-broken years at Mount Hope.

Within a year of that class photo, Elizabeth's wealthy Bishop grandparents, perfect strangers to her, would arrive in Great Village to take their granddaughter back with them to Worcester Massachusetts. There, little Elizabeth would be given everything money could buy and nothing that it could not.

Flossy stared out the window. She imagined the Bishops arriving from Boston in nice clothing, staying at the Ellmonte Hotel for a week and thinking nothing of taking the child away from everything she'd known. Of that time in New England with her grandparents, Elizabeth once said she'd got more affection from the servant and the dog than anyone in her father's family. Within a year, the child was gravely ill with asthma and eczema, and unable to go to school. She was also deathly unhappy.

Fearing for her life, Elizabeth's maternal Aunt Maude risked uprooting her once more to bring her to her own home in Revere, Massachusetts, where the youngster would grow up in a working-class Irish and Italian neighbourhood outside Boston. It meant she could return to Great Village for the summers, before going off to college.

If only the displacement and loss had ended there, Elizabeth might have found the footing necessary to limp along in her life but there was to be no such fate. There was no shortage of influential mentors and peers, like Marianne Moore and Robert Lowell, and concerned aunts in the wings, but the clouds of loss and mental illness that had hovered about her tender years would drift into the life she was making for herself. Friends lost their sanity, intimates took their lives, she fought her own losing battle with alcoholism, relationships disintegrated, homes were lost. She wasn't even — Flossy considered for a moment — granted a few hours to ready herself for her end.

She stopped. There had been a weight on her chest all morning, since she awakened before four. It seemed harder to breathe, she would have thought the air clearer after all that rain. She must stop thinking of Elizabeth Bishop; the sadness of that life could nearly drag Flossy down. She went through all the reasons why she might feel worried about this day. Was it Richard? Maybe Richard.

Was she herself ready for her end? A shiver went through her. "Nobody's ready," she muttered aloud, brushing the thought away as if it were a small cloud of gnats dancing in the dwindling August garden. No one was ready who wasn't already suffering a terrible illness and wanting to go. She'd lost her mother, Thomas, Patricia, David, her father, a couple of good students, other friends, her hearing, strength in her arms, balance. Though she had to admit there were other good things she'd lost too: patience for insufferable stupidity, any time for bigotry, willingness to waste precious time, need for approval. Age brought its own blessings. In all her years of teaching, she'd never met a stupid child but my-oh-my she'd met her share of stupid adults.

Bishop's death came back to her — though she tried to put it from her mind — the perfect non-negotiable, an aneurysm. Turning to leave the room, Flossy noticed the grandfather clock had stopped at two. She opened the glass door, retrieved the key and quickly rewound it. As the pendulum began to swing she reset the time and hastily swept superstition aside.

Had Elizabeth worried that she'd end up the same as her mother, maybe even expected it? Perhaps she was forever self-medicating depression with alcohol. Flossy often wondered if she'd feared the worm of suicide, what with Plath, Sexton, Berryman before her, all fine poets. Alcohol might even have been her way of covering the suicidal tracks, the slow noose, applied over decades, but without a doubt effective.

Flossy wondered if death might be quick and colourful, was there even pleasure in the final letting go, all those poets seemed to think so, the final pushing of the last door open, perhaps there would be nothing more than wide-shouldered terror. What would she feel in her last moment? Incredulity, she thought, no matter what age. She'd no doubt waste a good few final breaths in gasping denial, like finding yourself suddenly on the ground, having miscalculated a patch of ice or heaved sidewalk.

She thought of what was said about seeing one's life flashing before the eyes, the long tunnel, white light and the people who'd gone before. Dear Lord, she hoped not. There were a few she'd been happy to see cast off from these good shores for the next and had no desire to begin the conversation again. Would she be able to hear? They always said hearing was the last sense to go.

She'd asked Mealie about that once.

"Mighty Sakes, Flo, I think you'd have to be able to hear reasonably well in the first place." She could always count on a certain flat-footed practicality from Mealie.

The clouds were low and round-bottomed. Rain lashed grey against the windows, not thinking of ending anytime soon. Back in the kitchen, she bundled up the books and clippings and placed them all in extra plastic bags to keep them dry. The house was dark.

The lights were already on in Mealie's studio. Flossy had brought her paper in at four-thirty along with a drenched Oscar Wilde.

Why had she never talked to Elizabeth, adult to adult, about the mental illness in their families? Theirs were the two in the area most afflicted by it. Everyone knew this. And like a fresh death, it pains as much that no one speaks about it. In Elizabeth's case, it hadn't appeared in any other generation so perhaps the Bulmers and Bishops could allow themselves the comfort that Gertrude's illness was an anomaly. Nobody understood those things back then and each family carried the shame of it in private. Could she not have reached a hand across to Elizabeth? At least between them they could have spoken with more than curiosity, especially after Lota, her lover's suicide. Elizabeth had been a stranger to them, that was why. Taken away so young and only returning for visits, never long enough for either of them to get beyond their painful reticence.

Flossy stood watching out the kitchen window. It was a moody Maritime day. There was nothing so welcome after drought. Weren't people always waiting for something? For the rain to come, the rain to stop, the sun to shine, always waiting for something to pass and something to take its place.

As she stood there watching the rain dance on Mr. McNutt's roof, Flossy could not help recalling another time of waiting and watching and its terrible end.

"Get the goddamned into the goddamned boat." She felt the old weariness heavy on her chest. Could she never remember anything else, any tender words her father had said to her? After those three dreadful days, she could never do it again, could never stand at a kitchen window waiting and watching for anyone or anything, would sooner scrub the kitchen floor, clean out the refrigerator or move the entire woodpile from one side of the cookhouse to the other. Sweep out all the summer spiders. That memory of waiting was like another being taking hold of her sanity and pulling her inside-out. She'd been so young. And because of her innocence she'd found herself bound to her father's death far longer than she ever should have been, until she'd looked through that glass darkly and understood it for what it was.

Like everyone else during the hours and days that her father was missing, she had stood at windows not knowing what else to do, two days that bled to night that bled to day again; on some lonely sliver of a threshold between hope and despair, they'd all waited. There were people in the house who weren't normally there. Her mother's sisters had come and Uncle James was there. Flossy'd never seen her mother undone, never seen the strong, combative Lillian frayed and useless like a piece of discarded ribbon among the sweepings of the kitchen floor.

Only thirteen at the time, Flossy hadn't been able to keep her thoughts steady on anything but the fear inside her head chipping away at what would become a perfect statue of grief. She'd prayed and prayed over those three days her father was missing. Thomas had gone down to the water, spent the days walking up and down the shore as far as the tide would allow him to go in each direction. She and wide-eyed Jimmy watched each other across the room, neither spilling a word. After two days, she knew he could be counted on to keep their secret.

Had she done that to Jimmy? Dear Lord, Flossy sat down, her hand went to her mouth. She'd never thought of it like that before. Had she been the one to exact the unspoken promise to keep silent about the boat? Had she done that to him?

As the sun was setting on the third day, she remembered Mr. Fulton knocking and walking in through the door, saying to her mother as the room fell silent, feet shuffled and all eyes turned. "They found him, Mrs. O'Reilly."

Flossy was only a child; she hadn't raised the winds, the rain, the lightning or sent anyone out onto the bay. Nonetheless for years she felt it her fault, her own failing, that her father was dead.

And the other horror, the other "accident" only a year later, so suddenly split the scar of the wound that preceded it. The sequence played over and over again in her head like a musical round: her father, the Mumford boys, her father, those boys, her father. They'd felt cursed. Who'd be next? Was it three tragedies or three lives? People said they came in threes. She'd wondered that for years, was it over, or just waiting?

It had taken so many years, a decade at least, to forgive that Iago bay for what it had taken from everyone who'd meant anything to her, how it gouged their trust, their hearts, psyches, sheared them off clean like the entire length and breadth of the Chisholm farm. How many years had it taken to understand the bay's innocence, as innocent as Flossy herself, a small girl for her age, thirteen, refusing to get into a boat with her father? How many years had she thought it her fault, that he'd not come back because she'd refused to go with him? How many years had she, in her childish fantasy, imagined that she could have caught his arm, saved him, if only she'd gone with him in that boat? And what had Jimmy thought all those years?

Oh, she'd forgiven it. The bay was only water after all. When you turned those tragedies upside down and drained all the emotion from them, you could see that old tide was nothing more than indifferent Nature plodding like a tethered mule at the end of the moon's long lead. Nature hadn't lopped off the Chisholm farm, the baseball park and the old Spencer place because they deserved worse than anyone else along the shore. Nature wasn't punishing the Mumfords nor the O'Reillys for anything they may or may not have done. There wasn't the least thing personal about it.

The starlings were agitated today, making it hard to catch her breath as if she'd just finished climbing Hustler's Hill in one mighty rush. Her mind flashed back to that earlier time.

"Get in the boat," he'd said.

She closed her eyes, hoping the memory would pass.

A storm had blown up unexpectedly then too. The wind all morning had been slamming a barn door someone had forgotten to latch; she could hear the sound, creak-bang, creak-bang, creak-bang. From the house you could see the wind kicking up waves down by the shore. Sixty-nine years ago, you could fit a respectable lifetime into that.

It had been a Saturday too and the three children had gone out to the barn with their father that morning. After the chores were all finished, he told Thomas to go down to the feed mill and grind some bags of corn. It was a peculiar order as they still had some bags ahead but her brother was obedient and didn't question their father any more than would she or Jimmy. Wouldn't have done any good: once William's mind was made up, neither heaven nor high water could change it.

No sooner had Thomas harnessed the mare and pulled out of the lane than William told the rest of them — herself and Jimmy — they'd be going down to the bay. They, too, were obedient. When they got to the water's edge, the wind was fierce, whipping up the waves and thrashing the rain against them. Flossy and Jimmy had dressed to be out in the barn, not out in the wind with stinging, spraying water. Her legs were freezing and her feet wet from leaky boots. The tide was high and the choppy waves were crazed, crashing into the land. She was afraid.

Their father was a brooding unfamiliar sky that morning, had been all week. He was red in the face, reckless and in a rush. At the shore they were surprised to see he had a small boat, a skiff he must have borrowed from someone because the O'Reillys didn't have one of their own. He said he wanted them to get in with him to go fishing. Jimmy was used to their father's favours, the only one of them who was, and William lifted him right into the boat. Not so Flossy. Even at thirteen, she smelled danger.

"Come on, get in lass," he'd said warmly, as if she were only playing coy. The wind was tossing his hair all around that morning, knocking it down into his eyes, giving him a frayed, sinister look.

"I can't. Mah says I hafta sweep the kitchen after chores," she said.

"Don't be silly. You can do that later. Tell her I said so. Now come on, get in." His voice was gentle but urgent. He leaned into the wind blowing against him tugging his jacket and pants. They flapped against him like a flag. If it had been a warm summer day, that wind would have been festive and Flossy wouldn't have hesitated, but it was April, cold and ominous.

She didn't move and she wouldn't look at him either. The wind was catching her from every direction and she had to dig in and resist. She was soaked and shifted on her feet in a futile effort to keep warm.

"I'm your father, Flossy, get in the boat." This voice had lost the soothing undulation. It was a single repetitive note now and carried a warning as if he were a dog growling just low enough to make you wonder what it was you were hearing. It was the threshold at which fear always found compliance, the voice a child disobeys but once. Still, she did not budge.

Everything about this morning was wrong. The children, as a rule, didn't do special things with their father, like fishing in the middle of the day, especially this kind of a day. She wished Thomas were with them. Thomas would know what to do; he'd so long been the shield between the younger ones and their father.

Standing by the water's edge facing him, the bay tossing and churning, Flossy was scared. She wasn't sure she could have moved if he'd come near enough to pick her up. Her mother'd always warned her "never but never go down to that bay when the weather's stormy." They were freezing. Jimmy's hair was wet, he was red from the cold and his teeth chattering as much as hers. Besides, there weren't even any fishing poles in the boat. She didn't want to go out onto the rough water without her mother knowing.

"You don't have poles," she pointed into the boat.

William ignored the comment. "It's just the three of us," he said. "It'll be our little adventure, out for a wee sail, just us three. I know it's not very nice out but come on now, I only have the loan of the boat for the day." Flossy was equally fearful of angering her father. She'd seldom done so before without a strapping. Still, she didn't move.

Jimmy sat in the boat bobbing on the water as William held it by a rope. He couldn't let go to grab her because Jimmy would almost certainly have drifted off and Flossy stood just far enough away that William had to talk her into getting in.

"Come on, Flossy, we don't have all day. Get into the boat. Jimmy's all set. Aren't you Jimmy? You don't want to disappoint Jimmy, now. You know how he loves fishing." She didn't move and when he made a quick grab for her she jumped back well out of his reach. He almost lost the line and had to dash to the water's edge to step on it and haul it back. As he grabbed the rope, the boat gave a sudden kick and Jimmy was tossed backward off the thwart. While he didn't cry, the boy was losing the appetite for adventure.

"Flossy, get the goddamned into the boat." But the youngster was skittish now and her refusal caused Jimmy to have second thoughts. He scrambled back out, getting his feet wet doing so.

Sensing mutiny, their father calmed himself and changed tack, knowing he had to get Flossy first to get Jimmy again.

He raised his voice. "Don't you be going nowhere, Jimmy,

do you hear?" He turned back to Flossy and spoke softly again. "You know that smart blue dress you've been eyeing at the store? We'll go into town and get that for you, just as soon as Thomas is back. What do you say to that, now?"

Flossy was mute. When he took a step towards her, she stepped back.

"Didn't you tell Mama you liked that dress?"

"Yeah," she said cautiously, her head low.

"Well, we're going to get it for you, but first I want you to get into my little boat here." Flossy didn't move, but oh my how she'd wanted that dress, a store-bought dress. She could wear it to church tomorrow.

"I'm cold," she protested.

"You get in, you can sit by me. I'll warm you up," he said it tenderly and Flossy was close to giving in. He took off his jacket and held it out to her. "Here, put this on, you'll feel better." She hesitated. "Take it," he said with a smile, holding the jacket out lovingly like a delicious piece of candy in his outstretched arm. As Flossy cautiously approached to take the jacket, he let it drop to the ground and lunged at her but misjudged his footing in the sand. So nervous was she that she pulled back and drew farther away.

"You get the *goddamned* into the *goddamned* boat," he said through clenched teeth.

Seeing the old rage erupt into spitting demented wrath, the familiar beast rise up that gorged on its own, Flossy looked both ways and bolted back up the bank, and when she ran Jimmy ran too. The wind was behind them and so they flew.

Those were the last words she heard from her father, the only words that circled around and around again in her head. After they left him there at the shore, their father did not come home. When he wasn't back for supper, Thomas went to look for him. When he didn't come home that night or show up for chores next morning, Thomas went to tell Uncle James. When he wasn't back by nightfall, more people arrived.

The tide brought William back three days later and tangled him in Fred Corbett's weir. The children weren't allowed to go down. "He's gone, Mrs. O'Reilly, I'm sorry," Mr. Fulton had said.

The skiff made its way back too, though it pulled aground closer to Bass River and it was another full week before anyone found it with William's polished shoes wrapped in a gunny-sack and tied securely beneath the thwart. Doctor Rushton had already declared it an accidental drowning before those unkind shoes turned up to cast their several doubts.

HOW VERY LONG IT had been — years, Flossy thought — before she'd seen her father's adventure for what it really was: the puni-tive fist behind the accidental death, not an accident at all. He'd never meant to hurt them, she and Jimmy, no. In his delusional state he'd no doubt intended to take them with him, save them. It was the others, the ones left behind that William O'Reilly was desperate to hurt.

Flossy shuddered. She must get hold of herself. Memory was a dubious blessing. She was always amazed that details of what wouldn't amount to mental rubble from seventy years back could be burnished into the brain as tidy and fresh as this morning's preoccupation with milk gone off. It was as if the mind's attic had any number of dusty suitcases up there — stuffed with snap-shots, trinkets, smells, hair combs, grief and hat pins — ready to spring open at any moment and release their restless tide of recollection. Yet the details of a week ago Tuesday could be maddeningly elusive.

The young people had an hour before she'd call them to go off with Jimmy to the weir. Then, when they got back they'd all get ready for the Bishop's meeting at ten. Ruth would be up soon. She wasn't wasting any time sleeping late these days. Phil had stayed over to avoid getting a ride into town this morning but any little excuse served to keep him hanging around these days. She'd passed him in the hall in the middle of the night in his boxer shorts. He'd mumbled something but she had to tell him to hold it till morning; she couldn't hear a thing without her glasses. Even thirty years after she'd first heard of women's liberation, parents were considerably easier about their sons' night wanderings than their daughters'. She mustn't forget the raspberry tarts and rum balls. Ruth and Phil had both helped to make them. She gathered the tins of sweets and placed them in another plastic Sobeys bag. Was she forgetting anything?

From the kitchen window, she glanced down the Great Village terraces over Hustler's Hill to the church and watched a car coming along the highway from the direction of Parrsboro. It turned towards Truro. How satisfied she was with the summer. Uncanny the way things had turned out. Here she'd regretted saying yes to Marjory, had dreaded Ruth's coming right up until the hour of her arrival, even a bit longer, truth-be-told, and yet what a wonderful child she'd turned out to be, a wonderful young woman. The Campbells were overjoyed to meet their lost sister's charming granddaughter, another ancient wound all healed-up and haired-over. These things seemed long overdue. And in spite of the fits and starts, she'd be meeting her father and Richard Archibald his daughter today. Ruth Trotter-Schaeffer-Archibald, two dreadful hyphens, though they weren't bothering Flossy nearly as much these days.

It surprised her that Richard hadn't appeared before now but she thought Mealie might be right. He needed a bit of time. After seeing him in front of the house on Thursday, Flossy had called and left a message on his answering machine, which she knew he checked regularly. She'd offered the briefest apology, hoped they could talk soon and added Phil and Ruth's names to the registration list for the Elizabeth Bishop Society gathering. She felt sure he'd find a way to squeeze them in. She also suggested he might come by this morning to meet Ruth in private before their meeting began.

Flossy removed the plants and magazines from the top of the old black and white enamel *Enterprise*. She opened the stove's damper then lifted the lid and placed several pieces of crumpled newspaper inside with kindling laid carefully on top. She hadn't heard back from Richard, but she knew he was out there and maybe he'd come for dinner in the next few days, after the Bishop's conference was out of the way, when everything had settled down, have some quiet time to get acquainted with his daughter. Scraping a match across the box, she let its flame catch on several corners of the paper before dropping it onto the pile. For the next few minutes, she watched the fire build, placing bigger and bigger pieces of kindling on top. Finally, she chose a good-sized log from the wood box setting it on top of the small fire before closing the lid. There was nothing so comforting as wood-stove warmth.

Her mind drifted ahead to the coming meeting as the smell of burning wood drifted throughout the room. It was something immensely gratifying, finally there would be a Society for Elizabeth Bishop. After years of a few isolated admirers from here and there writing articles, raising banners, howling to the moon, it seemed there was at last going to be some recognition of her genius in this, one of her earliest homes, Great Village. If there were no other memory of its former shipping glory, the village would always be the place of Elizabeth Bishop's formative years, and for that, Flossy was convinced, it would always be great.

There was no doubt that the poet had tutored her ear and mined her memories from the early years in Great Village for some of her finest verse and prose — fishing, sandpipers, the shoreline, moose, milk-route bus rides to and from Boston. Perhaps the early Brazil years, when Elizabeth lived there with her lover, Lota de Macedo Soares, were as happy as any, but they were not to last either and even decades after she'd left Great Village, Elizabeth often found her Muse roaming the landscape of her early memories of Nova Scotia. A Maritimer to the core, she always migrated back to the East Coast: Nova Scotia, Boston, New York, Florida, Brazil.

Where did she come from? Her grandfather was a tanner, the aunts mostly nurses and teachers, as women were in those days, her uncle a tinsmith. There was nothing exceptional in her heritage but the Bishop had genius and could take her place among the best poets of the century. If only she'd had her old age to live out, if she'd had more years to write her poetry. Finish up all those unfinished poems. It didn't matter, though, what survived was of the finest cut and Flossy was grateful to have lived this long to see Elizabeth's creative genius celebrated right here in Great Village. It was another of those life circles closed and satisfied, Flossy's own finished couplet on the Bishop's life.

She looked once more down the road. There were a few cars gathering in the church parking lot across from the Legion. Some of the organizers were arriving. The meeting wouldn't start until ten. She looked across to Mealie's. She must have gone straight to work this morning. Flossy felt happy for her, too much afire to want her morning coffee and paper, a good sign. She could hardly wait to see these pictures.

Walking back to the stove, she inched the damper over.

Ironic what can grow up and flourish in the midst of a quiet village, any village and be entirely lost on all who come and go, have come and gone, brought in their hay and grain, chopped wood, paid bills, fed and clothed their children. Flossy was under no illusion that the vast majority of those in Great Village even today would have heard of the Bishop, read any of her poems, or been interested in the work they were doing to preserve her memory.

"Ya which?" Jimmy would ask each time Flossy'd mention the Society, though she'd talked about it a hundred times before. The poetry still wouldn't be studied in the senior grades of the local school. How many lost Donnes, Dickinsons and Shakespeares had there been down the ages growing up in obscure little villages just like this one, whose papers were used to start the morning fire of some resentful brother who'd have liked the poet a sight better if he'd spent more time at the barn? It was prodigal. How easy it always was for Flossy to sympathize with that older brother, with the Marthas of the world. The Lord knew she'd been long enough on the short end of that straw.

The Bishop, of course, was a flawed genius, were they not all? Were only the flawed able to look steadily enough into their own raw interior to then offer insight to the rest, expose their bloody hands, their sides for our curious fingers? She wondered. Flossy knew the lives of some of the best of them. She was sure she couldn't have tolerated the poets whose work she most admired. She'd have put them out in the woodshed. No doubt the few left in the village who had a personal interest in the Bulmer family had heard their share of stories over the years. The older families knew the fate of Elizabeth's mother, who languished in Dartmouth until her end. Then the Bishop herself, driven by alcohol. They wouldn't know what to make of the friends she brought home with her for visits over the years either. Such friendships between women might be fine in New York City but they were best unacknowledged in Great Village, as if a woman loving another woman, or a man a man, were anything new under any sun.

The time was creeping on. Everyone was sleeping in this morning. It must be the dark weather and so like these young people, not a wristwatch or an alarm clock between them. "What time is it?"

"It's summertime."

She'd give them an extra half hour, pour herself a nice cup of coffee and finish the last ten pages of Virginia Woolf's final diary in peace and quiet.

XXI

FLOSSY CLOSED THE BOOK AND SAT IN THE QUIET OF HER kitchen, save for the moaning wind and the crackling fire.

She felt nearly the same tempered sadness of a long vigil beside a dying friend. Virginia Woolf was gone. She shook her head. Leonard Woolf and her sister, Vanessa, had been concerned about her but just then everyone had their own preoccupations. It was the height of the war, with air raids and blackouts, and Leonard was doing volunteer night duty watching for fires. The day before her death, before she walked into the Ouse River weighed down with rocks in her pockets, he had taken her to see Octavia Wilberforce, a distant cousin of Virginia's who was practising medicine near them in Brighton. He'd spoken with Octavia about his wife in the weeks leading up to the suicide. In fact, Octavia was herself sick with influenza but agreed to see Mrs. Woolf nonetheless. She would say later, after it was all over, after they'd finally found the body, she thought Virginia had been haunted by her father. Flossy looked up and outside, could see the butternut tree trembling in the wind.

At that moment, there was a rap on the door, it opened and Jimmy limped in.

"Jimmy," she said, startled, jumping to her feet, "you're early. They're still in bed."

"Heh, heh, not *surprised*," he grinned, pulling a baseball glove out of a plastic bag. "The grandson's. Never uses it."

"Ah, that's much better than the one she's been using. We'll get it back to you. Have a coffee?"

"*Sure*, okay." Jimmy removed his jacket, hung it on a hook inside the door, put his cap on top of it and took his usual chair while Flossy poured him a cup. Oscar was curled on top of the wood box behind the stove. "Wasn't that a *beauty* last *night?*" he asked.

"The rain? We sure needed it," she said, dropping a teaspoon into his cup and placing it in front of him at the table. Her brother grunted acknowledgement.

After she got her own and poured some milk from the refrigerator, she stood at the window watching the rain and looking towards Mealie's studio. Jimmy was stirring sugar into his coffee, his back to her.

"Eighteenth of April, 1925," she said. "That's another one for Becky. I was thinking about that day this morning," she said wistfully, looking out into the curtain of rain, "down by the bay, with father. Was just like this, wasn't it?" He stopped stirring. She could hear the rain pelting against the roof. Her gaze followed a drop rolling down the outside of the window. It stopped abruptly as if it had lost its way, and, rolling away in two directions, dissolved into nothing. "When did you figure it out, Jimmy?"

He didn't answer and she began to wonder if he'd heard. He began to stir again, then stopped. "*London*," he finally said.

"In hospital?"

He nodded. She sat down near him at the table. "That war was hell on you."

"On a *lotta people*," he nodded his head again and stirred the coffee. "I *thought* I could *take a lot*," his old blue eyes looked pained. "You'd think *you'd forget* about it *by now*, you're forgetting everything else," he said. "I *think* about it *more* and *more*, Flo, all the time. When I *can't sleep* at night, I lie there and *count* off the *names* of my *mates* who were *killed*. I *never* get to the *end* of them."

"How many, Jimmy?"

"*Hundred* and *thirty-two*."

"Dear Lord, it's a wonder you survived surviving," she said. "It's a wonder you survived any of it — home, the war. Any of it. I, I don't ... I can only think that I let you down, Jimmy. I should have talked to you, helped you, let you talk about it."

He shrugged, looking down at his cup. "*Nobody* wanted to *hear*. Not just *you*." He took his glasses off and set them on the table. He shifted in his chair as if he were a man needing to settle into the words he was about to speak. "I *told Thomas*," his voice cracked. Flossy looked up at him. "A couple of weeks *before* he *died*, about *father* and us at the *boat*. I think it *must've killed him* ..." He swallowed hard.

"Oh *no*, Jimmy, dear God," she said, reaching a hand across and grabbing his arm. "It brought Thomas *back*, to *life*, couldn't you see that?" She patted him gently and shook her head. "You let him forgive himself, that's what you did. You *let Thomas go*. It was the kindest thing anyone could have done for him."

They sat quietly for a few minutes. Jimmy dug into his pocket, pulled out an old checkered handkerchief and blew his nose. How had she let him drift so far away, knowing he'd probably gone through hell and back in Europe? She'd not cared enough to ask, her own brother, had just not made the effort to let him talk. "I didn't think ...," she began. "I didn't think about how those things might have affected you. We should have talked about that, about Thomas and the Mumford boys, the war. All these things you've carried and I didn't help. It would have done us both good to talk. I should have been a better sister ... I'm so sorry, Jimmy."

He pulled his head back. "It *got* me *through*," he said, "a lot of things, knowin' *you saved* my *life*. I *would've gone* with him, Flo, in the *boat*, if it hadn't been for *you*."

XXII

FLOSSY CLOSED THE DOOR BEHIND HER BROTHER, RUTH AND Phil and leaned against it. The youngsters had straggled out of bed, the rain slowed and they were off, each with a piece of pie in hand, for an early trip to Jimmy's weir.

She took in a deep breath and exhaled slowly. This Elizabeth Bishop Society meeting had been years in the making. The date had been dragged forward for two full calendars and honestly there were times she thought she'd not live to see the day come, yet at this precise moment she wished for nothing more than a solitary few hours to walk along the shore or sit with her own thoughts in a big old chair. Dear old Jimmy. Oh well, perhaps tomorrow. She pushed off from the door and just as she did there was another quick tap and the familiar creak. She turned around fully expecting Mealie to walk in but instead Richard Archibald was there.

"Richard," she croaked, reaching back for the knob. She cleared her throat.

"Hello Flossy." There was a bit of strain showing in his eyes. A small indentation just above his right eyebrow was the very same as Ruth's, and showed when all was not right with the world.

"You're early. Come in, come in," she said. "I'm sorry, you've taken me a little by surprise. The kids have just gone off with Jimmy. They'll be back at nine ..."

"That's okay," he said, hanging his raincoat on a peg behind the door, the same one he'd used regularly every six months or so for the last twenty years. She noticed right away how trim he was this morning, like a bridegroom with a perfect shave, fresh haircut, a toffee-brown jacket with a mustard thread in it, blue shirt and neat taupe slacks. Still a trim man for a forty-year-old, he had the wiry build of a marathon runner, though Flossy thought he'd be hard pressed to chase her downhill to the general store. He took his glasses off to wipe a raindrop from them and Flossy saw how remarkably he resembled his daughter at the dark narrow-set eyes, almost a mirror to Ruth. He looked around the kitchen.

"I got your message, thanks," he said, "but I'm not here for that ..."

"Would you ...?" she began.

"I was ..." he said.

"... like some ...?"

"... driving ..."

"Sorry," she said, stopping.

"No, you," he bowed his head and turned his palm towards her, "please."

"Sit down, Richard. I'll get you a coffee."

"Thanks Flossy, no," he made no motion to sit. "I was just driving up from the bed & breakfast to take some things to the Legion," he pointed over his shoulder, "and there was an ambulance pulling out of Mealie's. Did you not see it?"

"Mealie's? No." She looked across at the studio lights. "Jimmy was here."

"It was headed for Truro," he said. "I stopped in. There's no sign of her. Has she been okay?"

"Well, I certainly think so. I haven't seen her this morning. Did you check the studio?" She looked across. "The lights are on. I thought she was at work already."

"I checked, she's not there. Doesn't she usually come for coffee?"

"Well yes, she does. Most mornings. I just thought ..."

"Unh?"

"She's been working all-out, getting ready for the show."

"I think we should go into the hospital, don't you? We've lots of time before the conference."

"I'll leave the kids a note." She reached for a pen and paper, then began to write:

Ruth & Phil,

Mealie's taken sick, so I've gone to the hospital with your father. We'll be back by nine-thirty. Wait for us.

F

They decided to take both cars, the Volkswagen and Falstaff, in case one of them had to stay. When they arrived at the hospital half an hour later and asked for Mealie, the nurse in the emergency department wanted to know if they were related.

"I'm her son," said Richard with no hesitation. "This is her sister, Mrs. O'Reilly."

Flossy glanced across at him then nodded. After answering as many questions as they could for Mealie's admission, they were told to take a seat in the waiting room. It would be a while yet.

Richard, they decided, should go back to Great Village to get everything ready for the Elizabeth Bishop Society. They'd catch up again at Flossy's place at nine-thirty where he would meet his daughter and they'd all go off to the Legion together for ten. Flossy looked at the clock. It wasn't quite six-thirty. Still early.

Settling into a wait at the emergency ward of the Colchester Regional Hospital, Flossy looked around at all the day's uncharmed: people coming and going with a variety of sprains, fevers, bloody hands wrapped in towels, rashes, wheezes and some ailments not discernible to the eye. A young mother, not much older than Ruth, was trying to comfort an inconsolable baby whose crying jangled everybody's nerves. Someone said there had been an accident on the Trans-Canada earlier that morning in the rain, a group of students from the Agricultural College at Bible Hill, and over the next hour frightened families would arrive and huddle, also waiting anxiously for news. Flossy didn't know what was taking so long, except that they'd been told the patients would be tended according to urgency, which she took to be a good sign.

Mealie was one of the healthiest people in Colchester County. She never went to the doctor. She was a big woman, though; maybe she had a heart problem she wasn't aware of. Maybe it was that swollen foot Flossy hadn't had a chance to ask about. It couldn't be too bad if she could call the ambulance, could it? It meant she could make a phone call. Why hadn't she called her? It was just like Mealie, not wanting to take Flossy away from the big Bishop day.

Waiting, that long, dreadful look into the unknown with a knot twisting in her gut, recalled for Flossy all the other waiting and watching. She could feel the old nausea creep back, a sensation building at the back of her throat as if she were an anxious bewildered child all over again. It was as if the body held memory that was all rushing back at her this morning. How could anything possibly be wrong with Mealie?

The hospital's emergency ward was a foreign land. It was unusual to get to eighty-two and not have darkened its door before. Of course, she'd not had children and all the fevers, earaches, broken limbs and stitches that went along with raising them. Thomas and her mother had both died at home. Flossy wasn't used to the monsters that could slip from the dark of the unknown, the innumerable possibilities of what and why. She'd never had to practise putting them out of her mind.

Outside, it was still raining. The waterlogged flowers of the peegee hydrangeas outside the hospital were weighed down this morning, bent towards the ground like some burdened and splayed old creatures. Flossy was to discover that emergency wards were a timeless warp: no information, no clue, no compassion or con- solation, no place to go and definitely no angels. She still didn't know if Mealie had twisted an ankle, slipped on the floor or fallen on a can opener. What could possibly be taking so long?

Flossy walked over to the admissions window again. She stood, waiting for about three minutes before the nurse looked up from her computer and sighed her impatience.

"I'm sorry to interrupt you," Flossy began, "but is there any news about Mrs. Marsh?" she asked.

The woman, a different one from before, overweight in a soft- pink uniform, looked behind as if someone might step up and offer just that.

"You family?" she asked with studied indifference.

"Sister."

"I'll see if anyone knows," she said. Flossy went back to her seat. She tried to concentrate on Mealie, not let anger get hold of this day, though every nerve of every soul in that room was taut. There was nothing to read and she didn't want to leave for a cup of tea lest they come looking for her when she was gone. Her few books were at home stacked upon the kitchen table, though she probably couldn't have concentrated anyway. How innocently she'd piled them there one on top of the other last night, happily setting Mrs. Woolf on top of Shakespeare, beneath Bishop, but now, this morning, they were cold comfort as she waited for word about Mealie. She certainly never expected to be spending the morning here.

The hospital clock made its indifferent rounds. She changed her seat so that she wasn't looking at it so often. She had waited the longest of any of those who'd begun the morning with her in the emergency ward. A whole new cast of summer calamities and illnesses had filtered in to take the seats of those already tended and sent on their way. That was either a good sign or a bad one. She put her hand to her chest to quiet the calisthenics inside. "No time for a heart attack, Flossy," she spoke sternly under her breath, coughing a couple of times to restore her heart rhythms. She could understand the value of prayer in such moments; it was something to do, something with which to push the fear back, to keep hope afloat when in every direction those lights were flickering out.

The rain had started again, a violent summer storm with thunder and lightning crashing and flashing at the same instant. She watched water bounce a foot off the pavement. The ambulance was pulling into the emergency bay again and people were dashing for cover. She hoped Jimmy and the youngsters would be having breakfast somewhere by now.

Eventually a nurse came over to ask the name of Mealie's family doctor.

"Doctor Morrow, on Prince Street," Flossy clutched her things. "Can I see her?"

"Soon," she smiled. "Don't worry, someone will come and get you shortly." But there was no news as the clock trudged around some more. A young man, weary and unshaven, who'd been sitting beside her for awhile and chewing his fingernails asked if he could get her a cup of coffee. She declined.

The nurse had said, "don't worry." That must mean there wasn't anything to worry about. Last night, she'd snacked on canned sardines and toast, read until eleven and noticed Mealie's light on but hadn't given it a second thought. It had seemed odd, though, wonderfully odd she'd thought at the time, that Mealie was working so late. Flossy watched another three patients disappear behind the emergency room doors. Was Mealie's light still on when she got up at four? Had she looked over?

Anxious and hungry, but not wanting to leave, she stood and stretched her legs, scarcely knowing what else to do as she waited. The chairs were terribly uncomfortable. A woman in a lab coat was standing by the nurse at the admissions desk. They were both looking in her direction. In another minute, she came over.

"Are you the family of Mrs. Marsh?" she asked.

"Yes." Flossy nodded.

"I'm Doctor MacGillivray," she said, extending her hand. She was pleasant and calm. "Why don't you come with me so we can find a little quiet."

Flossy gathered her purse and her raincoat and followed the younger woman through a set of swinging doors into the cluttered heart of the emergency ward. There were many people in all directions, nurses, doctors, technicians, aids, patients on gurneys, family members wandering about, crying children with parents, charts, computers, coffee cups and noise. She looked around for

Mealie but didn't see her. It was all very busy and she wasn't sure she'd ever be able to find her way out again. After a maze of hallways, they finally stepped into a quiet room. A brass plate on the door read "Chaplain." Inside the room, the young doctor ahead of her turned a dimmer switch on.

At that absolute moment, Flossy was truly amazed at the mind's capacity to know something yet refuse to hold it up and stare at it straight on, because as those seconds of waiting stretched into a minute, maybe two, she was not at all prepared for what Dr. MacGillivray was about to say.

"That's a little better," she said, taking a seat in a soft chair across from Flossy. She looked at the chart in her hands. "You are Mrs. Marsh's ...?" looking up at her.

"Sister," she said, "Flossy O'Reilly."

She looked down at the chart again, made a quick note and spoke with her head lowered, "Mrs. O'Reilly, I'm very sorry to have to tell you this but your sister didn't make it."

Flossy's hand went to her mouth as she collapsed with a moan she couldn't suppress.

"I'm very sorry," she repeated. "She didn't regain consciousness after they brought her in by ambulance and we lost her about an hour ago." They were both silent for two or three minutes until Flossy could speak.

"What happened?" she managed to push the words out in a whisper.

"Without an autopsy, I can only surmise that the blood clot in her leg may have become dislodged and caused a heart attack."

"Oh my Lord." She was feeling weak, perspiring, "I saw her leg and didn't think to ask. Why didn't I ...? Oh dear God." She shuddered and shook her head.

"Where was your sister being treated, Mrs. O'Reilly?" The doctor spoke slowly.

Flossy looked up. "Treated? I don't even know if she'd made an appointment with her doctor. You see I didn't ask her about it."

"For the cancer?" she asked. "We don't seem to have any record of treatment here in the hospital. Was she going to Halifax?"

She frowned, "*Cancer?*" Flossy leaned in as if she hadn't heard correctly.

The doctor looked up from her papers. "You didn't know?"

Flossy shook her head.

"Oh." Dr. MacGillivray pulled her clipboard up against her chest, closed her pen and slowly placed it in her pocket. "Well, this will come as a great shock to you too. Were you not close?"

"Close? Yes," she squeaked.

"Why was she not seeing her doctor?"

"I don't know. I didn't know there was anything wrong." Flossy could feel an ache creeping up into her jaw.

Doctor MacGillivray, a woman half her age, brown hair pulled back in a ponytail, did not meet Flossy's eyes. "Mrs. Marsh appears to have been in the latter stages of an untreated breast cancer," she said.

"Ohh," Flossy moaned again, putting her head into her hands.

"I'm sorry, Mrs. O'Reilly," the young doctor reached across and placed a hand on Flossy's shoulder for a moment. "I spoke with Doctor Morrow and she said Mrs. Marsh was diagnosed over two years ago but apparently declined treatment at the time."

"Why would she do that?" Flossy could barely speak; she looked away.

"I don't know," the doctor answered.

"Of course you wouldn't," she said. "Can I ... see her?"

"Yes, yes, of course. Is there anyone else you'd like to call?"

"No, no, Richard'll be back."

"Did she have any prior arrangements?"

"I don't know," Flossy replied. "Mattatalls would be fine, I'm sure."

Flossy stood, clutching her things. Her knees were weak, she turned the wrong way and had to turn back again. She couldn't think.

"I'll take you to her," the doctor offered. "Are you going to be okay?"

"I don't think so," she whispered.

XXIII

A NURSE SHOWED FLOSSY INTO THE DIMLY LIT ROOM AND asked her, kindly, not to disturb the body. The coroner hadn't arrived yet, she explained, and they would still need to take more blood samples.

Mealie lay large on a hospital gurney. The paramedics or emergency room doctors had cut her clothing from the neck down the front to her waist and there she lay, her big-hearted chest fully exposed. One of her arms was outstretched with an intravenous connection still attached to a vein. Flossy took a sheet crumpled at the foot of the gurney and pulled it up, right up to Mealie's neck. She didn't much care who she disturbed. She stared at Mealie's pale skin, her open mouth. There was nothing dignified about death. Flossy licked her thumb and gently rubbed a streak of charcoal from Mealie's cold forehead. She placed a gentle hand on the top of her curly grey hair, leaned her own forehead against Mealie's temple and wept there in utter silence.

After a few minutes, she straightened herself, caught her breath and wiped her own tears from Mealie's lifeless face. Flossy collected her things, walked out of the room and closed the door.

She checked her watch on her way back to the car. There was time to get home before the others. "Dear God, dear God. Mealie." A soft drizzle was still in the air.

She wouldn't even remember the drive home, later on, only that she'd had to pull off the road once, to lean against the steering wheel and cry like a baby in the privacy of old Falstaff. Turning up the Station Road, she couldn't bear to look at Mealie's house. Stepping back into her own, Flossy was flooded by the emptiness. The fire was out. What a dreadful absence: not at all like this morning when Mealie just hadn't come over for coffee and Flossy was imagining her too busy about her painting, too flat-out to interrupt herself. It was that other searing absence, the looming horror of gone, taken, the no-farewell absence that was pressing unbearably in on every side. She moaned and rocked in her chair. Oscar Wilde was scratching at the door. She let him in, her eyes watering up as she fed him.

Grief with no floor, it was flung beyond the continental shelf. What would she do without Mealie? Oh that it not be so. If only she could be taken instead, an old used-up cask of a thing, Mealie had so many more pictures to paint, colours to savour, sunsets to watch. Ready or not, Flossy would have gladly taken her place, walked into the waves that would wash her away to nothing, like Mrs. Woolf choosing the very stones to fill her pockets, weigh her frayed and fragile body down. Had she chosen carefully, had she picked the round ones, the soft shades of lavender rock Flossy preferred, the greens or reds that caught Ruth's eye? Perhaps she'd chosen irregular shapes with two or three colours burned in crevices, gold and green, purple-yellow with streaks of white, or rocks with no personality at all, do-the-job rocks, hard and hefty rocks.

Across the yards, through Mr. McNutt's orchard, Flossy could see the lights still on in the studio. "Mealie," she moaned, "it was supposed to be *me*." She put her head down on the kitchen table. She'd been a fool. All these weeks she thought the pull of death was hers, missing entirely that it was Mealie, Mealie who was dying. How could she have been dying? Such an intelligent woman, why didn't she have her cancer treated? How many years had Mealie come to share her morning hour, her dearest friend, and Flossy had talked senselessly about dead writers, Woolf and Shakespeare, even Bishop. She shoved the books away. She'd had flesh and blood beside her and missed her entirely for all those silly others, those long-dead others. Flossy, nose in a book, the world passing her by and there was Mealie burning her life right down to the wick.

All these years and years Flossy had simply observed from the sidelines as the world's parade passed her by. She'd done a job and that was it. She'd given her heart to nothing but lost causes and the ungettables of the world when all the while Mealie was right there, her constant, her companion, someone to watch for her, to get her jokes, to care for her, even scratch her back. It was so simple, so silly, but when it came down to it, the soul of a good life.

Now, she, Flossy, was going into the rest of hers as if into a darkened room. It wasn't supposed to be like this. "What will I do without you, Mealie?" No one would ever know her as well, nor care for her the same. She hadn't needed anyone else with Mealie near. What would she ever do without her?

Flossy could hear a car. She lifted her head and watched as Richard stepped out of his Volkswagen. What should she say? Flossy sat up, trying to compose herself. She reached for her handkerchief.

By the time Richard closed the screen door and she met his eyes, he knew. Flossy could not speak. Tears were rolling off her cheeks and she could only shake her head. She covered her face with her hands. Richard put his arms around her, muttering his sorrow, and held her long, until they could finally let each other go. Flossy found her handkerchief and blew her nose. Richard put the kettle on and Flossy told him about the cancer.

He poured the hot water into the pot, pulled the tea cozy off the magnet on the side of the fridge, stopped a minute to look at Ruth's school picture beneath another magnet beside it. "Was that always here?" he asked.

Flossy looked over, "Her photo? Yes," she said.

"All these years?"

Flossy nodded. Richard sat down at the table and poured milk into his cup.

"I thought there might be something, Flossy," he said.

She looked up. He'd taken his jacket off.

"She asked me if I'd take care of her affairs, about a year and a half ago. Remember when I was here at Easter? I said I would. She didn't offer anything more and I didn't ask." He poured the tea into their cups. "I'll go over a bit later and see if I can find any papers."

"I noticed her leg last week, Richard, and never thought to ask when she was sitting right there where you are now," she said.

The two of them sat in long trenches of silence. Now and again Flossy would lift an eye up to a desert landscape in her mind that she did not recognize, could not fathom, life without Mealie Marsh. She could hear Richard blow his nose now and again, then leave the room. Sadness and regret sat heavily in the space between them prompting little more than the odd word or two, neither question nor answer. Flossy talked half in a daze, like a patient emerging from an operation that could as easily kill as cure.

They were all they had right now, each other's slim estranged comfort, a broken pot put together with glue that was giving all over again.

She looked up, remembering Ruth and the day ahead of them. "I'm sorry, Richard, about Ruth, not telling you. I feel I abused your trust. I ... I wasn't a good friend to you."

"No, no, you were fine, Flossy, trying to be a good friend to everyone," he said quietly, as if they were talking about yesterday's weather, before there was any weather of any significance. After a long stretch, maybe three minutes, maybe fifteen, she had no sense of time, he said with some strength in his voice, "Marj said it was you who insisted she tell me now," he smiled across at her. "I'm grateful for that. I'm trying to dwell less on things missed and more on gratitude for her right now." Then his tone softened again, "But none of that seems so important just now, does it?"

Oscar Wilde jumped right up into Flossy's lap, turned around three times and curled up for a nap. "He's never done that before," she said, stroking the purring cat. "I think you'd better bring Oscar's tray back when you come."

Just then both heads turned towards the door as they heard Ruth and Phil returning from the weir. Jimmy had dropped them off, and between the two of them they were struggling with raincoats, boots and a full pail of fish.

Richard opened the door. As they came up Flossy's stairs, Ruth saw him and transferred the pail to Phil. She knew who he was. They stood looking at each other for a minute before he took a step towards her, closer but not too close.

Flossy was about to speak, then changed her mind.

"If I had known *anything* about you, Ruth," he spoke slowly and as a man holding back considerable emotion, "I promise you, on my life, it wouldn't have taken me sixteen years to see your first baseball game." He reached out to tenderly touch her face, she flushed and smiled up at him, taking one short dance step into his arms. Richard Archibald, Flossy thought, looked like a man who was never going to let that child go.

Phil set the pail down.

"How's the knee?" Richard asked.

"Good. It's just above the knee, actually," she peeled herself away from him and hoisted her long shorts to show him the blue and purple circle.

He bent to look more closely. "It's beautiful," he said, nodding.

"Thanks, I think so too," she smiled shyly as she covered it again.

"Hello." Richard held a hand out to Phil.

"This is Richard Archibald," said Ruth, "my father," adding quickly, "one of them." She smiled at Richard as she was turning towards Phil. "It's complicated." Then, looking back at Richard she said, "Phil's my cousin, through Mom, one of them. It's kinda complicated too."

Flossy had stopped hearing what was happening elsewhere in the room. The momentary joy she had witnessed and the satisfaction it brought had given way to the oppressive feeling inside her chest. In her mind's eye she was only seeing Mealie again, stretched out on a hospital gurney. Gone. She looked across at the empty chair and blinked to hold back the emotion that was building in her throat.

"What's the matter, Flossy?" Ruth stepped closer to her.

Flossy shook her head. "Something awful has happened, Ruth. Mealie was sick this morning and went into town by ambulance. Richard and I followed her into the hospital." She paused to still the tremble in her voice. She shook her head, "... but she didn't make it. She died this morning." Ruth rushed to her and she felt warm arms surround her. The young woman began to cry, great choking sobs that set all the rest of them off again. Richard, standing near Ruth put his arms around them both. Phil sat down in Mealie's chair swallowing hard.

After what seemed minutes but could have been an hour, the young people went outside to talk by themselves. Richard decided to go over to Mealie's to shut the lights off.

XXIV

TEN MINUTES LATER, RICHARD WAS BACK WITH THE CAT'S tray and a large manila envelope tucked under his arm. He turned it towards her and she saw their names in Mealie's handwriting.

"Sitting on the kitchen table," he said. He opened it, turned it over and two envelopes dropped out, one for each of them. "All her papers are here, in mine," he said. "She was ready, Flossy." He slid the other envelope across to her. "I'm just going to check on the kids for a minute." He poured her a little more tea before turning and walking out the kitchen door. He closed it softly behind himself, leaving Flossy alone.

She opened the envelope and unfolded two pieces of paper in Mealie's fine handwriting.

1994

Dear Flo,

   There are no regrets, for either of us.
   I learned of this scourge in May of 92 but it wasn't a

breast lump then, though it likely started out there. It was a bump beneath my arm. After more tests and prodding than a camel should have to endure, Doctor Morrow offered no guarantees, whether I took treatment or not. In her opinion, the cancer that was in the breast had likely already spread. You'll remember that both my parents went out with cancer, in their sixties, each endured the horrors of operations and chemo and both died within a year of diagnosis. I don't know how this is going to end but my hope is that I won't need to spend much time in hospital. I'm not one for people fussing over me. Until now I've been perfectly comfortable and Richard has offered that he can find someone on campus to supply me with marijuana if I should need it, though he doesn't know why. We all, in the end, have the occasional secret.

That is not to say that these haven't been the best years of my life and almost all of that has had to do with you, the comfort of your open door every morning, your sanity, love of a turned phrase, those Woolfisms you saved to read to me every day that brightened mine. I've always known that whichever of us has to go first, the other will suffer terribly. It's the bald-faced consequence of love. The living of a good life, as we've always said, has nothing to do with the number of years we clock. It has everything to do with the care we take with what we're given, the care we give to perhaps just one other human being along the way. You have been my rock, from which I could come and go, be fed each day and return to the studio to create. There has been nothing finer in my life, pure magenta, and it is all the reason why I returned to Nova Scotia and made it home.

*I have asked Richard to help you with the disposal of
all my things and the house. They are yours, if any of the
paintings should delight you, keep them and let the others
go. There is nothing I would have wanted more than to
offer you the same care and comfort you have given me in
my life, until the last day of yours. That I cannot, I leave
you, instead, my work, the better part of me and, I hope, an
enduring memento of the life we shared together every day
of every year.*

Ever yours,
Mealie

FLOSSY STOOD, BLOWING HER nose and looking across at Mealie's
studio. The rain had stopped; the sun was warm again. She could
see Richard talking to the young people in the backyard. She was
grateful he was here.

She was just about to shoo them off to the Bishop meeting
when another vehicle flew up the lane. Jimmy. He'd heard. The
truck rolled to a stop and he got out. He pulled the gate down
and from the box picked up a large bag of dog food and a bowl.
Logie danced around his feet.

"Onomatopoeia," Flossy whispered, shaking her head.

Jimmy pushed through the door, dropping the bag of dog
food and propping it up against the wall. "I *heard*, Flo, I'm
real *sorry* about Mealie." He pulled a handkerchief out of his
pocket and blew his nose before putting a big arm around her. "I
brought *Logie* to *stay* with you a few weeks, to see you through
the *worst*."

"Oh Jimmy," she shook her head, "bless you. Thank you, I
know what that means to you. You're a good brother, but I've
Oscar Wilde to take care of now. He'll keep me company. I

couldn't have the two of them in the house. I'd break my neck in the middle of the night." Jimmy located the handkerchief he'd just put away and blew his nose again loudly.

XXV

A LL THE LEAVES OF THE BUTTERNUT TREE HAD FALLEN
today.

Flossy had been watching for it these past two weeks. Leaves
began drifting down as she got up this morning and got herself
into her best clothes to go to Halifax. They dropped steadily as
Lottie Fulton pulled into the laneway to pick her up for the long
drive ahead. Though it was dark by the time they'd returned from
the opening of Mealie's retrospective at the Northgrave Gallery,
she could see the tree was bare with a harvest moon glowing
behind it.

After all the excitement, Flossy was weary and more than a
little empty. The show had been a great success, but it was just
another of the things to do for Mealie that was now behind
her. Soon, all those little things would be a pile of leaves beneath
Flossy's feet and there would be nothing left but the barren
limbs of loss. She had just closed the *Chronicle Herald's* full-page
spread on Mealie's life and work. Tomorrow she'd send it to Ruth
in Oakville.

Over the two months since her death, Flossy and Richard

had been sorting through Mealie's things, though it was clear
to them she'd done a lot herself. Ruth had wanted to stay in
Great Village, stay with them, but they packed her off to school
with a promise that she could come back at Christmas, if she
still wanted to, after she'd seen the Bishop's Step-Cousins Barnes
exhibit, for Mealie. Marjory had actually been almost helpful in
the weeks after Mealie's death. She was good in a crisis and she
and Richard were talking, at least.

Mealie's house had been appraised to put on the real estate
market when Richard offered to purchase it. Now he was keeping
a small apartment on campus and coming to Great Village on
weekends. He'd wander across for coffee most mornings when
he was there because he and Flossy had many decisions to make
and an art show for which to prepare.

Jimmy checked in on her as usual, bringing his squash, potatoes and beets, but now he was talking more about the girls,
the war and his own memories of their years living on the farm.
She had gone to her lawyer in Truro and transferred her share
of the farm directly to Jimmy and Noreen. They had both been
wonderfully kind over Mealie.

She stared at the painting Richard had hung on her wall,
Mealie's Remnant, her last finished picture as far as they knew,
the one Flossy had happened upon in her kitchen that hot day
in the summer, oh so long ago — the rugged olive of newly
turned earth, the blood-red energy at the heart of the painting,
the blue-purple stippling she adored. This one she wouldn't lend
to the gallery. It would stay with her. She stroked the edge of
the picture, closed her eyes and lightly ran her fingers over its
rucks and wrinkles, as if from the artist's Braille she might read
Mealie's thoughts when she was alive and creating it. But, alas,
it would not speak.

A great light had gone out from Flossy's life. All those other losses of the past, Thomas, David, her mother, they'd all been bearable because she'd had Mealie near. With her gone, Flossy had lost her language, her wall, her echo, her own Roger Fry. There would be no other who would ever know her as well as Mealie Marsh. Companionship like that didn't come by but once in a lifetime and that was a lucky lifetime indeed. Grieving was Flossy's study now, the delicate art of holding on and letting go. Meanwhile, life picked up and carried on for the people all around her. They talked about the weather again, the price of creamed corn, laughed in her presence once more, told jokes, forgot names, but some days Flossy could scarcely make sense of it all. She'd never realized that joy was fugitive too, like light and colour.

And yet she waited and watched. Walking the shore these days, bundled in her warmest sweater, each vibrant autumn colour tripping down to the tired earth, the sandpipers long gone to Argentina, she observed the restless salt waters rolling in and out. She felt incomprehensible comfort beside that vast indifference, the tides that would come and go long after she was gone and any trace of her. It was the Remnant that would endure, outlast the trifling details of any one life, that small, consistent courage to pluck a string, reach for a note, finish a poem, or, like Mealie, burnish one's spirit onto canvas. It was there that she spoke in colour, of her life, their life, any life, all life.

Flossy watched for that perfect lilac line on the far shore but the conditions seemed never precisely the same as when she and Mealie had last been there together. Other colours, though, mysteriously, seemed waiting for her to admire, some she'd never noticed before, never dared expect.

There were times when she looked out onto the bay and it

brimmed with manic cerulean waters, waves tumbling to shore like children out the doors on the last day of school. Other days, with rain and fog hovering, she could see only one beleaguered ribbon of blue far out in the middle of the saddest wasteland of red muck; still the most godforsaken beautiful place she knew.

ACKNOWLEDGEMENTS

GREAT VILLAGE is a work based on stories that have come down through the decades from Colchester County, Nova Scotia, along Cobequid Bay, though all have been fictionalized with the exception of Elizabeth Bishop, her family and friends, the Lighthouse Spencers, Hiram Hyde, the Moose River Gold Mine Disaster and, of course, the details of the life of Virginia Woolf. Many surnames used in this novel have been borrowed from those of early families that settled the Colchester region in the eighteenth century but all these characters have been fictionalized as well. There is a thriving Elizabeth Bishop Society that meets annually in Great Village, but its beginnings bear no resemblance to those described in this book.

The methodology used by Dr. Rushton to treat Thomas's illness is adapted from *Treatment of Neurasthenia*, by Dr. Paul Hartenberg, 1914 Edinburgh, Glasgow, and London. *Henry Frowde* and *Hodder & Stoughton*, translated by Ernest Playfair.

The author wishes to thank Sandra Barry and the other owners of Elizabeth Bishop's early Great Village home for the use of the house during the final weeks of research. Thanks to those who made suggestions to various drafts of the book: Donalda Nelson, Sandra Barry, Juliet Huntly, Margaret Canning, Jean Orpwood, Sara Street and Marilyn Vivian. Gratitude of a whole other order is due Heather Dau, Sally Harding, Marc Côté and Barry Jowett.